Also by Alexandra Amor

Cozy Historical Mysteries
Charlie Horse
Horse With No Name

Children's Animal Adventure Novels
Sugar & Clive and the Circus Bear
Sugar & Clive and the Bank Robbery
Sugar & Clive and the Movie Star
Larry at the Wedding (A Sugar & Clive Novella)

Memoir
Cult, A Love Story

Love and Death at the Inn

A Juliet Island Romantic Mystery

Love and Death at the Inn

First Print Edition: June 2016

Published in Canada with international distribution.

ISBN: 978-0-9948824-9-3

This is a work of fiction. All names, characters, and settings are fiction. Any resemblance to actual events, names, locales, organizations, or persons living or dead, is entirely coincidental.

Fat Head Publishing
Suite 218 – 2818 Main Street, Vancouver, BC V5T 0C1
www.AlexandraAmor.com

Love and Death at the Inn

A Juliet Island Romantic Mystery

Alexandra Amor

A Fat Head Publishing Book

For Steven

One

AT FIRST ELLIOTT SIMON THOUGHT perhaps it was a tarp or chunk of heavy fabric that had washed ashore on the rocky outcropping the locals called the Bird Sanctuary. The jagged rocks that stuck out of the Pacific were all planes and angles, black rock shiny from the spray of the sea. A few cormorant birds were standing sentry at the top of the outcropping. Lower three seagulls were fluttering around the dark shape that had caught Elliott's eye – and not in a good way. Whatever it was, Elliott could see it undulating between two pieces of the small island, half-in and half-out of the water.

The chatter of the tourists on board the Zodiac boat slid into the background of Elliott's consciousness. Surreptitiously, so as not to alert his guests that anything was wrong, he maneuvered the boat nearer to the island so that he could take a closer look. Until now he'd been narrating a commentary about the history of this part of the Salish Sea. The seven tourists with him, mostly Americans, watched him with alert and curious eyes, their chins disappearing into their life jackets to protect from the early morning chill. He'd always thought that life jackets made any wearer look as though they were nine years old.

There had been reports of an Orca pod nearby Juliet Island yesterday. The pod was one that had been in the news recently after a sighting of a calf. Imaginatively named K-20, the new calf was thought to be female and was a welcome addition to the small, endangered pod of Orcas that made its home here in the southern part of the Salish Sea. Late the night before, Elliott had volunteered to take a few guests out onto the water at daybreak to see if they could spot the pod, and the calf.

Elliott cut the engine, letting the Zodiac bob on the waves while he took a closer look at the mass on the rocks that was troubling him. The cries of the gulls were piercing and urgent.

Most of the guests in the vessel chatted among themselves. Although one, a man from Illinois who was seated on the chair directly in front of Elliott, turned toward the guide. He swiveled his whole torso in the restricted movement of a life-jacket wearer. Elliott thought his name might be Latimer.

"What do you think, Captain?" The man's intelligent eyes met Elliott's, his face still, his energy calm. This appeared to be a man who was not easily spooked.

"I'm not sure," Elliott replied, trying to keep his thoughts from registering on his face. Paying customers should not have to deal with what Elliott suspected he had spotted on the rocks. "I'm hoping it's just a tarp or a blanket."

Latimer was watching Elliott closely. Elliott briefly considered moving away from the small island and radioing for help.

Before he could decide, Latimer began to shift himself over from the port-side seat he had been occupying to the one beside him, starboard-side. "Give 'er a little juice," he instructed, "and see if you can't come up alongside, a little closer. You keep your eyes on those rocks there, and I'll have a look."

Elliott did as the man said, but he glanced forward at the rest of his guests. They were still chatting, pointing out seabirds to one another; thankfully oblivious to what was happening. The best case scenario would be that the ominous waterlogged object was just a piece of ocean trash. He tried not to think about the worst case scenario. Pushing the throttle up slightly, he turned the boat into the waves that were swirling around the tiny, jagged island. He overshot their target slightly, on purpose, and then cut the throttle, letting the boat drift back.

Suddenly the others in the vessel became quiet, seemingly aware that something unusual was going on. Out of the corner of his eye, Elliott saw six heads swivel in the direction of the rocky outcropping.

Latimer was leaning out of his seat over the side of the boat, grunting slightly. The light was not working in their favor. The sun had only been up for a half hour, and the boat was on the shadow side of the rocks. It was like trying to see a black dog in a cave.

Elliott took a chance and glanced away from the rocks to where Latimer was looking. Just as he moved his head, the water receded for an instant and the unmistakable form of a human leg wearing a hiking boot flashed to the surface. Latimer had seen it, too. He pushed himself up off the gunwale and turned to look at Elliott.

"Get on that radio of yours, son. I'd say you've got a situation here."

Two

"DO YOU WANT THE GOOD news or the bad news first?"

Maggie Archer hadn't yet climbed out of her truck, when her inn's front desk clerk and IT wizard greeted her with this question that no business owner wants to hear.

Before Maggie could answer, Ruby, her chocolate lab, pushed her way out the screen door and clattered down the wooden steps from the office, her tail sailing around in the air wildly with no rhythm or organization, as it always did when she was delighted. She dashed across the gravel driveway and threw herself at Maggie's legs. Maggie swung her legs out of the cab and crouched down, smushing her face into Ruby's face and neck; both the dog and the woman making little squeaking noises.

"Ruby, how's my girl? Were you good while I was away? Are you excited?"

The dog swirled around Maggie, almost knocking her over. Ruby pushed her broad forehead into Maggie's chest and lurched at Maggie's face with her ecstatic tongue.

"You'd think you'd been gone for six weeks, looking at the pair of you." Sparrow, the IT wizard, was a tall, willowy woman dressed in a blue smock-like dress over black tights and black ankle boots.

Maggie stood up and wiped the residue from Ruby's generous kisses off her face with her sleeve.

"How about you give me the good news while we're unpacking?"

"Okay. Well, we managed not to burn the place to the ground or drive away all the guests."

"Excellent. I knew I could count on you."

"Why are you home so early? I didn't expect you until lunchtime."

"The ferry made really good time. There was hardly anyone on board. Help me with these bags will you, please?"

Maggie opened the back gate of the old Suburban and lifted the window up to give them access to the bags and boxes stored there. The two women spent the next few minutes emptying the truck of its contents, carrying their packages into the kitchen and pantry of the Cormorant Inn.

Maggie was overjoyed to be home. Though it had been just twenty-four hours since she'd left the inn and Juliet Island, coming home was always sweet. As the inn's owner and manager, she never liked to be away for long. The last vacation she had taken had been two years ago when she spent a miserable week driving to and from a cousin's wedding in Summerland. Her motto was, 'When you live in paradise, there's no need to get away from it.'

From the kitchen, she could hear the gentle morning murmur of guests in the breakfast room helping themselves to the buffet of granola, fruit, oatmeal, fresh-baked banana bread, tea and coffee. Ruby sniffed every box that was set down and was shooed away repeatedly. When the truck was empty, Maggie closed the tailgate and made a beeline for the cappuccino machine in the kitchen. Sparrow had settled herself into one of the office chairs behind the inn's check-in desk. Ruby sat between her legs, getting her ears rubbed.

"How was the mainland?"

"Awful, as usual." The cappuccino machine hissed and whined as Maggie warmed her milk and ran beans through the grinder. "Every time I go into town, I swear the traffic gets worse. I used to be able to do so much more in a day than I can now. I spend most of my time sitting at stop-lights and circling in parking lots looking for a place to park."

"Better you than me!" Sparrow leaned down and kissed the top of Ruby's head.

Both women had been born and raised on Juliet Island, off British Columbia's west coast. The island was part of the archipelago called the Gulf Islands, and was home to about two thousand year-round citizens. In the summers that number more than doubled, swelling with tourists and those who owned summer homes. Though the winters were cool and wet, with more overcast days than not, the summers on Juliet, and the other islands in the chain, were the envy of the rest of the country; warm (but not too hot), and dry with cool nights filled with fresh sea air that made it easy to sleep. Maggie's home and business, the Cormorant Inn, sat on a bluff, facing south and overlooking the Salish Sea. The seventeen-acre parcel of land that included two beaches and a small meadow had been purchased years ago by her parents, before the island had become a tourist destination. In fact, when Maggie's father, Reg, had told his brothers he was buying the land, they'd all shared that they thought he was completely off his nut. Not too many years later, when the inn was built and the tourism industry started its upswing, they grudgingly conceded that perhaps it had been a wise investment. If they knew how the inn's financial statements looked now, they might feel smug again.

Maggie set her coffee mug down on the reception desk and collapsed into the second desk chair beside Sparrow. "I'm ready," she said reluctantly. "Give me the bad news."

"The Millers canceled the wedding."

"What? Shit. Really? I just spent $300 on new linen tablecloths. Why didn't you call me while I was over there?"

"They just called five minutes ago. Sorry, Mags."

Maggie stretched her head back, leaning her neck on the back of the chair. "Fucking hell." She blew out a long breath and then raised her head and looked at Sparrow, "We'll have to give them their deposit back."

"Yep. Already working on it."

"Is there enough in the account to do that?"

"Just."

"Goddammit. Did they say why they were canceling?" Maggie could hear the whiny tone in her voice and didn't like it.

"They did not. But I called Rachel over at Timmon's Marina as soon as I hung up from the mother of the bride. Rachel is the bride's cousin, remember? And was going to be one of the bridesmaids…"

"Excellent work. I love it that you always have a source."

"…and she said the groom broke it off two days ago."

"Oh, dear."

Sparrow held one hand up beside her mouth, palm flat and vertical and leaned toward Maggie conspiratorially. "And just between you, me and Rachel?"

"Yes?"

"He ran off with the maid of honor and they got married in Vegas yesterday."

"No!"

"I swear."

"Okay, well, now I don't feel so bad about them canceling. Poor bride. That sucks."

"It totally does."

"Can you please update the online booking system then, opening up that weekend?" Maggie thought out loud, "Maybe we'll get lucky and get a last-minute booking. That's the August long weekend. It should be in high demand."

"Already done."

"You are amazing. I don't pay you enough."

"No, you don't."

"Maybe we could put a little do-dad on the web site saying we have an opening for that weekend. What do you think?"

"Do-dad?" Sparrow turned from the computer and eyed her boss. "Is that the official web-marketing term?"

"I believe it is."

Sparrow sighed, "Yes, I will add a 'do-dad' to the side bar with a mention of dates available for weddings."

"Thank you. By the way, while we're talking web stuff, how are the Trip Tips reviews these days?"

"They're good. We got two more five star reviews yesterday, and one four star."

"Why did the four star people ding us?"

Sparrow turned and with a few clicks of the mouse, brought up a web browser and then the Trip Tips site. She entered 'Cormorant Inn, Juliet' in the search bar and a photo of the inn taken from the sea, with its wide cedar beams and glass-fronted great room came onto the screen. "Let's see…they said…" Sparrow's eyes scanned the screen, "Here it is, 'Our stay at the inn was excellent. The cozy atmosphere – from the river rock fireplace and comfy couches in the great room to the sound of ocean waves lapping below our room at night – made us feel at home immediately. The staff is superb, every face friendly and welcoming.'" Sparrow made a little flourish with her hand, "'Our only complaint was that we could not dine at the inn on the Friday night of our stay, as the dining room only seats twenty and tables are booked up months in advance. If we had been made aware of this when we booked our stay, we would have asked to reserve a table, as apparently the inn's chef is the best on the island. Other than that, our stay was perfection.'"

"Perfection! But they couldn't leave a five star review?" Maggie scrunched up her face.

"You can't please all the people all the time, Mags."

Maggie poked through a pile of mail, sipping her latté and separating the envelopes into two piles; bills that absolutely had to be paid today and ones that could wait. Two of the inn's guests, Ron and Karen Arnold, dressed in matching green Gortex jackets and dark blue jeans, walked by the front desk, each eating a banana.

"You're back, Maggie. We missed you at dinner last night." They leaned up against the counter, chewing.

"Thanks, Ron. It's good to be home. Why don't you have Tyler with you on this trip?"

"He's a young man, now. He's got his own life. He said he'd rather go on a river kayaking trip with some of his friends than hang out with his parents on 'the island that time forgot,' as he calls Juliet."

Maggie uttered a fake gasp and then smiled, "The island that time forgot? I'll take that as a compliment."

"Please do." Karen popped the last bite of her banana into her mouth and then talked around it, "We love the rustic atmosphere here, Maggie. Don't ever change it."

The innkeeper held up three fingers of her right hand in a Boy Scout salute, "I promise. What are you guys up to this morning?"

"A long walk down on Wellington Beach." They turned to go and then turned back, "Hey," Ron said, "May we take Ruby?"

At the sound of her name, the dog got up off her foam bed under the counter and trotted around the reception desk, wagging her tail and smiling at the Arnolds.

"I dunno," Maggie said, "I don't think she looks very interested in that idea."

"C'mon Ruby." Karen tapped her thigh and the trio exited the lodge through the wide, cedar doors, Ruby rudely pushing ahead of her companions.

Maggie stood, grabbing her coffee cup. "I'm going to go have a shower and get tidied up to face the day."

Sparrow was hunched over the computer keyboard, a page of what to Maggie looked like hieroglyphics on the screen. She grunted and continued tapping on the keys.

As Maggie turned to leave, looking forward to her hot shower and clean clothes, the front doors opened again and she turned back, assuming the Arnolds had forgotten something. Instead, coming toward the desk was a tall figure in an RCMP uniform, his heavy boots making a clomping sound on the wide plank wood floors.

Sparrow looked up from her computer, "Hey, Brandon. How's it going?"

"Morning Sparrow. Morning Ms. Archer."

"Brandon, you make me feel old. Call me Maggie, please."

"Yes, ma'am."

Maggie groaned. 'Ma'am' was worse. *When did I stop being 'Miss,'* she wondered. "What's up, Constable? I can call you 'Constable' now, right?"

Brandon blushed, and Maggie wondered if his shyness and innocent ways were suited to being an officer of the law. At least he had been posted back to Juliet Island where the crime rate was officially almost zero. He wasn't likely to have to arrest drug dealers or gang members here. The previous year had seen exactly one robbery – which turned out to be a case of intoxication. The 'victim' had actually broken into his own house when he couldn't find his keys and had then put his computer in a 'safe place' (the oven) so that it wouldn't be stolen while he was passed out – as he knew he was going to be. The crime had been solved two days later when his wife arrived home and went to bake two loaves of bread, only to find a strange metallic smell coming from their oven. The MacBook Pro had survived the incident, although the marriage had not, the wife saying she was tired of living with not just an alcoholic, but a stupid one.

Brandon answered Maggie's question, "Yes, I've officially graduated and been sworn in." He beamed.

"Well done. How can we help?"

The young officer's face fell and Maggie reflected that it was so easy to read; it shifted so quickly and transparently, depending upon what thoughts he was having. It was like watching a silent movie. Maggie wondered how the boy would correct this trait. "I need you to come down to the station, Ms., er, Maggie."

"Me? Why?"

"I'm afraid I can't say, ma'am."

Maggie stood up taller, straightening her spine, "Brandon, I was up at 4:30 this morning to catch an early ferry. I need another very strong latté, and I have an appointment with my water pic that I need to keep. You'll have to tell me why or I'm not coming."

"Um. Well. I'm not sure..."

Without looking up, Sparrow admonished him in her best big sister voice, though the officer was not actually related to her, "Just tell her, Brandon. You're not James Bond."

Maggie watched the boy consider his options. He was staring at a wall of two stubborn women, and he knew it. He cut his losses, "We need you to identify a body."

Three

THE SUN WAS SLANTING THROUGH the wide storefront windows of Dr. Maeve Freeland's offices, creating soft shadows and oddly-shaped prisms on the carpeted floor. Elliott, seated in one of the waiting room chairs, leaned his elbows on his knees and tapped his palms together, gently. With every moment that passed, his regret at taking the early morning boat out to see if they could find the K-pod deepened. The whole incident could create a serious delay in his plans for leaving the island.

Frank Nelson, the island's senior RCMP constable, stepped into the waiting room from the hallway and took his seat opposite Elliott in one of the other hard, plastic chairs.

"Sorry about all the interruptions, Mr. Simon. The finding of a body is not a usual occurrence over here, as you can imagine, and we're just wanting to make sure we do everything by the book."

"No problem, Constable," Elliott said, though he didn't mean it. So far the whole event had been a huge problem. The loudest protestations had come from the owner of the Balena Whale Watching Tours, the outfit Elliott was temporarily working for. Gerry Stewart had not appreciated being radioed at 8 a.m. alerting him to the presence of a dead body washed up on Sea Bird Island and discovered by one of his crew members. He seemed to take the occurrence as a personal affront with no thought to how the body that was being pulled out of the ocean might have felt about the situation.

Elliott had guessed correctly; Frank Latimer, the guest on the boat who had helped him with the body, was a career naval officer. The big man from Illinois had laughed and shaken his head at the description Gerry had given of what he planned to do to Elliott with a spare fishing rod and a fillet knife. The swearing that had come through the Zodiac's radio while they waited for the Coast Guard would have made a prison warden blush. "Not one of them candy-ass kitchen knives, you understand." The crackling from the radio wasn't enough to prevent the entire boat from hearing Gerry's rant. The two ladies seated in the bow blanched and raised their eyebrows. "A knife sharper than my Nana Murphy's tongue. You will not sit down for six weeks, my friend. Every time you think of Juliet Island – hell, every time you think of the ocean – you will flinch and bleed a little from your anus. Comprendé?"

"Roger that, Gerry. Thanks for your support. I can see the Coast Guard vessel now. We'll be back to the dock as soon as we can."

"Sharp, Simon. Do you hear me? Razor sharp."

Elliott had turned the radio down at that point and worked to ignore Gerry's threats of sodomy. The Coast Guard took charge, followed soon by an RCMP vessel, with Frank Nelson aboard. He had called in two fellow officers from the nearest island, and despite the tragedy of a dead man in the water, Elliott could sense the men's keen interest in the event. It was much more intriguing than handing out parking tickets to summer visitors. Elliott turned the whale watching Zodiac back toward Juliet Island before the officers began pulling the body out of the water. That was not something he thought the tour guests should see.

It was hours later now and Elliott was tired. He'd been up since long before dawn and was not sleeping well on his sister's pull-out couch, which he never actually bothered to pull out. He just fell asleep each night with his head on one of the arm rests, still clothed, the TV throwing a blue halo in its dark corner of the room.

Even though Elliott had been through his story twice before,

Nelson wanted him to repeat it. "I need to make sure I've got all my facts straight," he said.

This was clearly not Nelson's first rodeo. Elliott wondered where the man had been stationed before he came to Juliet Island. His eyes had the weariness about them of all long-serving officers, and his face stayed impassive and without warmth during their interview. He had asked Elliott to meet him here after he and the boat of tourists had been sent away from Sea Bird Island. The short voyage back to the marina on Juliet's north side had been fraught with anxiety and tension. Two of the women on the boat had started to cry. Their husbands comforted them, but Elliot had seen on their faces that they were rattled as well. Even the stoic Mr. Latmier had looked shaken by what they'd discovered.

Gerry had met the group at the dock, his filthy straw hat jammed down onto his head, almost covering his eyes, and his dark blue flannel shirt buttoned wrong. Gerry was as rattled as any of them, but tried to hide it with bluster, blue language and efficiency. He chivalrously helped all the ladies out of the Zodiac, something Elliott had not seen in any of the previous trips he'd guided. He then escorted them up the dock to the tour office, handing them over to his wife, Adele.

"Full refunds, of course, folks," he helped a woman named Susan with bright red hair and cats eye glasses off with her life jacket and threw it at Elliott with some force behind it, as though the discovery of a body was somehow Elliott's fault. "And a coupon for a free trip any time in the next year. Let me get you settled in with Adele and she'll sort you all out." As the group started to trail off down the dock, Gerry hissed at Elliott, "You stay right there, sir. I've got a fillet knife with your name on it."

Elliott smiled to himself and tidied the boat. He had been warned by his sister, Libby, not to ever take anything Gerry Stewart said personally.

When his chores were done and the zodiac was tidy and

refueled, Elliott walked the length of the marina dock and then across the gravel parking lot and climbed into his SUV. He had been instructed to report to the doctor's office as soon as possible. The drive across the island with the sun shining and the new green on the deciduous trees would have pleased him had it not been for the grim discovery that morning.

Elliott had shared the chain of events that had led them to find the body with Frank Nelson as clearly and concisely as he could. No, he didn't recognize the body. No, they hadn't tampered with the body in any way. No, they hadn't tried to pull the body off the rocks. They had left it in place because the person was clearly dead. (Or, in the less delicate words of Petty Officer Frank Latimer, "That unfortunate gentleman is chum.") Elliott hadn't wanted to upset the ladies on the tour boat or interfere with a possible crime scene.

"A crime scene?" Frank put his pen down in the crook of his notebook and reached for his coffee cup when Elliott said this. He feigned relaxation, but the tension in his neck and chin belied his true feelings, "What makes you say crime scene?"

"Just trying to be respectful, Constable. However the body got into the ocean, whether he fell off a boat or intentionally swam to his death, I assumed you wouldn't want a bunch of civilians messing up what evidence there might be. If there had been the slightest chance he was alive, of course, we would have tried to rescue him. But the way his head was cracking against those rocks, and the interest the gulls were showing in him, told me his body had long since ceased to house a soul."

Nelson put his cup down and changed topics, perhaps trying to unseat Elliott. "What is your permanent address, Mr. Simon?"

Elliott looked down at his hands for a moment, "I don't really have one. I'm staying at my sister's at the moment. Above the bakery."

"Your sister is Libby Simon?"

"That's the one."

"My God." Nelson got a dreamy look in his brown eyes. "Her chocolate croissants make me want to put my head in her lap and cry. How does she get the pastry so damn soft and flaky?" Nelson shifted from bad cop to good cop without hesitation. Elliott suspected this was more his true nature. Being a hard-ass did not come naturally to him, as it did to Gerry Stewart.

"I have no idea." Elliott smiled, "you'll have to ask her."

"Oh, believe me, I have. She is tighter with her pastry secrets than a nun's arsehole. I'm a bit of an amateur baker myself. I had to do something creative in my spare time to get my mind off the job when I was in the city. I have never been able to duplicate her results. Maybe I should try more butter and less salt…" Nelson drifted off for a second, his eyes pointed at the far wall, obviously seeing visions of pastry nirvana. He was interrupted when Dr. Freeland came out of an examining room and poked her head into the waiting room.

"Frank?"

Nelson jerked back to the present. "Yes?"

"Can you come in here for a second?"

Nelson stood up, "Stay here, please Mr. Simon. I don't have too many more questions for you and then I can let you go."

The constable disappeared down the hallway to the examining rooms, where, given the absence of a hospital on the island, the deceased's body had been brought temporarily. It would stay here until it could be transferred to the closest medical examiner's office, which was in Victoria, on Vancouver Island. Elliott leaned back in his chair, and rolled his shoulders, trying to loosen some of the tension. He glanced at the end table beside his chair and the low stack of magazines on it. There were three rumpled and creased issues of Honeybee, a magazine he remembered reading as a child, and an issue of Vanity Fair with an unnaturally beautiful actress in a slippery looking gown on the front that declared, "The Prime of Miss Jean Cody." *Clever*, Elliott thought, sarcastically.

He heard the crunch of tires on gravel and looked up and out of the windows. A second RCMP cruiser was pulling in beside Nelson's. It stopped, and a man so young he seemed like he should still be in short pants got out of the driver's side. The passenger door opened, and a woman climbed out of the vehicle.

Later, when he was lying on his sister's uncomfortable sofa, listening to Steven Colbert interview an actor he'd never heard of but who was supposed to be a Very Big Deal, Elliott allowed himself to remember the moment as the woman closed the car door and turned to face the clinic windows. At the time, as his eyes fell on her face, he had heard a soft fizzing in his head. It was like a muted version of the sound a wooden match makes when brushed against the striking surface on the side of the matchbox. The sound was subtle, but clear, and he had wondered for a second if he was having a stroke.

But he knew he wasn't. He knew it was her.

She was tallish for a woman, almost as tall as the officer with her. At least 5'7". Her brown hair was tied in a messy but thick braid that was falling over one shoulder. She was wearing jeans over what looked like black boots with a low heel, and a light blue puffy vest over her long-sleeved t-shirt. The young officer and the woman walked together across the gravel lot and approached the doctor's office. She walked with the long strides and erect posture of someone who was sure of themselves. The officer pulled open the clinic door and they stepped through. Elliott felt a sudden desperation to know her whole name, first, middle and last, and the nicknames her parents had called her when she was a child. He needed to know her shoe size and her favorite scent, her favorite color, and whether she preferred silver or gold jewelry.

Get a grip on yourself, man, he thought to himself.

He watched her come across the threshold.

She met his eyes and sort of grimaced at him. Not a smile; but a strange, awkward acknowledgement. Her cheeks were flushed, and she had her hands jammed in the back pockets of her jeans.

Elliott began to stand up, to hold his hand out and introduce himself. Just as he began to rise, he heard Frank Nelson's voice down the hall, "Ms. Archer. This way please." The woman disappeared from view down the hallway. Elliot sank back into his chair, almost breathless.

Nelson's head appeared around the wall, "Thank you, Mr. Simon, you can go. If I need to ask you any follow-up questions I can find you at Libby's bakery, correct?"

Elliott nodded and then added, "But only until tomorrow. I'm starting a new job on Monday so I'm heading over to the mainland to get settled into my new apartment tomorrow."

The rest of Nelson's body appeared around the door frame and he took a few steps toward Elliott. "I'm afraid I'm going to have to ask you not to leave the island, Mr. Simon. Until we know more about what happened I'd appreciate your cooperation with that."

Elliott frowned. "I can't not show up for my first day at a new job."

"If you like I can call your employer and tell them why you're delayed."

"Because *that* will look better? Having an RCMP officer call my new bosses and tell them I'm part of the investigation of a death?" Elliott was standing now. He jammed his hands into his jeans pockets and frowned.

"It should only be a day or two at the most. I promise I'll let you know as soon as you're clear to leave." Nelson disappeared and Elliott realized he wasn't being given a choice.

He walked out to the parking lot, anger swirling around in his brain and guts. As he felt the sun hit his face, the image of the woman he'd just seen in the office flashed through his mind, and he was cheered ever so slightly.

Four

"HAD YOU EVER SEEN A dead body before?"

"Just my parents, to say goodbye."

"What's it like?"

"Sparrow! Morbid. Please don't."

"It's okay, Carol," Maggie said, "I don't mind talking about it. It might help me to process it." Maggie shifted in her chair and hugged her coffee cup closer. "It's really strange. The closest word I can use is surreal. We're used to seeing human bodies with life force in them, but when that's gone, it's really peculiar." She shivered slightly. "It was unpleasant. He was bloated from the water, and his skin was a really odd color. It made me sad for him."

Sparrow was sitting cross-legged on top of the reception desk, in between the other two women who occupied the desk chairs.

Carol, the inn's bookkeeper and assistant manager, not to mention Maggie's best friend, reached over and rubbed Maggie's knee briefly. "How soon did you recognize it was Arthur?"

Maggie grimaced, "Right away."

"How was he?"

Maggie pulled her eyebrows together, puzzled, "Dead."

"No, I mean, how did he look? Was he…" she searched for a word, "injured?"

"Oh. A bit, yes. He had quite a few bruises and scrapes on his face. He was still wearing his coat and clothes and stuff. I guess they were going to leave him as they found him and transport him to the ME's office. He was dripping water onto the examining room floor."

Carol shuddered and took a deep drink of her coffee. Maggie looked at her friend, perhaps seeing her for the first time that day, "You look like shit."

"Thanks."

"Another late night?"

Carol looked at once pleased and chagrined. "Yep."

"Who with this time?"

"Shut up. Aren't you supposed to be finding out where Arthur's wife is?"

"Oh, right." The deceased, Arthur Brier, and his wife, June, were regular guests at the Cormorant Inn. "Sparrow, can you look and see when Arthur checked in?"

Sparrow picked up the computer keyboard from where she sat and began typing on it, reaching down to use the mouse that was positioned beside her leg. "Arthur arrived on Wednesday. There's a note that says June is arriving today. Oh, no." Sparrow looked up at her boss. "Doesn't she know?"

Maggie shook her head. "They've tried calling their home and her cell and couldn't reach her. At least, that's what Frank said when I left the doctor's office. He may have reached her by now. Do you guys remember seeing him around this week?"

"Who, Frank?" Carol was fishing around in one of the desk drawers.

"No, Arthur Brier. The Tylenol are in the next drawer over."

"You're the best!" Carol fumbled with the bottle, trying to hold her coffee cup at the same time, but the safety lid defeated her.

"Give me that." Maggie took the bottle out of Carol's hands, opened the lid and handed it back to her. "Sparrow, did you see Arthur this week? Did you notice anything different about him?"

"I think I saw him yesterday at breakfast."

Carol swallowed her tablets and took a sip of coffee, "I saw him walking on the beach yesterday. He was in dress shoes."

"That's kind of odd." Maggie reached for the bottle of Tylenol, replaced the lid and threw it back in the drawer.

"It was a little strange. It was clearly not easy for him to walk, his soles were giving him hell. He was sliding all over the place."

"Anything else? Anything either of you guys remember? Frank Nelson is going to question you, so you might want to search your memories for any information you can give him. Speaking of which, is Greg around?"

Carol snorted, "Are you kidding? It's not noon yet."

"Well, Frank's going to want to talk to him, too. And Amy."

A guest approached the reception desk. Sparrow hopped off the chair and turned to face him while he asked about maps to island hikes. Maggie stood up, "Let's take this conversation somewhere more private, Carol. I need to ask you a few questions."

Carol stood as well and the two women walked through the doorway that led to the inn's kitchen. There was no office at the inn. Carol did her bookkeeping work at the second computer at the reception desk. All the paperwork for the inn was kept in Maggie's cottage, in the spare bedroom she used as an office. Carol looked at Maggie for guidance about where they should talk. Maggie glanced outside through the kitchen's back door and nodded her head in that direction.

"Ruby," Maggie called. The dog leapt up from her usual post under the reception desk and followed the friends out of the kitchen. The trio trailed across the side yard to the staff picnic bench that sat, faded and cracking, under an old spruce tree. Ruby sniffed the familiar ground and moved around the yard in a weaving pattern.

"You really do not look great, Carol," Maggie said as they sat down.

"Thanks. I feel about as good as I look."

"Who's the lucky fella?"

"Fuck off."

"Okay." Maggie smiled.

Carol rarely revealed the names of the men who were the cause of her late arrivals and early departures from work. She was thirty-four going on seventeen and had the body to match. A natural blonde, which not many women could actually say, she had cornflower blue eyes that, admittedly, were tinged with a bit of cynicism now. As much as Carol played the field, Maggie had a secret belief that her best friend had always wanted to find someone to marry and raise kids with. Carol didn't have a maternal bone in her body, and she possessed the trifecta of characteristics no one wanted in a girlfriend – jealousy, wild mood swings and zero intimacy skills – but somewhere in the deepest reaches of her heart, Maggie suspected her friend ached for a picket-fence life. Carol would never admit to this, of course.

Maggie had known when she hired her friend to help her run the inn that there would be conditions involved; first, she could never expect Carol to keep a regular schedule or working hours, and, second she could utterly depend on her friend to devote herself to the inn's cause as though it had been her own family's project. Carol was loyal like no one else Maggie had ever known. And though Maggie was no slouch in the brain department, Carol had intelligence and a memory that would rival most computers. That she didn't put that intellect to its full use was none of Maggie's business, she had finally realized. Carol made it very clear that she wanted to stay on Juliet Island and spend her life doing the inn's books and having the occasional fling, and that was all there was to it. Several years earlier, Maggie had stopped leaving self-help books on Carol's coffee table and emailing her inspirational articles from Oprah's magazine.

Ruby dropped an old tennis ball, almost black with dirt and covered in pine needles, at Maggie's feet and backed away several steps. Maggie pinched the ball between thumb and forefinger and threw it into the woods that led down to the beach. Ruby charged off.

Maggie came to the point, "This is not going to be good for us."

Carol had her eyes closed and her face turned toward the sun.

She knew that Maggie was referring to the death of one of their guests. "No. It is not."

"How is the revenue situation?"

"Terrible."

"Worse than last year?"

"Yep."

"Fuck."

"Yep."

"How can it be *worse* than last year? We're more focused this year. We've trimmed costs. We even took out a couple of ads in those Tourism BC magazines. My parents never did that stuff. Cripes, they employed practically everyone on the island just to be kind. I'm not doing that. I'm barely paying you or myself."

"As I am painfully aware. But you have a big debt that they accumulated that you're trying to dig yourself out from underneath. And they left you with that great whacking roof repair bill."

Ruby returned, panting around the ball in her mouth and dropped it on the ground. Maggie threw it again and wiped her hand on her jeans.

"And," Carol continued, "there have been those negative Trip Tips reviews. That really hasn't helped."

"No kidding. I wish I could figure out who's doing that. I feel like it must be another resort on the island, but I just can't fully bring myself to believe that."

"Has Sparrow been able to find out anything online about the identity of the people who are posting the bad reviews?"

"No. She's trying but so far that's a dead end." Maggie sank into deep reflection about her situation. She threw the ball automatically when Ruby returned it again, but her mind and heart were elsewhere.

Her father had built the Cormorant Inn. It had always been his dream to own and operate a small hotel in a quiet place. In the mid-1970s, before Maggie was born, he and Maggie's mother had come to Juliet Island on a holiday and had fallen in love with the island, the people, the laid back atmosphere, and the wild ocean that surrounded them. When a seventeen-acre parcel of oceanfront land came available a few months after Reg and Betty's first visit, they leapt at the chance to own a piece of what they referred to as Paradise. Their friends and family all thought they were nuts. At that time, British Columbia's Gulf Islands were a backwater place, sparsely populated with farmers, cheese makers, those who had dropped out of society during the 1960s (and had forgotten to drop back in), and the refugees of life; those who were on the run from something, or someone. Or themselves.

Reg and Betty slowly built the inn by hand, with a bit of help from local craftsmen. They used reclaimed timber when they could and the result was one of the most beautiful and rustic inns on the west coast. Reg was an artist when it came to design, and Betty was a wizard with a sewing machine and had a designer's eye. The inn's popularity had grown over the years. While Maggie was growing up surrounded by woods and ocean, the Archer's added several free-standing cabins to the land. Eventually they also built their own home, tucked away close to the beach and out of sight from all the other buildings on the property. All the cabins and buildings had cedar shakes, rough-hewn cedar siding, plentiful windows, most with views to the water, and a small porch at the front door.

However talented Reg and Betty were about building and creating an inn with a homey atmosphere that would rival any small inn in the world, they were, by their own admission, terrible business people. Betty loved employing local teenagers to clean the rooms and do other odd jobs around the property, but her soft heart caused her to hire more people than she needed simply to give them a good start in life and to ease the burden on their parents. And though Reg was a design genius, he was not an organizational expert. His projects tended to go over-time and over-budget, though he didn't mind, always wanting the best for his guests. These factors combined to leave the coffers in a continuous almost-empty state, though the inn was busy and popular, especially once eco-tourism entered the lexicon. The island offered endless opportunities for back-to-nature experiences, including whale watching, kayaking, hiking, mountain biking, beach combing and storm-watching in the winter months.

Maggie had never known any other life. By the age of five she was 'helping' her mother set up the breakfast area in the dining room before school. She did her homework sitting at the reception desk while her mother did office work. All the locals knew Maggie and considered her one of their own.

And so, when Maggie's parents fell ill and passed away within six months of one another, they left their only child a business with a reputation as one of the best inns in the Salish Sea, and with a debt load that practically made Maggie swoon when she thought about it. But she knew no other life, and couldn't conceive leaving the island and getting a 'job' anywhere else. She had no other skills. She had deferred her university education for several years after high school, saying she wanted to be really clear about what she took so that it wouldn't be a waste of time. Two years turned into five, then ten, and she finally admitted, even to herself, that all she wanted was to continue to do what she was doing; being the owner and operator of the Cormorant Inn.

It was harder work than she'd ever imagined, even after watching her parents do it for decades. They had had each other, and so far Maggie did not have a partner or spouse to share the load. Carol, Sparrow and the other employees were a huge help, but all the decision-making, all the worrying, all the friendly hosting-even-when-you-weren't-in-the-mood fell to Maggie. She didn't know it, but her employees were worried she was burning out.

Carol laid down on the bench seat on her side of the picnic table, the crook of her elbow covering her eyes, her knees bent and her feet flat.

"There was a guy at the doctor's office today." Maggie said this casually as if it was no big thing, just an aside.

"What guy?"

"I don't know. I didn't recognize him."

"He was there with the body?"

"No, he was out in the waiting area."

Carol was silent for a few seconds and Maggie thought perhaps she was falling asleep. Then Carol's head appeared above the line of the table as she raised herself into a sitting position, placing her hands flat on the tabletop. "Wait a second. There was a *guy* at the doctor's office?"

Maggie closed her eyes and turned her face toward the sun. "Yes. That's what I said."

"A cute guy?"

Maggie's lips curled up a bit at the ends, "Maybe."

"Are you kidding me? This is amazing! You *never* say, 'There was a guy'. Ever. I've never heard you say that. I thought you were dead from the waist down."

Now it was Maggie's turn to be rude, "Fuck off."

"Who is this guy? I need details. What did he look like? How do we find out who he was? Oh! Frank will know. I'm calling Frank." Carol leapt up from the picnic bench and sprinted for the kitchen door, startling Ruby who bolted to her feet and started barking.

"No! Carol!" Maggie froze at the bench. Eventually she stared down at Ruby who had stopped barking, but was standing at high alert, ears perked, tail and legs stiff. The dog looked at Maggie, her brown eyes full of questions. "Dammit," Maggie said to Ruby, "I should have kept my mouth shut."

The sun warmed Maggie's back, and she started to feel drowsy. She realized she'd never gotten a chance to take a shower and was running on less than five hours of sleep. She took Ruby back to the lodge and made herself a sandwich. When she popped her head into the reception area, Frank Nelson was there, sitting on the second desk chair, questioning Sparrow and Carol about the drowning victim, Arthur Brier. Carol made a face at Maggie, and in the way that close friends can convey paragraphs with just a raised eyebrow, Maggie knew Carol had been thwarted so far in asking Frank who the stranger at the doctor's office was.

The law man noticed Carol's mugging and looked up.

"Hey, Frank. Do you need me? If not, I'm going to go home and get cleaned up."

"Just one more question. How well do you know the deceased's wife?"

Maggie thought for a moment. "Not very well. She tends to keep to herself when she is here. I definitely had more contact with Arthur."

"Okay, thanks. I think I have everything I need from you. I do need to talk to Greg though. When does he get in?"

Carol looked at her watch. "It's close to one now. He should be in any time to begin prepping for dinner."

Maggie mock-saluted the group and left the lodge by the screened kitchen door. She walked through the woods on the well-worn path to her cottage, chewing her sandwich as she went.

Her home was a miniature version of the main lodge building. It, too, was built using wide, square cedar beams, hardwood floors, plentiful floor-to-ceiling windows that caught every drop of sunlight available. The abundant windows were very important in a climate that saw more than thirty-five inches of rain every year and the overcast skies that went with that. The couch and chairs were left-overs from her parents' days, soft and comfy and perfect for napping on Sunday afternoons. Not that Maggie ever had a chance to do that. The heart of the home was the living room/kitchen which looked out over a small bluff that dropped down to the ocean. There was a wrap-around porch that circumnavigated the entire home, and each room had French doors that led to the covered outdoor space. On hot summer days, Maggie could leave all the doors open and received the benefit of the ocean breeze. The cottage almost felt as though no one lived there. Maggie spent so little time in it there was no clutter anywhere, except the spare-bedroom office. A few photographs of her parents stood on the mantelpiece above the river rock fireplace, but there were no magazines, no coffee cup-stained books lying around. For Maggie, life was work.

She stripped off her vest and hung it over one of the bar chairs at the kitchen island as she came into the house. Ruby headed straight for her round, foamy bed and crashed, exhausted from so much ball chasing.

Fifteen minutes later, feeling clean and refreshed from a shower and a change of clothes, Maggie stood in the living room, hands on hips, looking out at the water, wondering what to do with herself. The shower had woken her up, and she didn't feel the need for a nap any longer. She was troubled, and she was never able to relax when that was the case. The inn was in desperate financial straights, and the tragic drowning of one of her guests was not going to help the inn's reputation. She and Carol had done everything they could think of to pull the inn out of the financial death spiral it seemed to be in, but every time they seemed to be getting ahead, another mishap would set them back. The roof repair that Carol mentioned was a good example, as was the wedding cancellation, but those were only the latest ones. The taint of a death at the Cormorant Inn could be the final nail in the coffin.

Maggie paced around the living room slowly, absently touching the back of the couch and the tops of the chairs. Ruby watched her with one eye.

Eventually, Maggie turned and faced her dog, "Well. Mooning around isn't going to help. I need to take my mind off things. Maybe some creative expression will make me feel better."

After rummaging around in her bedroom closet for a few minutes, first on the shelf above the hanging clothes, and then on the floor behind old shoe boxes and a Rubbermaid container full of Christmas decorations that she'd made as a child, Maggie found what she was looking for. Calling Ruby, she left the cottage and, with more purpose now, marched back through the woods the way she'd come and up to the inn's back door. She opened it and shooed Ruby through.

"Sparrow?"

"Yup," came her voice from the reception area.

"I'm leaving Ruby with you. I'm going out to take some photographs."

"Roger that."

Maggie, walking the length of the inn toward the water, slung the camera strap more comfortably over one shoulder and trotted, eagerly now, down the wooden steps that led to the inn's dock and boathouse. She untied the bow line of the small aluminum boat and then stepped in. A few tugs on the starter rope and the outboard motor roared to life and then settled into its soothing putt-putt rhythm. Reaching onto the dock, she untied the stern's rope and pointed the vessel out to sea, keen to catch the late afternoon light. She smiled and breathed deeply for the first time in hours.

Five

THE DIFFERENCE BETWEEN PILOTING A Zodiac filled with tourists and paddling alone in a kayak was similar to the difference between driving a car through a landscape and walking through it. In the kayak Elliott was so close to the water he almost felt he was part of it. He could feel the rocking of the ocean underneath him, which was both pleasing and soothing. In the Zodiac he drove roughshod over the waves. Now, he was at their mercy and he liked that. He liked feeling smaller than nature. It was the natural way of things, though, he reflected ruefully, mankind seemed determined to prove that law wrong. He didn't think that battle was going to end well.

"Paddling solo in a double kayak. If that's not a metaphor for my life, I don't know what is," he said out loud to the sea.

Feeling restless and uncomfortable after Frank Nelson had let him leave the doctor's office Elliott had taken himself home. He'd had a lunch of ham and cheese croissant with Libby in the back of her bakery and then wandered upstairs to his temporary apartment. But dissatisfaction was floating through the very air. He wasn't normally a TV watcher. Turning it on at two in the afternoon on a Saturday, he'd found he couldn't get interested in any of the sports that were on, and reality TV certainly wouldn't ever be his choice. He'd thought of going for a walk on a beach somewhere, but wished he had a dog to take with him. He'd circled his apartment for a while, swiping shallow canyons through the dust on the bookshelves. Finally, he'd wandered down the outside staircase to the bakery and watched Libby ice a cake.

After a few minutes she'd noticed her brother. "What?"

"Nothing. I'm interested in your work. How do you get those swirls so even?"

She kept her eyes on the cake in front of her, "The piping bag does most the work. Wait. Why are you asking me about icing? What's wrong?"

"Nothing's wrong."

"Bullshit. Tell me."

Elliott tapped the heel of one of his boots against the toe of the other and crossed his arms in front of his chest. "I'm bored."

"Ah ha."

"Gerry didn't know if I'd be available to guide this afternoon, so he assigned Phil to this afternoon's trip and now I don't have anything to do."

"So, go for a walk. You won't be on the island much longer. Enjoy some free time before your start your new job in the city." Libby kept spinning the cake in front of her on its little pedestal. Elliott thought it was starting to look like there was more icing than actual cake.

"I don't have a dog," he said petulantly.

Since Libby and Elliott had been raised with a succession of dogs in their family home, she understood completely why this was a legitimate reason not to go for a walk.

"Go to the marina and scrape barnacles off boats or something. I'm sure Adele could find you something to do."

"I've already had one telling-off from Gerry today. I don't want to be around him until he cools off."

"He's mad at you because some guy drowned?"

"You know Gerry. He's irrational at times."

"No kidding." She pulled the pastry bag away from the cake with a final flourish and examined her handiwork, her eyes critical behind her black-framed glasses. Then she looked up at her baby brother for the first time since he'd walked into the kitchen. "What about kayaking?"

"Hmmm," Elliott thought about this.

"That's not a no. Amber!" Libby called to the front of the store.

A face appeared at the doorway that divided the kitchen from the front of the store. It was a young and lovely face, marred, Elliott thought, by several piercings that looked both painful and awkward. Above the face was blond hair tied up loosely in a very messy, cascading arrangement on the top of the head in question, liberally laced with purple, green and blue accents. "Yes?"

"Give Elliott here," she jerked her thumb at her brother, "directions to Mike Reasoner's place. Then call Mike and tell him my brother is going to come down and borrow his kayak for a few hours. Okay?"

"Yes, boss." The colorful head disappeared.

"Go," Libby said. "Get outside and have some fun. And try not to drown."

Which is how Elliott ended up suited in a life jacket that was slightly too large for him, paddling a double kayak just off Juliet Island's southernmost tip. Libby had been right. This was the perfect activity for him today; he loved the feeling of using his upper body muscles after days of inactivity. The fresh ocean air and quiet was just what the doctor ordered after a stressful morning that included a drowned stranger and an undeserved bollicking from his boss.

He hadn't spent enough time in nature since coming to the island, he realized now. He had thought that filling in as a whale watching guide for Gerry and Adele would provide him with the connection to nature that he needed. But now, as he silently slid past a kelp forest that tickled the bottom of the kayak, he realized that was not the case. He needed more direct connection.

His previous job as a Parks Canada ranger had allowed him to spend days and weeks, sometimes months at a time, hiking and riding horses through virtually untouched territory. He had never been happier than during those times when he was charged with exploring land to turn into parks. Which, as it turned out, didn't please his wife all that much. She had married him knowing full-well what his job description was and that it took him away, especially in the summer, sometimes for an entire season. She had said before they married that she was fine with that, but, as with so much in life, once the day-to-day reality of living alone for months at a time hit her, she was far from fine with it.

Even more unfortunately, her way of dealing with her frustration was to have an affair with an ex-boyfriend.

After discovering the affair, which Elliott was sure Heather had wanted him to, they submitted themselves to months of counseling. The end result of that experimental torture had been that Elliott had volunteered to quit his beloved job and try to find new work that kept him closer to home. The marriage dissolved anyway, and Elliott was left jobless and homeless. Thank God for big sisters with spare rooms over their bakeries.

A seal popped its head up out of the water, eyeing Elliott with a glassy, indifferent expression, and then sank below the surface, disappearing. In the far distance, he could see one of the larger ferries traveling east to Tsawwassen. Closer in, he could also see a small outboard boat putting away from him, about fifty yards out. He pulled his paddle out of the water and closed his eyes, listening to the quiet; the water lapping gently against his boat, the squawk of a seabird high above his head. He thought he also heard a yelp, but that must have been the seabird as well.

He continued paddling, letting thoughts and feelings roll through and around him. This was the first moment he'd been truly alone since Heather had kicked him out, permanently, finally. He imagined that what he was thinking and feeling needed this kind of space in order to surface. He let it come, imagining that the sky and sea around him were big enough to handle whatever he might feel.

He could blame Heather for ruining his life, but the truth was that he was just as complicit. He had married her knowing he wasn't in love with her. She had been his mother's choice, and at the time, he thought that was a good way to choose a wife. His mother, Mary, was not an easy person to please, and Heather had charmed and befriended her from their first meeting.

"Heather is the right kind of people," his mother had said after their first dinner together as a foursome. Elliott knew that what she meant by 'right' was monied and well positioned. Heather was a lawyer from a family of lawyers who lived in the 'right' neighborhood in Vancouver. She worked at a firm in a glassy tower downtown, golfed in Point Grey and had gone to Queen's University with one of Mary's country club friend's daughters. This had been enough to start Mary on a campaign to have her son wedded to Heather as quickly as possible.

And it had worked. For a while. Elliott sighed as he paddled, remembering the controlled chaos of the wedding preparations. Mary and Heather had bonded even more deeply over silk gowns, centerpieces and stationery. Elliott sometimes wondered if they should have been the couple getting married. They were perfect for one another. He also remembered wondering if he should have felt more. He'd admired Heather; she was smart and funny and well-read. That she wasn't very kind was something he thought she might grow out of. But he knew he didn't love her. He'd tried talking to his dad about this one day at the driving range, but Joe had only looked at him with puzzlement and kept repeating, "She's a great gal, E. You'll be fine."

But reassurance wasn't what Elliott had been looking for. He had been seeking the truth from someone who had traveled the road of a long marriage. But, knowing his dad would be uncomfortable being pressed for how he really felt, Elliott had left it.

Before he knew it, he and Heather were back from their honeymoon, decorating a two-bedroom, two-bathroom bungalow in Dunbar that Heather was already complaining was too small, even though it had cost the equivalent of the gross national product of a small third-world nation.

And now, the damn house wasn't even his. He'd quite liked it, even though Heather always referred to it as their 'starter home'. The backyard was huge and faced south. He was able to build some raised beds and grow a few vegetables, getting a neighbor to water them when he was away because Heather thought gardening was 'icky'. As soon as the divorce was finalized Heather had put the house up for sale and moved to a pink pseudo-mansion in Kerrisdale with her ex-and-current-boyfriend. *The new house suited them*, Elliott thought somewhat bitterly. It was hideous and without soul. Perfect.

He had been paddling automatically, his arms moving in a smooth rhythm, muscle memory kicking in from his days paddling off Spanish Banks. But then was jerked out of his reverie. It was another yelp. He was sure of it this time, and certain that it was human and not avian. He turned his torso in the kayak and looked left and right. The ferry boat had almost disappeared from view behind an island. He dipped one blade in the water and turned the kayak in a circle, looking back toward the beach where he had put into the water, but there was no one there. His view to the right was somewhat blocked by a small outcrop of jagged, marine rock, similar to the one where he'd discovered the body this morning, although much smaller. He decided to paddle around it in case what he was hearing was coming from behind it. Ears attuned to the sound now, he paddled swiftly around the rocks, taking care not to scrape the kayak bottom on anything that might be just below the ocean surface. Just as he came around the outcropping and saw the vista that stretched over acres of water to the next island several nautical miles away, he heard another yelp, this one distinctly louder. Paddling faster, he disturbed two murrelets who hurled abuse at him as they flew off the rock where they had been standing. He could now see where the yelps were coming from. There was a woman standing up in what looked like a small outboard fishing boat. She was very clearly sinking.

He dug in, dipping his blades with force and moving as swiftly as he could toward her. The wake of the ferry arrived soon, and though it was diminished by the distance it had traveled, he still cursed under his breath because it was slowing him down. The woman was up to her knees now in water, bailing furiously, something weighted hanging around her neck. She saw him then, and raised one arm, waving, and yelled something. He couldn't hear her words, but he lifted his paddle out of the water and held it aloft, signaling to her that he could see her.

For a long time, it felt to Elliott like he was paddling in one of those exercise pools that push a current against you. You paddle or swim as hard as you can, but you're not actually going anywhere. His shoulders and biceps began to burn with the strain.

"Left now a little. Faster! Come on, come on! You can do better, Simon. Push it. Look out there. Rock. That's it," Elliott encouraged himself.

After what felt like hours of frantic paddling, though must have only been about five minutes or so, he was getting closer but could see that he wasn't going to reach the woman before the boat sank. The water was up to her mid-thighs now and he knew that at any second the boat would be totally swamped and she would have to tread water until he got to her. He hoped to hell she could swim.

His eyes were entirely focused on her, and he was starting to believe he'd reach her soon. And then the fishing boat was gone. One second it was there, the next there was nothing. The woman disappeared with it.

Six

ELLIOTT CAUGHT HIS BREATH AND stopped paddling for an instant, wondering if she couldn't swim and had simply sunk. But no. There she was. Her head bobbing just above the waves. He was close enough that he could see that she was also holding one arm above her head. He thought she was trying to make sure he knew where she was, but then noticed she had something in the hand she held aloft.

"What are you doing?" he muttered to himself, paddling frantically now, "Save yourself and forget whatever's in your hand."

Looking back, he would remember the incident as noisy. But truthfully it was silent except for the voices in his head. The water, the islands, the trees were all oblivious to what was going on. They stood sentry, as they ever had and ever would, over man's petty concerns. The roaring Elliott heard was all from his mind; racing thoughts and frantic instructions to himself.

He was almost there now and deliberately slowed down so he wouldn't run the woman over. He eased up to her, turning the kayak sideways so that she could pull herself up and into the second seat. When he got close enough to see the features of her face, he realized with a shock that this was the woman from the doctor's office that morning. Her hair was wet now, but still in a braid, and her eyes that had taken his measure with intelligence while he sat like an oaf in the waiting room were now strained and ringed with fear.

He stopped the kayak beside her. She was treading water with her right arm and still had her left arm stretched up in the air. In that hand was a black camera, the strap trailing down into the water.

"Take the camera." She held it out toward him.

"Forget the camera, lady. Get up on the damn boat. Your lips are blue."

"No! Take it. Take it, please." She somehow maneuvered herself with her right arm close enough that Elliott could grab the camera. He set it on his spray skirt and used the paddle to steady the boat as she grabbed onto the kayak's body near the seat in front of him.

"Climb up," he said, "I'll counterbalance so we don't tip."

"Give me a second." Her breathing was deep and gasping. *She probably needed a moment to settle herself mentally as much as physically*, Elliott thought.

They sat there quietly for a moment, the yellow kayak bobbing and drifting. Elliott heard her sniff and he wondered if she was crying. He looked away, not wanting to make her any more self-conscious that she must already be, and noticed his horizon was now filled with Juliet Island. The kayak must have swung around during the struggle.

Several minutes passed and her breathing slowed. He started to get nervous she would end up hypothermic, so he prompted her. "Come on. Let's get you up into that seat."

She sniffed once more and then looked at him, meeting his eyes fully for the first time, "Nice day for a swim, don't you think?" she said and grinned at him.

Funny that after almost drowning, what a person needs most is a shower. The hot water coursed down Maggie's body, warming her up and settling her down. She closed her eyes and tilted her head back, letting the water flow through her hair and down her back. She was still shaking a bit, but assumed that was adrenaline and that it would pass. The water changed temperature slightly and she wondered if she was emptying Libby's tank. She turned and shut off the taps and stepped out onto a dark green bathroom mat that had a bleach stain on one edge.

Elliott, for that was how he'd introduced himself once they got onto dry land, had brought her to his sister's bakery and up to his apartment to shower and get out of her wet clothes. He had insisted they do it this way because she was chilled to the point of teeth chattering, her lips were blue (as he'd mentioned when she was still in the water), and Libby's store was closer to the beach where Elliott had left his truck than her inn was. She didn't have the strength to argue, so she let him guide her up the outside staircase to his apartment.

"Well," he hesitated as he opened the door, "it's really just where I'm staying for now. It's usually my sister's office."

He had left her there, saying he would meet her in the bakery downstairs when she was done. "Less creepy that way," he had said, and she laughed despite her exhaustion.

Now, wrapped in a towel, with another around her head, she left the bathroom to find a pair of sweatpants, a pair of grey socks, a white short-sleeved t-shirt, a grey long-sleeved t-shirt with the UBC Thunderbirds logo on it, and a long-sleeved flannel shirt that he'd left out for her on the coffee table, along with a note.

'Garbage bag to transport your wet clothes home. Camera safe and sound.' And sure enough, there was a green garbage bin liner under the clothes and her camera sat beside this pile.

Thoughtful guy, she thought, and then heard Carol's voice in her head, "But is he cute?"

He was cute. And tall; taller than her, which she appreciated because it made her feel slightly less hulk-like, with dark brown hair that was a bit curly at the ends. It was left slightly longer than a businessman's haircut and was pleasantly messy, although that might have been due to the fact that he was kayaking. His eyes were brown and soft, *like Ruby's*, she thought, smiling to herself, and he had one canine tooth that looked a little crooked, which was completely adorable.

In his truck, he had fussed over her. He found a blanket in the backseat that smelled slightly of gasoline, but he put it over her anyway before he got into the driver's seat and whisked her away from the beach, cranking the heat in the truck up as far as it would go.

"I'm fine. I'm fine," she kept saying, even though she wasn't. He wasn't having any of her protestations.

"You don't want to mess around with hypothermia, uh..."

She realized he was searching for her name, "Maggie," she said through blue lips, "Margaret Archer, technically."

"Fine, Margaret Archer, no more guff from you. We're getting you into a hot bath as soon as possible." He said it sternly but took his eyes off the road momentarily to give her a quick smile, taking the edge off his tone.

It was only when he led her into his bathroom that he realized he didn't have a tub.

"Shit. I totally forgot that there's no bathtub. I've only been here a week."

He looked embarrassed and she found herself wanting to soothe what must be his frazzled nerves. "This will be fine. I'm warmer already just from being in the truck and under this blanket."

Which was how she found herself pulling on a stranger's sweatpants and t-shirt early on a Saturday evening in May. Everything was too big for her, of course, so she rolled up the hem of the sweatpants and pulled the drawstring as tight as she could. The sleeves of the flannel shirt had to be rolled up as well, the layers of t-shirts under it making her feel very cozy. She took the green garbage bag into the bathroom and threw her soaking clothes into it, including her bra and panties. Her black Blundstone boots were there too, also soaked, of course. She decided not to put them back on, and threw them in the bag as well. She figured she could make it from Elliott's truck to her cottage in her sock feet when he drove her home. She hung the towels to dry and ran her fingers through her hair, smoothing it out as best as possible.

She glanced around the apartment as she left, noticing the pillow on one end of the couch and a blanket folded neatly at the other end. She guessed correctly that Elliott wasn't pulling out the sofa bed to sleep every night. The room was not as untidy as some bachelor pads she'd seen. It didn't smell, at least. There was a pizza box on the coffee table and two empty beer cans. She had noticed coffee cups in the sink in the bathroom when she first went in, but Elliott had whisked those away as he left her.

His suitcase was lying on top of the desk that was pushed against the windows that looked out over the parking lot. The lid was closed but part of the leg of a pair of jeans was hanging out. She guessed that he'd grabbed the clothes that she was wearing out of this very case, and felt grateful. He was obviously not a man with many possessions, and she wondered briefly what had led to him living above his sister's shop in an office that barely functioned as an apartment. Thinking this, she turned and realized there was no kitchen. How did he cook? A person couldn't survive on pizza, beer and coffee.

Suddenly feeling conscious that she was invading his privacy, Maggie picked up the garbage bag and her camera and headed downstairs, closing the apartment door behind her.

The staircase that led down from Elliott's suite, ended at the back door to the bakery, which led into the heart of the operation, the kitchen. Maggie was only halfway through the door when Libby launched herself at Maggie, hugging her and choking back tears.

"Maggie! What the hell?" She stopped hugging and held Maggie at arms-length, peering at her, her own eyes glistening with tears, "Are you okay?"

"I'm fine. I'm fine." Maggie's chin quivered a bit with the sudden rush of emotion that she actually was fine, so she covered this up with a laugh that sounded more a cross between a grunt and a choke, "Thanks entirely to your brother here."

"Oh, Elliott, thank God you were right there!" Libby flung herself at her brother who hugged her, resting his chin on her black hair. He winked at Maggie over Libby's head, and Maggie found herself feeling suddenly shy.

Libby detached herself from her brother and started swooping around the large kitchen. "Come, come, sit, both of you." She materialized two bar stools from somewhere and placed them on one side of the stainless steel industrial table in the middle of the room. "I've got bagels coming out of the oven in," she peered at the timer on one of the huge ovens behind her, "two and a half minutes. We've got freshly sliced roast beef in the fridge, and cheese. I might even have a few beers."

Elliott shrugged at Maggie and sat down on one of the stools. "You might as well surrender. She isn't often this nurturing, but she's always this determined."

Maggie had known Libby for almost exactly two years. As soon as Libby had moved to the island to take over the bakery from the elderly Norwegian couple who were selling it, she had approached Maggie about providing the inn's bread and deserts. It was an offer the inn owner leapt at because it meant she didn't have to employ a bakery chef, and yet she could still provide her guests with the best bread and sweet treats the island had to offer. Plus Maggie loved supporting the local economy, not to mention a local businesswoman. Libby was indeed determined; she blew through most situations like a small force of nature. She didn't exceed five feet by much but with her jet-black hair, pale skin, black eyeglasses and forthright manner, she was difficult to miss. It was usually one of the teenagers that Libby employed who brought the bread and goodies to the inn every day, but on the occasions that the baker did herself, she and Maggie always had a chat and a cup of coffee. Maggie knew that Libby had grown up in Vancouver, the daughter of a wealthy family who wanted her to use her considerable brains in a traditional way; lawyer, doctor (preferably brain surgeon), stock broker or the like. But Libby never walked anyone's path but her own. She had discovered early on that she had a head for business and took delight in marketing and finance. After rescuing a down-and-out restaurant in Gastown just after finishing her business degree, and turning it into the new 'It' restaurant in Vancouver, she began to understand that she also had a flair for making businesses thrive when no one else could see their potential. The Bakeri was her latest project but wouldn't be her last. She moved around the province, finding businesses to rescue, doing so and then reselling them when they had been turned around. Maggie knew Libby wouldn't be on Juliet Island much longer; The Bakeri was already an enormous success.

Libby set out mayonnaise, mustard, butter and cheese on the island, as well as knives and small plates, and demanded that Maggie tell her story. "I've heard Jethro's side of the story but I want to hear yours. What in the hell were you doing out on the water in a leaky boat?"

Maggie laughed. "Jethro?"

Elliott rolled his eyes and his cheeks turned slightly pink, "It's a nickname left over from childhood."

"If I tell my side of the story then you have to tell me how you acquired it."

"Deal."

Maggie explained that she'd gone out to take some photographs. She had been certain that the motor was full of gas because it was a rule at the inn that anyone who used any of the boats, filled up when they were finished.

"Just like at Gerry's," Elliott chimed in, taking a swig of his beer.

"Exactly! Thank you. It's just one of those things you do with marine vehicles. And anyway, I think I was the last person to use the boat. So I'm nearly 100% positive the tank would have been full." Suddenly Maggie jumped off her chair, "I have to call the inn! They won't know where I am."

"Relax." Libby waved her oven-mitted hands in a calming motion. "Already done. I called them as soon as Elliott left you upstairs."

"Thank you Libby. I'm such a nit." She climbed back up onto the stool, "Where was I?"

"Outboard motor. No gas." Elliott smiled at her. He had the beginnings of smile lines at the corners of his eyes, which Maggie was finding very sexy. She was very conscious of his presence and also that she was wearing his clothes.

"Right. So I left the dock thinking the tank was full. Within fifteen minutes the engine started to splutter. I messed around with it for a bit and then it cut off fully and I couldn't get it restarted. Inconvenient for sure, but not dangerous. I wasn't too far from shore and we always have oars in that boat so I would've just had to row myself home. I would have been sore, but no harm done."

Libby handed Maggie a bagel, "Leave it for a second, it's still pretty hot. And…then what? When did you start to sink?" She handed her brother a bagel as well.

"Almost immediately. I was just getting the oars into the locks when I noticed water in the bottom of the boat. I didn't think anything of it, sometimes that happens, and I started rowing. But the water level started rising and that's when I realized there must be a leak. I started bailing but it did no good. The water was coming in faster than I could get it out."

"And then you saw Elliott?" Libby asked.

Maggie turned and met the man's eyes, feeling her stomach drop a bit. "Yes. I had stood up to see if I could see anyone around. I had a vague idea that I'd seen a kayak earlier, but I couldn't see it anywhere so I started yelling in case anyone could hear me."

"I was behind some rocks," replied Elliott.

Maggie used the bread knife Libby had slid across the island and cut open her bagel, and then passed the knife to Elliott, "I figured.

I didn't know what to do. I wasn't going to just lie down and let the ocean take me. So I bailed and I yelled and the water kept coming. And then I spotted you again. I saw you wave your paddle."

"Could you tell where the leak was coming from when you were bailing?"

"No. Not at all. It seemed like it was coming from everywhere."

"That probably means the hole in the boat was right in the bottom."

"Is the boat gone?" Libby spoke through a bite of her bagel-wich.

Maggie nodded and swallowed, "It is now resting comfortably somewhere at the bottom of Tyee Bay."

Libby took a sip of her beer, "You are lucky to be alive, young lady."

"I am." She turned to Elliott, "I haven't thanked you yet, so… thank you. It sounds melodramatic, but I think you saved my life."

"Well, you certainly couldn't have swum to shore just using one arm. What is the deal with saving your camera when your life was at stake? There are other cameras out there that you can buy, you know." Elliott didn't mean to sound harsh, but he realized his tone was affected by his concern for this woman he'd known less than two hours.

"My dad gave me that camera. It was one of the things we used to do together – take photographs – and it was probably my favorite father-daughter bonding activity. We'd go out on our own on hikes or boat rides or drives and we'd take pictures. He started taking me with him when I was really little, and eventually he gave me my own camera. This one," she patted it where it lay on the island in front of her, "he gave me for my 35th birthday." She paused, remembering, "which was just a year before he died."

"I'm sorry."

"So thank you for saving me *and* my camera. It means a lot to me."

"You are very welcome. It's all a part of the service here at The Bakeri. Right Libs?"

"If you say so, Jethro. I've never had to rescue anyone from the sea, though."

"Jethro!" Maggie laughed again, "Okay, I shared my story and got all sappy about my camera. Now you have to tell me where that name came from. Fair's fair."

Seven

"When Elliott was a growing boy," Libby said, beginning the story of her brother's nickname.

He interrupted her, "Please don't embarrass me more than completely necessary."

Maggie glanced over at him; he had a shy and nearly fearful look on his face.

"Hush, you big baby," Libby said, "let me finish."

Elliott looked over at Maggie, "She's the older of the two of us. Can you tell?"

"Go on, Libby," Maggie said, grinning. "I can't wait to see what it is that's making your brother so uncomfortable."

Elliott groaned.

Libby began again, "When Elliott was a growing boy, he ate everything in sight. When he was between the ages of fourteen and eighteen, our mother couldn't keep food in the house. If it wasn't nailed down, he ate it."

Elliot walked over to the fridge and got himself another beer. He stood at the end of the counter, his head hanging down a bit, listening and occasionally sipping from the bottle.

"When mum sent him to school, she'd pack him two or three sandwiches, a juice box, a stack of cookies, an apple, a banana. And he would still come home hungry."

"Okay, let me just say..." Elliott tried to jump in but Libby kept going.

"Finally the lunches got so big, she had to buy these extra-large paper bags so that everything would fit into them. Sometimes, he'd just use a plastic grocery bag. So our dad took to calling him Jethro, after the character in that TV show The Beverly Hillbillies. Have you seen it?"

Maggie shook her head, "No, but I've heard of it."

"I guess it was on TV when our parents were kids. Jethro was the big, galumphing nephew of the main character." Libby walked around the table and put one arm around her brother. She had to look up into his face. "There. That wasn't so bad was it?"

Elliott looked down at her and then over to Maggie. "In my defense, I was a growing boy. And I was on the soccer and rowing teams."

Maggie liked how comfortable Libby and Elliott were with one another, and how close they seemed. As an only child, Maggie had never known the type of sibling connection this brother and sister pair clearly exhibited.

"Time to take Maggie home, Jethro," Libby said. "She looks like she's had enough excitement for one day."

Elliott watched his passenger out of the corner of his eye as he drove. She seemed to be deep in thought; her eyes stared unseeing out the passenger window, and she was entirely still. He didn't know her well enough to know if this was normal, but he suspected it had something to do with the events of the afternoon.

He took a chance and asked, "Penny for your thoughts?"

"Oh," she kind of shook herself, like someone coming awake from a deep sleep, and turned to smile at him. Her face was already familiar to him, and he found himself resisting the urge to put his hand on her knee. "I was just thinking about the boat sinking."

It seemed to Elliott that there was more underneath what she was saying but he wasn't sure if he was entitled to probe or not. So he tried saying something neutral, "Was it insured?"

She chuckled softly and brushed a strand of hair away from her face, "I suppose so, yes. I'll have to dig out the insurance policies, but yes, I'm sure it was insured. It probably wasn't worth much. It was pretty old. So was the motor." She grinned at him. Clearly he had amused her.

"What?" He was mystified.

"That's such a guy thing to ask."

"It is?"

She made her voice deep, imitating him, "Was it insured?" and then laughed again.

He felt chagrined by her teasing but also pleased that she was joking with him. The little frisson of intimacy caused him to be brave enough to ask, "So you weren't thinking about insurance. What were you thinking about? You were pretty lost in thought."

"Hmmmm, yes." She looked out the window again, and then turned back to him. Later he would think of this moment and describe her expression to himself as her 'frank face'. She was about to be totally honest with him and he could see it instantly. He loved that she was transparent to him. "That's not the first inexplicable accident at the inn." She stared at him, waiting for his reaction.

"What do you mean?"

"I mean," she took a deep breath and let it out, "that other stuff has been happening at the inn that's weird and unexplained."

"Like what?"

She thought for a moment. "Like...one week we had three guests with flat tires. Three separate cars. Another time, about three weeks ago, there was salt in all the sugar bowls in the breakfast room." She paused briefly, thinking and then continued. "Although that could have been Greg's fault. He does smoke a lot of pot."

"Who's Greg?" Elliott asked.

"Greg Alder, the inn's chef."

"Okay. Continue."

"Then a month or so before that, two of the canoes from the boathouse went adrift. It was just coincidence that Carol happened to be down on the beach and saw them so we could go out and retrieve them. It was dusk and if we hadn't caught them before dark, who knows where they would have floated to overnight."

Elliott stopped his truck at a T-intersection, "I take a right here, correct?" He was still learning how to get around the island.

"Yes, down to the end of this road and then left."

The vehicle made the turn, and Elliott settled into his seat a bit deeper, thinking about what Maggie was saying, "Anything else happen that you're…concerned about?"

"I know I sound paranoid." She looked at him with a bit of defiance in her eyes. "And of course, stuff happens with any business like this. Things go wrong. So it's not that the problems have happened exactly…" She broke off and squirmed a little in her seat, thinking.

"Yes?"

"I'm going to sound crazy – I don't even know why I'm telling you this – it's just that something about all this stuff has my Spidey senses tingling. I'm *positive* I filled the motor on that boat. And I'll have to double-check but I don't think any of the staff would have used it in the meantime or left it without a full tank. They all know the rules and are pretty good about following them. Well…except for Greg. He's a bit of a rogue."

A small island deer popped up out of the ditch beside the road and trotted across in front of the SUV. Elliott slowed down until it had disappeared into the woods on the far side of the road. "I'd trust your Spidey senses."

"You would?" She sounded surprised.

"Yes, I would. As a man, I'm not quite as privy to that kind of intuitive information that you women are. Our mother always told Libby and I to trust ourselves when we had that kind of gut reaction to something." Their eyes met and he gave a little nod to emphasize his point. "She's a big believer in intuition and I am too. It saved me from more than one dangerous encounter with a bear."

She turned sharply and looked at him, "A bear?"

"Yep. I worked for Parks Canada for years and that's when my mother's advice about intuition came in handy. More than once I would have a bad feeling about a particular trail or hillside that I was hiking, so I'd change my route. Later, if I took that trail back – 'cause I felt okay about it then – I'd find fresh grizzly scat."

"Wow. That's amazing. And surprising coming from someone so…" she looked over at him and grinned, "tall."

"What does height have to do with intuition?"

"Well, tall and manly, I guess is what I mean. I think you're mother's right that men don't trust their gut as often as women do."

He felt ridiculously pleased that she'd called him 'manly'. He drove in silence for a few minutes, enjoying the feeling.

"And the toilets," Maggie suddenly said.

"Pardon me?"

"We had a stretch where all the toilets kept backing up. That was the other thing I thought was weird. Someone was putting paper towels down them, even though we have signs posted in every bathroom saying to only put TP in the toilets. Island septic systems are not like city ones."

"So you think that might have been deliberate?"

"I'm not sure. I can't decide if I'm being paranoid."

They came to the end of the road and he turned left. The entrance to the inn's driveway appeared beside the big, carved wooden sign that announced 'The Cormorant Inn. Juliet Island's most peaceful resort.' Elliott's tires crunched along the gravel drive that wound through pine and spruce trees. The sun was low in the sky and glinted through the tree trunks now and then, like a blinking orange flashlight. As they pulled into the inn's small drop-off parking lot they spotted an RCMP cruiser.

Maggie had her seatbelt unbuckled and her door open almost before Elliott put the vehicle in park.

Constable Frank Nelson must have been just inside the front

doors, for he pulled them open and stepped out onto the front porch as Maggie mounted the steps, still just in socks. "Maggie. I heard you had an incident on the water."

"I did. Elliott here was kind enough to rescue me."

Frank nodded at Elliott, acknowledging him, and then looked back at Maggie. "Everything okay?"

"I think so. I'm in one piece anyway, but…" she looked over her shoulder at Elliott and then back to Ed, "the boat sinking got me thinking. I'd like to report some other 'accidents' here at the inn." She used finger quotes around the word accidents.

Frank was wearing what Elliott had always thought of as the officer-of-the-law mask. Growing up, he had seen it on every Vancouver Police officer he happened to encounter. It was a mixture of skepticism and mental and emotional distance that they all wore. Out of necessity, Elliott had assumed. The amount of crazy, not to mention tragedy, a police officer has to deal with on a daily basis in a large city must be mind-boggling. You'd have to learn to detach or you'd go nuts yourself, Elliott had always thought.

"I need you to come down to the station anyway," Frank said, "so how's about you fill me in about your accidents while you're there."

"The station? Why?"

"I need to take your statement about the victim. Also, we have not been able to contact June Brier, the victim's wife. I need to ask you about her."

"Why there though? Can't you just ask me your questions here?"

"I'd rather you came to the station, Maggie. That way we'll make sure we follow procedure 100 percent."

"You interviewed the other staff here, didn't you?"

"We did. But you're the owner of the establishment where the victim was staying. I need you to sit down with me and tell me everything you know."

Elliott saw Maggie's shoulders sag a little. He was about to intervene but then from behind Frank came the sound of the lobby door opening and closing, and a woman Elliott didn't know stepped onto the porch. "She's not coming with you today, Frank. Stop being an idiot."

Elliott stifled at laugh at the woman's frankness as she came around to Maggie's side and put her arms around her friend and began to lead her into the lodge.

Frank protested, "It needs to be today, Carol," although most of the edge of authority had left his voice.

"For fuck's sake, Frank! She almost drowned a few hours ago. And where's she going to go? This is an island, for Christ's sake, not East LA. Get off your high horse and calm down. She'll come into your precious station tomorrow morning and give you a full statement."

"What about the victim's wife?"

"What about her? We gave you all the contact information we have for her. If you guys can't find her, that's your problem." Carol yanked open one of the wide lobby doors by its curved iron handle and ushered Maggie through it, letting it fall closed behind them.

Frank watched them go and then turned back to Elliot. "I never should have slept with her. Now she pushes me around even more than my wife did."

Eight

"You smell like pot."

"Shut up. I do not."

"You do! I could smell it when I came in through the kitchen door."

"That's Greg, not me."

Maggie flopped down onto the empty desk chair beside Carol, "You're saying you didn't smoke with Greg before he started prepping for dinner?"

Carol looked up from underneath her eyelashes, "I'm not saying that exactly."

"I thought so."

After dismissing Frank and Elliott, Carol escorted Maggie to her cottage and tucked her into bed. The inn's proprietress was asleep before Carol left the room, and she slept deeply and dreamlessly for four hours. Now it was nine p.m. and she was wide awake and troubled more by her adventure with the fishing boat than she had been immediately after it happened. The danger of it all had had time to sink in. She felt herself quivering a bit inside, the after-effect of her adrenaline surge. After lying awake for a half hour, she'd given up on getting back to sleep. She pulled on a coat over Elliott's sweatpants and shirts, stuffed her feet into an old pair of hiking boots, and drifted, like a homing pigeon, back to the inn.

Carol took a sip from a wine glass and turned back to her computer screen. "June showed up."

"She did! That's awesome. When?" Maggie stood up and

disappeared briefly into the kitchen, returning with a wine glass and poured herself a decent measure from the open bottle Carol had tucked beside her monitor.

"Just after you went for your nap."

"What happened? Did you tell Frank?"

"You betcha. I checked her in without saying anything and texted him as she was filling out the registration form. I fiddled around a bit and deliberately messed stuff up to keep her here as long as possible and she was just going up the stairs to her room when Frank arrived."

"Well done. You did all that while stoned?"

"Thank you." Carol made a mock bow, ignoring the jab, "Frank escorted her up to her room and told her about her husband's unfortunate demise there. Then he took her to identify the body."

"I thought I had done that."

"That was probably not an official identification. They just needed to know who he was at that point. But I imagine they need a next of kin to confirm who the person is. That's how they do it on CSI, anyway."

Maggie gently spun her wine glass around on the desk by its stem, "You're probably right. Where is she now?"

"In her room. I took her some tea after Frank brought her back, but she asked for wine instead."

"Poor lady. How did she seem?"

"Not great. Pale as marble. Her hands were shaking when I gave her the wine. I asked if she wanted me to stay with her but she said no. She wanted to call her family."

"Do they have any kids?"

"I don't know. They've never brought any with them when they've stayed here, have they? But that doesn't mean there aren't any."

Maggie sighed and sipped her wine. "What a shitty thing, all the way around."

The quiet clink of cutlery and gentle murmur of voices floated out to the front desk from the dining room. The sound reassured Maggie that all hope was not yet lost.

Greg, the chef, appeared at the entrance to the kitchen, wiping his hands on his apron. "Hey, boss. How are you doing? I hear you went for a swim today."

"I did. But I survived."

"Nice outfit."

Maggie looked down at herself. She felt like a lumberjack who'd been shrunk in the dryer. "Get a glass, Alder, and join us."

Greg didn't need to be asked twice. He disappeared and quickly reappeared with a glass and a folding chair. He settled himself in the kitchen doorway, and Carol poured wine into his proffered glass.

"Cheers." The three friends clinked glasses.

"While I've got you both here," Maggie said, "let me ask you this. Did either of you use the fishing boat since last Tuesday?"

"Not me," said Carol, shuddering. She had a fear of open water, which made living on an island a little inconvenient. Whenever she took the ferry to the mainland or Vancouver Island she always stayed in her vehicle on the car deck, refusing to acknowledge that she was on a boat. As far as Maggie knew, Carol had never used any of the inn's canoes or fishing boats.

"Me neither," Greg sipped his wine. "Why?"

Realizing she hadn't shared the story of the boat sinking with her colleagues she told them the whole tale. The motor running out of gas, the attempt to row back to land, the water in the boat, the bailing and then the sinking.

"Jeez, Mags, you easily could have died."

"Don't remind me. You always fill up when you use the boats, right Greg?"

"I rarely go out on the water in the inn's boats, but yes, if I do I always fill up afterwards."

"When was the last time you used that little fishing boat?"

"Oh," Greg absentmindedly swirled his wine in his glass, "last fall probably."

Maggie smiled, "Okay then. Well, you're off the hook, since I used that boat earlier this week." She thought for a moment, "Who else might have used it?"

Carol pulled open a drawer under the desk and pushed the hanging files in it around a bit, "Let's check the sign-out sheet." Finding the file she was looking for, she opened it on the desk and ran her finger down the sheet on top, "Let's see. March. April. Here we go: May. May 2nd. May 4th. When did you have it out?" She looked up at Maggie.

"Last Tuesday. What was that? The 5th?"

"None of the guests officially signed it out after that. The last sign-out was the 4th. Bernard Hiller."

"Right. He uses it all the time when he's here for fishing. But he always leaves it filled with gas. How long did he stay?"

Carol turned to the computer and bought up the guest registration program. Doing a search by Hiller's name brought up a list of his stays. "He checked out on the 5th."

"Okay, well, that solves that. It wasn't him."

"Do any of the other staff use the boats?" Carol asked, putting the file folder away and closing the drawer.

Greg and Maggie looked at one another. "Not really, I don't think," Maggie said. "Sparrow goes out in one of the canoes occasionally but I don't think she uses the power boats. I can't see Amy taking the fishing boat out." Amy was the inn's housekeeper. "What about Chris or Taylor, Greg?"

"I wouldn't think Chris would. His parents have at least one powerboat that's really nice, so he probably uses that if he wants to go out on the water. Ask him." Greg jerked his head toward the kitchen.

"Chris!" Maggie called into the kitchen, where she could hear the hiss of water and the occasional thump of a pot on the counter. Chris was the kitchen's dishwasher, bus boy and general dogsbody.

"Yeah?" came the teenager's voice from the area of the sinks.

"Can you come out here for a sec?"

The boy appeared, all spots and self-consciousness, as anyone who has survived being seventeen can remember being. "Yeah?" He said again, looking around from Maggie to Greg to Carol.

"Chris, do you ever take the fishing boat out from the dock?" Maggie asked.

"No." The boy had a look of guilt and defiance on his face, which could not have been easy to achieve.

"It's okay if you do. I'm just trying to find out who might have used it before I did today."

"I heard it sank."

"It did. With me in it."

"Jeez." The boy wiped his hands on the seat of his black pants and swiped at his sweaty forehead with his arm. "Nope. Wasn't me. I never use those boats."

"What do you mean it wasn't you?" Maggie made sure to keep her tone light, though Chris' phrasing made her nervous.

"I dunno. I just mean it wasn't me. Whatever it was that happened, I didn't do it. I never go near the boats here. I have enough of my dad dragging me out to go fishing on his stupid boat."

"Oh, okay. So you've never taken one of the boats out from our dock?"

"Nope."

"Okay. Thanks Chris."

As the teen walked back into the kitchen, Greg raised his eyebrows at Maggie.

"What do you think?" she asked, sotto voice.

Greg shrugged, "Hard to tell. I've never experienced that kid to be a liar. But… he is a teenager. They lie just to get the practice in, don't they?"

Carol pushed the toe of Greg's Crock with her toe, "That was just you."

"Oh. Right." Greg grinned and drank some wine.

Maggie returned to the subject at hand, "What about Taylor?"

"She's been off since last weekend. She had that wedding to go to in Penticton, remember? Tonight is her first night back."

"Oh, right. Who was covering her shifts?"

"Sparrow."

"Ah. Okay. Well, that's a dead end then." Maggie chewed lightly on a thumbnail, thinking. "I can't think of anyone else who would have used the boat, can you guys?"

"Not unless a guest took it out without signing it out." Carol finished her wine and poured herself some more.

"Right. Dammit. We're back to square one."

"Yep."

Greg stood up and threw back the last of his wine. He grabbed the chair, folded it, and tucked it under one arm. "I better finish cleaning up. Otherwise I'll be here all night." He bumped Maggie's shoulder with his hip as he passed her, "Glad you're okay, boss."

Maggie looked up, distracted, "Thanks, dude." She yawned and stretched her arms high above her head, arching her back. "I'm going back to bed. It's been a hell of a day."

"Good idea. Sleep well. I'll see you tomorrow."

"See you then." Maggie kissed the top of Carol's head and shuffled away, her boot laces dragging.

The Juliet Island RCMP detachment was housed in a one-story building that sat by itself just off Schooner Road in roughly the middle of the island. The land around it had been cleared of trees and was now just patchy, stubbly grass, mixed with moss. Beyond the edge of the lawn surrounding the detachment was the edge of the island's native forest.

Maggie pulled into the parking area and left her old Suburban looming between two police cruisers. Though it was Sunday, the front doors were unlocked and Maggie found Frank Nelson sitting with Julie, the receptionist, behind the front counter. He opened the half-door at one end of the counter for her and ushered her to his office.

"Thank you for coming in today, Maggie. You look a lot better than you did yesterday."

The constable's office was a clear reflection of the man himself; mostly tidy, with a casual air about it and a decorative focus on taxidermied fish. Frank was close to retirement. He had been an RCMP officer since he graduated near the top of his class from the academy in 1985. Through his career, he had been posted all over Canada, serving in places as diverse as Halifax, Yellowknife, Vancouver, Regina, Flin Flon, and Prince George. Divorced and counting down the days to retirement, Frank had been the perfect fit for a posting on Juliet Island. He was experienced enough to know when to let things slide and also commanded respect from the locals due to his experience. The fact that he topped 6' 3" didn't hurt, either. He was a keen fisherman, as the three rods propped up in the corner of his office testified to; as did the glassy-eyed samples of marine life that were mounted and hung here and there on the walls. When he wasn't in uniform, you could usually find him on or near the water with a fishing pole in his hand.

Maggie smiled and sat down in the guest chair Frank motioned toward. He sat down in his black swivel chair and leaned back, placing his hands behind his head, locking eyes with Maggie. He wasted no time getting to the point.

"Did you know the victim was a developer?"

Maggie furrowed her brow, "A developer of what?"

"Land. Hotels. Buildings."

"No, I didn't know that. I just knew him as a guest."

"The victim and his wife, June."

"Yes."

"So you didn't know that Arthur Brier ran one of the most successful construction and development firms in the islands?"

"That's what I just said." Maggie's tone became defensive.

"Okay." Frank leaned his head back even further, his chair creaking a bit under the strain. He was quiet for a few seconds, and then he popped forward, rounding his shoulders and placing his clasped hands in front of him on the desk. "He didn't approach you about developing your land?"

"No, why would he? It's not for sale."

"How are your finances Maggie?"

She was taken aback by this question, having not expected it. She stalled for time, "Finances? What do you mean?"

"I mean, how solvent is your business? How much money is the inn making?"

"None of your business, that's how much."

"Look, Maggie, you know I cared about your mom and dad very much. But the truth is that while they were great at fostering good will and being genial hosts, they were not fantastic at the financial side of things. I imagine they left you with a good deal of debt when they passed on."

Since it wasn't a question, Maggie kept her mouth shut and held Frank's gaze.

After a moment of this staring contest, Frank continued. "So, it wouldn't surprise me if you were thinking of getting out of the hotel business. And I'm wondering if Arthur Brier was helping you consider your options."

Now it was Maggie's turn to lean forward onto the desk. She bored her eyes into Frank's. "I just told you. I didn't know the man was a developer. Most people come to the Cormorant Inn to leave their working lives behind. I make it a policy never to ask people what they do for a living. First of all, it's none of my business, and second of all, I don't care! Our guests come to Juliet to relax, be pampered, walk on beaches, sleep in and take naps. They do not come to discuss business. We didn't even have WiFi until three years ago." She had worked up a head of steam and found her voice was raised, "What is this about Frank? Are you asking me if I had something to do with Arthur Brier's death?"

Frank paused for a moment, thinking. "What I'm doing is my job – I'm just trying to fill in the of background on our victim and make sure there was no foul play involved. It's most likely that he simply fell off one of the bluffs up near the inn, or out of a boat we haven't found yet, but when I found out that he was a land developer, I had to ask if you were aware."

"No, I wasn't aware. End of story." Maggie sat back in her chair, tense, her ears ringing with anger.

"Okay, good. That's great. That's all I needed to know. Now," Frank's energy shifted perceptibly, like changing the font on a computer screen, "tell me about this accident of yours yesterday."

Maggie took a deep breath to steady herself. She didn't like Frank knowing about and prying into her financial situation. It was embarrassing enough to be scraping by, watching every penny, and having Carol juggle bills, deciding which ones to pay each month, without the local police being all up in her business. But she knew that he was doing his job and that he always had her best interests at heart. He was a good man, behind the gruff police exterior. Despite their ten year age difference, he had been one of her father's closest friends over the last few years. She supposed that was how Frank knew more about the inn's finances than she would have imagined or expected.

So she told him about the boat sinking and then carried on, mentioning the other accidents and weird occurrences that had been going on for the past few months. The same ones she had shared with Elliott the day before.

When she finished speaking, Frank rubbed the tops of his fingers under his chin. "The boat is gone, correct? Sunk?"

"Yes."

"And the other things you noticed were," he counted off on his long fingers, "flat tires, salt in the sugar bowls and plugged toilets."

Now that he'd summed it up like that it sounded pathetic even to Maggie's ears. "Yes?" she said.

Frank smiled at her, "Is that a question?"

"It sounds a bit silly when you say it like that but…I dunno…" she lost her nerve a bit, "I feel like *something's* going on. I just don't know why or even what it is."

"Okay. Well. I'm not sure what to say, Maggie. There's nothing I can do, really. Especially with the boat sunk in Tyee Bay. We have no evidence that it was tampered with."

Maggie nodded. He was right.

"But here's what I'll do. I'll ask young Brandon to make sure he swings by the inn daily on his patrol. Okay?" Frank stood up, dismissing her.

"Sure. Thanks, Frank."

"No problem." As he ushered her through his office door into the reception area, he asked, "Is Mrs. Brier still at the inn?"

"She was when I left to come over here."

"Do you know when she intends to check out?"

"She hasn't said. I kind of assumed she'd go home today, unless you need her for some reason."

"I would rather she stayed until we've done a bit more investigating. I did ask her to let me know when she's leaving, so hopefully she'll do that."

Maggie said good-bye and crunched across the parking lot, deep in thought. She was slightly disappointed that there wasn't more Frank could do about her concerns about the inn. She understood that there wasn't really anything to investigate, and, at the same time, wished the situation was less ambiguous.

Or am I being paranoid? she thought. *Maybe I'm just being overprotective of the inn. Or overly sensitive to problems.*

She sighed as she walked. The air was full of the scent of pine trees and grass that was slightly damp from a light rain shower in the night. Maggie absently chewed one of her cuticles. The conversation she'd had with Elliott returned to her. "Trust your gut," he'd said.

"He's right," Maggie said out loud, though there was no one around. She realized that if anyone was going to find out what was going on, it would have to be her. "And so what if I look into the accidents and they prove to be nothing? At least then my mind will be at ease."

Resolved and relieved at having made a decision, she climbed into the cab of her old Suburban and pointed it toward home.

Nine

THE CRASHING OF CAKE PANS and cookie sheets was almost deafening. Water splashed over the edge of the industrial-sized sink and soaked the front of Elliott's apron. He scrubbed vigorously, teeth clenched and jaw tight, mumbling angrily under his breath.

Libby pulled a tray with loaves of French country bread on it out of the oven and slid it into a spot on the tall cooling rack. "Okay, okay. Hulk angry. I get it."

Elliott turned from the sink and waved his soapy hand at his sister, "What in God's name do I have to do with it, for fuck's sake? I was just in the wrong place at the wrong time. So now I'm a *dishwasher?"* His face was screwed up with anger and frustration.

"Hey, at least you have a place to live and a roof over your head, thanks to your amazing and generous sister. The fact that you can make yourself useful while you're here is just a bonus."

Elliott made a rage-like noise and turned back to the sink, grabbing a bread pan and tossing it into the water. A tsunami of suds rolled onto the countertop, "Goddam power hungry asshole. How would he like to be told he was trapped on this godforsaken island and couldn't leave?"

After his conversation with Maggie, Frank Nelson went to the bakery and found Elliott packing in his make-shift apartment.

Frank had requested that Elliott not leave the island until new developments in Arthur Brier's death were resolved.

"What new developments?" Elliott asked, standing over his suitcase, three pairs of socks in one hand and a shirt in the other.

"I'm not at liberty to say, Mr. Simon."

Elliott had argued that he had nothing to do with the man or his death, and that he had, in fact, provided the authorities with a service by reporting the body and staying with it until said authorities had arrived.

"And we appreciate that very much, sir. But for now, we have a few questions that are unanswered and as the primary witness to the body's location and condition when you found it, we would ask you to stay here until such time as we feel it would be appropriate for you to leave."

"Are you placing me under arrest?"

"No, sir. We are not."

"I'm not a lawyer, Constable, but I think you have two choices. You can either arrest me, or not. If you don't arrest me, then I think that means I'm free to do whatever I want, including move to Vancouver where there is a job waiting for me."

"That is true, Mr. Simon, and we have no desire to arrest or detain you. I'm asking you to stay out of your sense of civic duty, just for another forty-eight to seventy-two hours. By then we should have all of our questions answered."

Nelson stood, impassive as a hundred-year-old oak tree, his hands tucked neatly behind his back, his face quiet and calm. It was unusual for Elliott to have to look up at anybody and that, almost as much as being asked to delay his plans for leaving, was pissing him off.

"You're doing the right thing, bro. It's just few days. You could possibly be in Vancouver by Tuesday at noon, if you're that anxious to start your cubicle nation job."

Libby's refusal to be pulled into Elliott's storm gradually calmed him down, although his cheeks remained red. But that could easily have been the heat from the ovens.

The bell on the door of the bakery tinkled pleasantly all morning. Sundays were The Bakeri's busiest day, with locals stocking up on bread and weekenders doing the same plus buying treats and handmade sandwiches for the ferry ride home. Libby had been up since 3 a.m. and would continue baking all day to meet the demand. She loved Sundays.

Amber appeared at the wide door that separated the front of the store from the kitchens at the back, "Someone to see you, Libby."

Maggie appeared behind Amber carrying a canvas bag with the Juliet Island logo on it.

"Hey! How are you? Recovered from yesterday I hope?" Libby walked around the kitchen's center island, holding her hands up like a surgeon about to perform brain surgery, "I'd hug you but I'd get you all floury."

Elliott looked up from his dishwashing and felt his stomach tighten at seeing Maggie. Today she had a fresh-scrubbed look about her; her braid was tidy and seemed to have a small leather tie at its end. She was wearing jeans and boots, as she had when he'd first seen her at the doctor's office, and a black leather jacket that had lapels like a man's suit.

"Have a seat," Libby said.

"No, thanks Libby. I don't want to disturb you guys. I just came by to drop off Elliott's clothes." She held the canvas bag aloft and smiled at him. "Thank you again, so much, for rescuing me. And for taking care of me after. These are clean, by the way. Freshly washed this morning." She smiled again and laid the bag on one of the bar stools.

Out of the corner of his eye, Elliott saw Libby watching him and Maggie, her head swiveling back and forth just slightly from one to the other.

"Hey, how about this?" Libby said. (*"Here it comes,"* Elliott thought.) "Maggie would you please do me the huge favor of taking my baby brother out of here? He's had a rough morning and I think he could use some fresh air and some company other than mine. Besides, he's about to ruin my best baking dishes and get himself fired. What do you think?"

Maggie looked stunned by the request, so Libby kept talking before Elliott could brush away the request, "You probably need some time off too, right? You had a helluva day yesterday. Why don't I buy you guys lunch? My treat. Amber!" she rushed on, bellowing.

The rainbow hair and piercings popped into the doorway again, "Yo."

"Grab two twenties out of the till please, and give them to Elliott. Thanks, hon."

Almost before he knew what was happening, Elliott was stripped of his rubber gloves and apron, shoved into his coat, and he and Maggie were standing on the sidewalk outside the bakery, Libby and Amber waving at them through the front window.

He looked down at the bills in his hand and then back up to Maggie, "Um. I'm not sure what to say. My sister is a serious force of nature. You don't have to come to lunch with me if you don't want to."

"Are you kidding?" Maggie looked up at him, her eyes twinkling, "Time off, a free lunch AND your company? How could a girl refuse?" She swiveled around on the balls of her feet and looped her arm into his. "Let's go."

Though the day was warming up, it was still mid-May and summer wouldn't arrive in full force for another six weeks. Maggie said she'd like to sit outside, but she kept her leather jacket on.

The patio at the Bluenose Pub had few guests. By Sunday at noon the weekenders had mostly gone to catch their ferries home, and the locals were busy, as usual, with chores and napping. There were just two other tables occupied on the patio, and as often happens when restaurant staff is bored, the service Elliott and Maggie received was sporadic, when it wasn't downright neglectful.

This did not upset Elliott in the slightest. It meant he and the beautiful woman in front of him were hardly interrupted. And she was beautiful. Sitting across the table from her, the sunlight bringing out the copper in her hair, he saw what he had first noticed in the doctor's office. She was physically attractive, yes. Her eyebrows were full and very expressive on her face. She used them to emphasize questions or express dismay. Her brown eyes were flecked with a color he couldn't describe. It was like amber, but both darker and lighter at the same time.

But she had no idea what a stunner she was. That was clear. Elliott had spent five years of dating, engagement and then marriage to Heather, and was around quite a few women (mostly her friends) who knew they were attractive. He recognized the signs: the head positioning to ensure the best angles possible; the hair tossing; the swift checks of their appearance in any and every reflective surface; the constant fidgety straightening of clothes and hair. He had known early on that his wife was only ever hearing a small portion of what he was saying because most of the noise in her head was about herself and how she looked. Her beautiful girlfriends were like that, too. When Elliott and the other husbands from Heather's circle were together they joshed one another about their beautiful wives and how lucky they were, but those conversations always left Elliott feeling sad. Running underneath the bravado and pride was the persistent sound of loneliness. Once he and Heather separated, he resolved never to be in a relationship again where he felt invisible.

Maggie seemed entirely oblivious to her cheekbones and her skin that looked so soft Elliott had to clasp his hands together under the table to keep from touching it. She snorted when she laughed. She crossed her eyes and made funny faces when she was making a joke. She talked with her hands, waving them around and drawing pictures in the air or on the table. When she ordered a burger, fries and a pint of beer for lunch he almost swooned. In all their years together, he had never seen Heather eat anything resembling bread, let alone a deep fried potato.

When their waitress finally set their plates down in front of them, Maggie looked at her lunch with delight.

They were talking about the one thing they had in common. The mysterious death of Maggie's guest, Arthur Brier.

"Tell me about your meeting with Nelson," Elliot said, "Is he always so…immutable?"

"Hmmm," Maggie chewed a fry and thought, "kind of. He's the big man on the island, the only real measure of authority. That gives him a bit of a standing in the community, which I think he's pretty comfortable with." She grinned at Elliott, "Bonus points for 'immutable' by the way, Mr. Parks Canada."

"Hey, I had a good education, thank you very much. I'm not all backwoods and pickup trucks." His tone was light and he grinned back at her, "Did I use it right?"

She laughed, "Exactly right. He is immutable. And also fair. And stoic. And a great infielder."

Elliott gave her a questioning look.

"Island softball team," she said, succinctly.

He nodded, "So, the good news is that he didn't accuse you of pushing Brier out of a boat or anything."

"Right. Although he did manage to make me uncomfortable."

"How so?"

"He kept coming at me with questions about Brier. Did I know he was a developer? How was it that he'd never mentioned that to me? Etcetera." She waved her hand in a circling motion and then picked up her burger and took a bite.

"Did you know he was a developer?"

"No, I honestly didn't." She chewed and swallowed, "But..."

"Yes?"

"I didn't exactly tell the truth about the inn." She looked at him with the full power of her brown eyes, no blinking.

"What do you mean?"

"I didn't lie or anything. But he started poking around about the inn's finances and whether developers have talked to me about selling and I didn't exactly answer him. I don't know why I'm telling you all this. Stop me if I'm boring you."

Elliott looked at her, wondering what to say, but she carried on before he could form a question.

"Developers have been poking around the inn for a while." She looked like she'd just confessed to stealing the crown jewels.

"And?"

"And...that might have been information I should have shared with Nelson."

"Did he ask about that specifically?"

"No."

"Then you have no obligation to tell him your private business. It has nothing to do with Brier's accident. Right?"

She picked a piece of lettuce off her plate and chewed it thoughtfully. "I guess not."

"What are you thinking?"

"Well, I'm just wondering about the weird stuff going on at the inn that I told you about yesterday, and then my thing with the boat and Brier's death and the truth is, a couple of developers have been coming at me pretty hard, wanting to buy the inn and the land it's on. So when Frank told me that Brier was a developer I kind of...I dunno. It made me wonder what's going on. Last night while I slept I kept thinking about it all. Do you ever do that? Think while you sleep?"

"Sometimes. If something's really bothering me."

"What if," she continued with her last thought, "the accidents at the inn are someone deliberately trying to drive me out? What if – and I can't believe I'm saying this – they were planned and orchestrated to get me to sell?"

"How many developers have approached you?"

"Lately? Two, I guess, in the last six months. But I always shut them down immediately. That's my family's place. There's no way I'm leaving."

She picked up a french fry and bit it, gazing out over the water.

The Bluenose's dock was wide and deep, set on tall pilings that were sunk into the shoreline at Moon Bay. The sun glinting off the water sparkled, and offshore the occasional sailboat drifted past, silently. Beyond the bay, in the distance, Elliott could see one of the other gulf islands and a few houses built at the water's edge. He reflected that it was almost as quiet here as it was in the parks that he'd patrolled and made his home in for so many years, although the island was much more occupied. In the parks, if he was in a remote area, he could go weeks without seeing another soul.

Elliott turned his attention away from the water and back to Maggie. She was watching him, sitting with her arms leaning on the table in front of her. They looked at each other without saying anything for a long moment. She had a small mole on one of her earlobes that he felt a pressing need to nibble.

"What were you thinking about?" she asked.

"Quiet."

She glanced out at water again and then back to him, "It's one of my favorite things about living here. I've spent time in cities, of course, but I grew up here, and I honestly don't know how people can stand all the noise in a city. It never stops."

"It never does," Elliott agreed.

Their waitress came to collect their plates, breaking the bubble they were in. When she was gone, Elliott asked Maggie, "So? What are you going to do about the stuff that's making your Spidey senses tingle at the inn?"

She looked a little surprised, "Oh. Well. Nothing, I suppose. I'm not sure what I could do. It's all a little strange and unexplained but it may be nothing. Maybe I'm just being paranoid…" she trailed off.

"I don't think you are."

"You don't?" She scrunched up her nose at him.

"Nope. Remember what I said about my mother's faith in intuition? I think it beats logic most of the time."

"You might be right." But he could tell she still wasn't convinced she should do anything.

"What if I helped you dig around a little bit? See what's going on."

She sat up a little straighter. "Really?"

"Really. I'm a man without a project or purpose these days. My job as a guide at the whale watching outfit is part-time at best. I'm anxious to leave the island," (Did her face fall a little when he said this?) "but Constable Nelson wants me to stay for a few days. Frankly I'm bored and frustrated. What if together we looked into your idea that maybe a developer is trying to force you out? That piece of land you've got is prime real estate and would be worth a fortune to someone who wanted to put a fancy hotel there. Crimes have been committed for far less."

She was very still for a moment. He could see the pulse in her neck throbbing a bit. He wondered if she said no, how he would be able to make excuses to see her before he left the island. But in the end he was saved from such a fate.

She stuck out her hand. "Deal."

His grin was broad as they shook hands. "Deal."

"Am I Sherlock or Watson?" she asked, and grinned at him.

Back at The Bakeri, Elliott and Maggie parted ways, she back to the inn and he to his late afternoon guiding shift at Gerry's whale watching outfit. He arrived a few minutes early and thought this might be an opportunity to get some background from his bosses on the Cormorant Inn and the Archer family. Gerry and Adele had lived on Juliet Island as long as Maggie's parents had and Elliott thought that they had probably known the other couple.

The wooden building that housed the whale watching outfit's office was painted a happy turquoise blue. Elliott suspected that this was Adele's choice; he couldn't imagine Gerry caring about paint colors enough to make a choice, let alone choosing a color as bright and cheery as turquoise blue. He stepped through the office door, closing it behind him. Adele was sitting in front of the dusty computer she perpetually stared at. Elliott brought her a cup of Libby's coffee in a take-out cup, knowing full-well how terrible the coffee was in the office.

She looked up when he handed it over the monitor to her, "You didn't!" She was pleased.

"Two creams and one sugar."

"Never leave me, Elliott. Stay here and take care of me." She sipped the coffee through the hole in the lid and closed her eyes in ecstasy.

"If Frank Nelson has his way, you might get your wish."

She opened one eye and peered at him, questioningly.

"He wants me to stay on the island for a few days until he can get everything sorted out about that dead guy I found yesterday."

"Huh," she grunted and took another sip, cradling the paper cup in both hands. "Frank treats this island like his own personal fiefdom sometimes, Elliott. If you don't want to stay you don't have to, I'm sure."

Elliott sat down in one of the plastic chairs that lined one wall and sipped his coffee, "Sense of civic duty I suppose."

"You're a good man, Charlie Brown."

The clock that hung between the two windows that overlooked the marina told Elliott he had five minutes before Gerry would show up and start yelling at him to get the tour boat ready. He plunged in, "Adele, you knew the Archers over at the Cormorant Inn, didn't you?"

She pushed her wheeled chair away from her desk a bit so she could have a better view of Elliott and crossed one leg over the other, settling in for a chat. "I did. Betty and I were good friends for a long time."

"Tell me about the inn and their running of it."

"What do you want to know?" She paused for a second, eyeing him sharply, "And why?"

"I've been talking to Maggie Archer, and she's concerned about some accidents and things that have been going on at the inn. Not to mention the untimely death of one of her guests. I had lunch with her today and offered to help her look into things to see if perhaps someone is trying to drive her out. I know the inn is one that you recommend to your customers so I wondered if you had some insight into the place that might help me understand it in the context of the island."

"What specifically do you want to know?"

"Well, first, how did the Archer's do financially?"

"Terrible." She sipped her coffee again.

Elliott waited but she didn't seem to be about to expand on that word, so he prompted her, "In what way?"

"In every way, son. They were lovely, lovely people and Betty was one of my closest friends. I still can't get over the fact that she's gone. They were both kind and generous and community-focused. They did so many great things for this island. But," she emphasized the word, "they sucked at financial management."

"How?"

"Oh, heavens. They were generous to a fault, hiring staff they didn't need just to be kind. They hadn't raised the prices at the inn in probably fifteen years at the time they died. They were often so focused on the work around the place that they'd forget to do the books or pay their taxes, so they'd end up with a huge bill from

Revenue Canada. And Reg liked his toys. He was always buying a new boat or car or chainsaw to tinker with. They had so many boats there at one point, they had to pay for moorage at two marinas on the island. Maggie at least had the sense to put a stop to that almost the instant she took over."

Elliott thought about this for a moment, sipping his coffee, "It's such a great piece of property. You'd think it would make money without any effort from them."

"You'd think so. It is probably the best location on the island. But Reg and Betty were just terrible business owners. Like I said, lovely, generous, amazing friends and members of the community, but not a lick of financial sense between them."

"And now they've left Maggie with a mess to clean up," Elliott quipped.

"It's true. That poor girl. She seems to have more of a sense of fiscal responsibility, but she may be too deep in the hole to make a go of it."

"Do you think she'd ever sell?"

"Nope," Adele said, definitively, "Not a chance. She'll have to be forced out. She will never voluntarily leave that place. It's all she's ever known."

Elliott thought about this for a moment, "Do you know anyone who's interested in the property, Adele? Anyone who might stoop to causing accidents that would make Maggie consider selling?"

Adele tapped one manicured fingernail against her coffee cup, thinking, and then answered Elliott's question with a question. "Do you think someone deliberately sabotaged her boat yesterday?"

"You heard about that?"

"Of course I did. News travels faster than the speed of light on this island. It's all anyone is talking about."

"I don't know for sure if Maggie's boat was tampered with, and we can't check since it's at the bottom of Tyee Bay. But, just between you and me, she says it's not the first time something inexplicable has happened at the inn."

"Huh. Interesting." The click, click, click of her nail continued, while Elliott waited patiently, leaning his head back against the wall behind him. He could feel his shoulder muscles were tight from the strenuous paddling he'd done the day before and he took a bit of pleasure in the feeling.

When Libby had hooked Elliott up with the Stewarts a week ago for this part-time guiding gig she had told him that Adele and Gerry were a couple of the longest term residents on the island. And that they saw and heard everything that went on. "They know everyone," Libby had said, "And their customers bring them news from all over the island; from all the different hotels and restaurants and inns. Adele's true genius is extracting information from people without seeming like she is." Libby had snorted, ruefully, "I told her about my divorce within five minutes of knowing her. And you know me. I never tell people that kind of private shit. Hell, I didn't tell you'd I was divorced until six months later."

So Elliott was prepared to wait for Adele's insight about, or assessment of, who might not have Maggie's best interests at heart. He waited and after a few minutes her finger stopped tapping. He raised his head and looked at her, hopefully.

"You know the one person that comes to mind?"

"Who?"

"Well, it's a few people I guess. The Keith brothers; Michael, Trent and Bill."

"Why them? And who are they?"

"For a few reasons." Adele said, answering his first question. She put her coffee cup on her desk and crossed her arms in front of her. This was serious business. "First of all, they own a competing hotel. Keith Point Lodge over on Wild Rose Road. And they are never shy about running down any of the other inns and B&Bs and hotels on the island. Where most other people who own a place like that have a 'live and let live' approach and know that variety in the types of accommodation that's offered on the island is only good for the island economy, the Keiths think the opposite. They are a 'kill or be killed' family. They spread rumors and gossip about the other inns and hotels, they take any opportunity to cut fellow hotel owners down, they treat every encounter with their fellow hotel owners like it's a fight to the death."

"Wow. Charming."

"Oh, it gets better. They have a property, like I said, on Wild Rose Road. 'Keith Point Lodge' which is a hilarious name because it's not on the water. It's not on the 'point' of anything, although it is about a five minute walk from Spirit Lake. But it's a nice enough place. They bought it years ago when the Eastern family was selling it. Changed the name, of course. But that wasn't enough for them. There was a waterfront B&B about a five minute drive from them, owned by a couple named Bob and Ellen Tozer. Bob fell ill with cancer, poor man, about five years ago, and while Ellen was dealing with all that, the Keith boys were on her like a duck on a June bug and basically bullied her into selling the B&B. Bob was in hospital in Vancouver, and Ellen was trying to run the B&B and going back and forth to Vancouver General a couple times a week. Bob was seriously ill and Ellen didn't think he would survive; she was terrified about losing him, naturally. He had been the driving force behind owning the B&B, so when the Keiths started talking to her they played up the fact that she could be left all alone saddled with the business and no one to help her run it."

Elliott shook his head in wonder.

Adele continued. "Ellen panicked. She didn't say anything to Bob because she didn't want to worry him. She up and sold the place to the Keiths while Bob was still in hospital. And then," Adele sighed and shook her head, "Bob got better. He beat the cancer and was like a new man. Ellen had to tell him that she'd sold his business out from under him to those leeches, the Keiths."

"Oh, no."

"Oh, yes. And the worst part is they convinced her to sell it for way below its value. They got her to sell it to them privately, without using a real estate agent, and the price they got it for was criminal. They should be in jail for that."

"Wow. These Keiths sound like a treat."

"They're a piece of work, that's for sure. Several of us who knew Bob and Ellen tried to convince her not to sell. Gerry and I kept having her over for dinner to talk to her. But she wouldn't hear anything about it. She was panicked. Terrified and not thinking straight at all. The only future she could see was one without Bob, with her holding the bag on a business she liked but wasn't invested in if Bob wasn't around." Adele sighed again. "She thought the Keiths were doing her a favor."

"Good God."

"So," Adele picked up her cup again and took a sip, "if there was one family that could be behind any dirty deeds going on at Maggie's inn, I'd say it is more than likely the Keiths."

The office door flew open and crashed into the wall behind it. Gerry came into the room, cigarette dangling from his lips, rubber boots squeaking on the floor.

"Where's that fucker, Simon? We've got customers waiting."

"No smoking in the office, Gerry." Adele pointed one finger at her husband. He turned and threw his cigarette out the door onto the dock, where it fell through the slats into the water. When he turned back, Adele said, "Elliott's right here."

Gerry spotted Elliott in the guest chair, "There you are, you useless tit. Three of the passengers are here, so get your ass down to the Zodiac and saddle up."

"Aye, aye, captain." Elliott stood and walked to the door, winking at Adele as he passed, "Thanks for your help."

"Anytime, hon. You bring Maggie by for dinner. I'll make my special Salt Spring roast leg of lamb for you both."

"I won't be here long enough to keep that date, I'm afraid, Adele. But thank you very much for offering."

Elliott crossed the office threshold and walked down the sloping dock toward the little crowd waiting beside the tour boat. Adele, lost in thought, whispered to herself, "I don't think you'll be leaving anytime soon, sweetheart. You've got it bad for Maggie Archer, whether you know it or not." She looked up at her husband who was rifling through some papers tacked to the cork board across from her desk, "Remember when we first met, Gerry?"

He spoke without turning around, "I sure do. You had an ass like a ripe peach."

Adele gazed out the open door, lost in thought. Then her husband surprised her for the first time in about ten years. He spun around and marched over to her desk. Grabbing her office chair by its arms, he pulled it toward him, until he was standing right over her. He bent and kissed her gently but firmly on the mouth. Then he whispered in her ear, "And you still make my heart leap every time I see you."

Ten

THE MORNING LIGHT CAME RUSHING through Elliott's curtainless windows. He rose to consciousness slowly, like a swimmer seeking the surface. Before he opened his eyes he noticed that he was filled with pleasant feelings. In his semiconscious state he examined these and found Maggie at the heart of them. He replayed their lunch from the day before in his mind, remembering her laugh, her face that seemed incapable of an expression of guile, and the ketchup spot she'd had on her cheek that he hadn't told her about until they were ready to leave because he'd thought it was adorable.

Layered in with these feelings was something else he didn't recognize at first. He prodded and massaged the mystery feeling and was able to identify it as purpose. He had a mission to accomplish. For the first time in over a year, since he'd left his parks job and begun the futile effort to save his marriage, he had a purpose. He had a reason to get up that morning, and not just so that he could steal a chocolate croissant from his sister.

He stretched his feet out over the far end of the couch and his arms high above his head. The blanket that had been partly covering him slipped off onto the floor.

A half hour later, showered, shaved and dressed, he took the stairs two at a time down to the ground floor, whistling all the way. He grabbed the backdoor handle and pulled, but the door resisted him, standing still in its frame. He peered through the window into the kitchen. The lights were off, the ovens dark. He realized it was Monday. Libby closed the bakery on Mondays.

Even the absence of chocolate croissants couldn't dampen the man's mood. He turned and went to his truck. Climbing in, he pointed it toward a greasy spoon diner he'd heard mention of, still whistling.

Keith Point Lodge greeted him impassively as he drove down the gravel driveway, having found the place with Adele's specific directions. The main building was two stories with a green metal roof, grey vertical siding, exposed beams at the roofline and lots of wooden framed windows looking out onto a picnic and barbecue area. There was an additional building attached to the main house by a covered breezeway. This was clad in identical style, although it was single story and slightly less imposing. Elliott parked his truck in an area marked 'Guest parking'. He walked through the two-story building's entrance, which had cedar poles at least four feet in circumference supporting the roof over the entryway. There were huge clay pots on either side of the doors, filled with grasses and other perennial greenery.

The inn's lobby was silent. Through a doorway Elliott could see what looked like a living room or perhaps a common area for guests. Two green loveseats sat facing one another, a coffee table squatting between them. The reception desk stretched across the lobby on his left. A computer monitor shared the desk surface with scattered papers, a notebook liberally covered with stickers of what Elliott assumed were the names and logos of bands he was too old to be familiar with, and several half-empty coffee mugs, milky clouds floating on the surface of the brown, deeply unappetizing liquid inside them. The desk was unmanned so he spent some time poking around near the spinning shelves that held postcards and greeting cards. There was a small bookcase against one wall that held books that seemed, at a quick glance, to be focused on local travel and the history of the Gulf Islands, and Juliet Island in particular. One book, called *Pioneer Island,* he had seen in several stores and businesses during his short stay here. It must be the most famous literary offering from Juliet. He picked it up and flipped it over. The black and white photograph of a woman with a generously sized bun on the crown of her head, a cameo broach pinned to her blouse at her throat, and the unsmiling expression of photographs taken in the late 19th and early 20th centuries stared out at him.

Behind him a voice said, "Can I help you?"

He turned and found a teenager looking at him, somewhat resentfully. She was wearing a t-shirt that was a little small for her breasts, which seemed a little large for her frame. Her jeans looked the way a boa constrictor looks when it unhinges its jaw and swallows an animal whole – stretched almost to the bursting point – so Elliott wondered if 'two sizes too small' was the look she was going for. She had more makeup on than he'd possibly ever seen on a woman, let alone one so young. He wondered briefly why she would want to cover up her flawless, youthful skin so thoroughly. There were many women in Hollywood who would have traded their souls for her skin. He thought she might also have false eyelashes on but he couldn't be totally sure without asking her to tilt her head toward a light. Her expression was one of pained exasperation. He imagined she was the daughter of one of the owners, pressed into service for the family business, whether she liked it or not. She did not appear to like it.

Elliott put the famous island pioneer back on the shelf and said, "Yes, you can help me. I'm looking to speak to one of the Keith brothers."

She jerked one of her thumbs over her shoulder, "Out back."

Elliott waited a moment, but there was no other information forthcoming. "Thank you," he said and left through the front doors. He blinked in the sunlight and said a silent prayer of thanks that he'd survived his own teenage years in essentially one piece. It wasn't easy.

Elliott strolled along the length of the lodge, following a gravel path. He spotted a couple of wood and iron benches placed strategically to take advantage of the view. The lodge sat on a high point on the island, and though it wasn't waterfront, it did have spectacular views. Looking down through the pine trees, Elliott could see the now familiar vista of the dark Salish Sea in the foreground and humped, forested islands in the background. He kept wandering, still enjoying the feeling of purpose that had brought him to this place. He realized that for a while he'd been hearing the slow but steady sound of a hammer driving nails home. Following his ears, he eventually found a man standing on a ladder that was propped up against a small, windowless shed, nailing shingles onto the shed's roof. Elliott wondered if this was one of the Keith brothers, or just an employee.

"Excuse me?" he said, looking up at the top of the ladder, hands in his jeans pockets, hoping he had a disarming look on his face.

The man stopped between hammer strikes, turned and pulled a few nails out of his mouth, "Help you?" His face had the lined and worn look of someone who spent most of his time outside. Elliott imagined that's what his face could look like in ten years, after all the sun damage it had received during his parks days. The man's eyes were hooded by brows pulled together and there was an air of exasperation about him, as though Elliott were a three-year-old child who was constantly interrupting.

"I'm looking for Michael Keith."

"You found him. What can I do for you?"

Now that Elliott was in front of the person he'd been looking for, he realized he hadn't planned what to ask. He couldn't come out and say, 'Have you been sabotaging The Cormorant Inn?' so he made up a lie on the spot. "My name's Elliott Greg," he fudged, using his middle name as his surname. "I'm looking to buy an inn or a B&B on one of the Gulf Islands. I'm spending this week touring around, doing a bit of research, and I wonder if I could ask you a few questions." Keith's eyes stayed cold and unwelcoming, and Elliott belatedly remembered what Adele had said about the family not being helpful to their fellow hotel operators. He quickly added, "I understand that this is one of the most successful properties on Juliet Island, so I thought you'd probably know quite a bit about the market and the opportunities available here or on another island."

Keith's eyes softened almost imperceptibly, and Elliott mentally breathed a sigh of relief.

"Sure. I can tell you a bit." Keith drove another nail into the shingle he was holding down. "Do you mind if I keep working? I've got a hell of a lot to get through today."

"Not at all," Elliott smiled but to no effect. The hotel owner kept his eyes on the shingles. "I suppose that's one of the downsides, isn't it? All the constant work."

"You can say that again. We own two properties – that's me and my brothers – and, let me tell you, not a day goes by that I don't have a list as long as my arm of stuff I gotta do. It never ends." He drove another nail home with force.

"How long have you owned this place?"

"Oh, I guess about fifteen years now. And we own another, smaller one over on the east side of the island. That one's waterfront."

"Nice." Elliott tried to sound impressed. "Do you have plans to keep expanding? Any more properties you're interested in?"

"Not officially, no."

"But unofficially?" Elliott squinted up at Keith and almost batted his eyelashes when the man glanced down. He felt a surge of adrenaline and wondered if this was what it was like to work for the CIA.

"Well, unofficially I guess you could say we always keep our eye open for new opportunities. This is a big island with lots of room for growth, and I don't think the tourist market is tapped out yet. We sailed through the recession in '08 and for the next couple of years after that, even though so many businesses folded. I think that in a place this beautiful you'd have to be pretty stupid to screw up."

Elliott heard voices to his left and turned his head. Coming along a walkway that led back toward the front of the property was a middle-aged couple dressed in spring jackets, jeans and hiking boots.

Keith followed Elliott's gaze and nodded at the couple, "Mornin'. How was your hike?"

The couple stopped and looked up at Keith, "Spectacular, Michael. Thanks for the recommendation."

"Glad to hear it. You could try the Silash Trail tomorrow if you're looking for another walk. It's a little longer, and a bit steep at times, but it goes out to a waterfront park, which is nice."

"Maybe we'll give that a try," the husband said. They both smiled at Elliott and then kept walking, their feet crunching on the gravel path.

Elliott waited until they were out of earshot and then started to speak again, but Keith beat him to it, "That's another thing. You gotta be all things to all people in this business. If a guest is friendly and wants to chat, you gotta chat to 'em. But if they want to be left alone, you gotta respect that, too. It's a people business."

Keith didn't seem like a people person to Elliott. He had a hard shell that was almost visible, like his flannel shirt, although it had faded into the background slightly when the hikers had approached and talked to him. Elliott expected that he knew how to turn the charm on for his guests.

He tried to get Keith back to the topic of being a hotelier, "Is there a lot of competition when inns and B&Bs go up for sale?"

"It is an island, in case you hadn't noticed." Keith's tone was sharp, and Elliott suspected this was his true personality coming through. "So when the land is gone, it's gone. But we're a ways away from that yet."

Elliott played with a rock near one of his boots, attempting to appear casual, "I guess all the waterfront land is gone, though, hey?"

Keith brought his hammer down with another whack and reached into his tool belt for more nails, "You got that right. Decent waterfront property is harder to find than whores at the Vatican."

Charming, Elliott thought. "Are there any waterfront properties that you think might be coming up for sale soon?"

Another nail slammed home in the shed roof and Keith glanced down at Elliott, perhaps sizing him up for the first time. "Now why on earth would I share that with you, fella? I keep those cards close to my chest." He tried to make it sound lighthearted but his voice was without warmth or friendliness. Elliott suspected he had just about played out this man's tolerance for talking.

Elliott asked a few more vague questions related to the weather and the ferries, subjects he thought wouldn't raise any red flags with Keith. Then he excused himself and walked back to his truck, mulling over his experience of Michael Keith. Was this a man who would deliberately sabotage another island business? He wished he'd had more time to talk to the man, to size him up. An impression formed after five minutes could not be relied upon. "Nice try, Hercule Poirot," he muttered to himself as he climbed behind the wheel of his truck.

Eleven

"Have you seen June since yesterday?"

Having come around from the great room, Maggie was leaning, peering over from the guest side of the reception desk. Sparrow looked up from the computer screen with wide, distracted eyes.

"Whaaa?" she said, playing with the beads around her throat, her multiple silver bracelets clinking together.

"Have you seen June Brier today? Did you notice if she came down for breakfast?"

"I did not notice. I've kind of had my head buried here. I'm having an issue with Word Press."

"With what?" Now it was Maggie's turn to look puzzled.

"The back end of our website. I'm trying to get it to do something it doesn't seem to want to do."

"I'll take your word for it. Is Taylor around?"

"No, it was Melissa on breakfast this morning. I can hear her in the kitchen." Sparrow motioned with her eyes toward the kitchen door.

Dragging her hand along the smooth wooden countertop, Maggie walked along the length of the desk and then around its corner. She spotted Melissa, the other part-time waitress, loading the dishwasher with breakfast plates and bowls.

"Melissa?"

"Maggie?" Melissa mimicked Maggie's questioning tone.

"Did you happen to see June Brier this morning at breakfast?"

Maggie grabbed a handful of dirty cutlery from the plates on the counter and added them to the silverware basket on the dishwasher's pullout tray.

"June Brier?" Melissa said, thinking, "Blonde? Tiny? Slight case of LA face?"

"What's LA face?"

"You know." Melissa put the plate she was holding in the dishwasher and put her hands up on either side of her own face and pulled back so her skin stretched over her bones.

"Oh," Maggie lightly slapped Melissa's hands down from her face, "yes. Okay, I get it. That's her. Stop. She just lost her husband."

"My bad." Melissa bent again to add more dishes to the machine.

"Have you seen her today?"

"No. Not today, I don't think." Melissa scrunched her face up a bit, thinking, "No I'm almost positive I didn't see her down here today."

"Okay, thanks." Maggie went to the buffet table and grabbed a clean plate from the stack put there for breakfast. She grabbed a croissant from the basket with the tongs, and then a packet of butter and one of jam. Moving down the table she placed a small bowl on the plate and scooped some fruit into it. She set the plate down on a tray at the far end of the table, and poured coffee from the carafe into a mug. Adding two creamer containers and two sugar packets to the tray, she picked it up and turned to go upstairs.

June Brier was staying in one of the Starfish Suites. Both suites looked out over the cliffs and down to the ocean below. They were the largest suites in the inn, with spacious bathrooms that included soaker tubs, a separate glass shower stall with two shower heads, a sitting area with two chair-and-a-halfs set at a ninety degree angle and sharing an ottoman, a queen-sized bed and unimpeded views of the ocean and islands beyond Juliet.

Maggie knocked at June's door. She could hear some quiet noise inside and then the door opened to reveal the widow. She was dressed in perfectly fitting boyfriend jeans and a blousey long-sleeved t-shirt that looked like it might be made of hemp or bamboo or some other exotic fiber. Wrapped around her neck several times was a thin, pink scarf.

"Oh. Maggie. I thought you might be Frank Nelson."

"Um, no. It's me," Maggie was thrown off slightly. June's face was fully made up and every blonde hair was in place. She even had lipstick on her overly inflated lips. Maggie thought her eyelashes looked a little too full and long to be authentic. "I was worried because I hadn't seen you downstairs for breakfast. I thought I'd bring you something." She made a little offering motion with the tray she was holding.

"I never eat before noon."

"Oh. Okay. Well." There was nowhere to put the tray, so Maggie stood with it in front of her. "I just wanted to see how you were doing. Are you okay?"

June's blue eyes searched Maggie's for a second and then what was perhaps her social mask fell a bit, "No, I'm not really okay. I'm sorry for being rude. I just…I don't quite know how to handle this." She touched the corner of one of her eyes with a French manicured nail.

"I'm so sorry, June. I don't have any idea how you're feeling but I want you to know that anything we can do for you would be our pleasure."

"Well, the least I can do is invite you in." June smiled wanly and stepped aside so Maggie could enter.

The suite was untidy; clothes strewn here and there, a suitcase lay open on the bed, clothes spilling out of it. Maggie glanced into the bathroom and saw towels and underwear scattered across the floor. She set the breakfast tray on the bed and motioned toward the suitcase, "Are you leaving?"

June flopped down in one of the comfy chairs by the window, "What? Oh, no, I was just looking for something."

Maggie stood with her arms folded across her body, not sure what to do or say now that she was in the room. June looked at her with something like contempt in her eyes, but Maggie chastised herself for judging this woman who had just lost her husband. She decided to broach the subject she was most interested in. As gently as she could, she asked, "June, was Arthur a land developer?"

The widow pulled her feet up onto the chair and crossed her legs, sitting yoga style, "Sort of. Why?"

"I had a chat with Constable Nelson yesterday, and he was interested in the fact that Arthur was a developer. He wondered if Arthur was interested in the Cormorant Inn."

"I didn't really pay too much attention to Arthur's work. He was always going on about whatever his latest project was. But yes, I think he was interested in this…" she looked out the window past the balcony and down to the ocean, "place." She made it sound like a four-letter word.

Maggie noticed her back go up. June had managed to be insulting without really saying much. It was conveyed in her superior and angry attitude. It felt to Maggie as though resentment was floating through the air in the room. But she pressed on, not knowing when she would get another chance to ask June these questions. "So was he looking into the inn because he was thinking of buying it?"

June turned her head back to Maggie, and the look in her eyes made Maggie's blood cool a bit. June was looking at Maggie the way a snake looks at a mouse. "Not him," she finally said, "but some of the people he works with. They tend to buy beat-up old resorts or hotels and spruce them up and turn them into profitable businesses."

Now Maggie was positive June was trying deliberately to be insulting. Grief did funny things to people. She took a breath and kept a lid on her indignation, speaking through slightly clenched teeth, "The Cormorant is a viable business now."

"Really? Because every time we've been here there's been some problem that needs to be fixed."

Maggie felt her ire rising but she didn't want to get into an argument with June. Especially not forty-eight hours after the woman's husband had died. She decided it was probably best to cut her losses and get out. She picked up the breakfast tray. "Please let me know if there's anything we can do for you today, June. Again, I am so sorry for your loss."

"Thanks." June picked at something on her pant leg.

"Should I ask the front desk to prepare your bill so you can check out as quickly as possible?"

June looked up and frowned at Maggie, "Check out? I'm not checking out."

"Oh! Sorry. I made an assumption you'd want to go home as soon as possible."

"Nope," she looked out the window again, "there's nothing for me there. I might as well stay here and see if Barney Fife and his men learn anything more about my husband's death. Speaking of which," she brought the full force of her blue eyes onto Maggie again, "why would Arthur go out on the water? Had he done that before when he stayed here?"

"That's a great question. I don't have an answer, but I will find out. We ask the guests to always sign out the boats when they use them. And sign a waiver. I'll go back through our records and see when he had signed out a boat before."

"He usually arrived a couple of days before I did when we stayed here. He'd come over on a Wednesday or Thursday and then I'd come over on Saturday morning. I didn't feel the need to spend as much time here as he obviously did."

Again Maggie felt as though she'd been insulted. She turned to leave and, balancing the tray on one hand, reached for the door knob on the room's door.

"Can I ask you something?"

Surprised, Maggie turned back around to face June. "Sure."

"Have you ever been married?"

This was pretty personal coming from someone who seemed to be intent on hurting Maggie's feelings, but she answered anyway, "Um. No. I haven't."

"Why not?"

Now we're besties? Maggie thought. "Never met the right guy, I guess." It was her standard answer and it was usually enough to mollify those who asked that particular question.

June, however, seemed to need more this morning. "You never felt the need to have a man around? Especially running a place like this on your own?"

Maggie almost smiled at this. "Well, no, actually. I haven't ever felt that need." She tried to keep the defense she felt out of her voice as she explained further. "First of all, I'm not on my own. I have amazing staff who help me out with everything. And also, my mother raised me believing that I'm as capable and strong as any man. She happened to be married when she was running the inn with my dad, but she always made it clear to me that being fully myself was more important than being part of a partnership, even though she and my dad had an amazing marriage. They were best friends and strong partners their whole time together. In fact, I think that's why they died within six months of one another. Once my dad was gone, my mum just couldn't conceive a life without him. They called it heart disease but I think she died of a broken heart." Maggie paused for a second, thinking, "So actually, that's a third thing. I can't imagine being in a relationship that wasn't as good and mutually supportive and loving as theirs was. It was a great model for me. And I've never met a man who I felt I could hold up to that standard."

June looked at Maggie as though she'd answered in a strange, foreign tongue, her brow slightly furrowed, her head pushed forward on her neck a bit, "But…aren't you, like, lonely?"

"Sometimes," Maggie said, "but most of the time, no, I'm not."

June shook her head slightly, a tiny motion of disbelief and dismissal. Maggie realized that the moment of intimacy she'd just shared had been wasted. She didn't think June had understood any of it.

She turned again, and pulled open the suite's door, telling June again to let them know if they could do anything for her. June didn't acknowledge that Maggie had said anything. She was staring out the window again, slowly coiling a blonde lock around one of her index fingers.

"How did it go with Princess Buttercup?"

Maggie had been sitting at the front desk, going through the mail and other correspondence for the inn. She looked up as Sparrow folded herself into the other desk chair and set her cup of coffee down beside the computer monitor. "Who?"

"June Brier."

"What did you call her?"

"Princess Buttercup. Doesn't she strike you as someone who believes in the very core of her being that it's the rest of the world's purpose to serve her and make her life easier?"

"Stop being rude."

Sparrow poked Maggie's ribs with her bare toe. "You agree with me."

"I do but you won't get me to admit that under oath. She's our guest and she's out of her mind with grief."

"Do you think so?"

"I do. She is definitely in the throes of deep grief. She's angry and bitter and…being more rude than usual."

"Ah! See. You do think she's a princess."

"Shut up and tell me about the new brochures. How are they looking?"

Maggie sipped her coffee while Sparrow, the in-house graphic designer and technical guru, front desk attendant and purveyor of handmade organic essential oils, walked her boss though the changes to the inn's brochures. Sparrow had printed up an example of the new Cormorant Inn rack cards and trifold brochure.

"The rack cards are for the ferries, right?"

"Yep."

"And you added the new rate information to the brochure?"

"Yes, boss."

"You're a marvel, sweetheart. Thank you." Maggie leaned over and kissed Sparrow's cheek. "I'll proof read these today and then they can go to print."

"Do you want to see the website changes I made?"

"I do. Let me get a fresh latté." Maggie trotted into the kitchen and whipped herself up a foamy, highly caffeinated mug of joy. She returned to the front desk and pulled her chair closer to Sparrow's so she could view Sparrow's monitor. She sipped her drink and made a small groan of pleasure.

"You don't need a boyfriend. You've got that cappuccino machine."

"Damn right. Okay, show me."

Part-way through the website demo Carol arrived, cradling her own mug, which declared, "It's not a hangover. It's wine flu."

Maggie looked over her shoulder at her friend, "You're here early."

"Couldn't sleep. Figured I might as well work on last quarter's tax filing. What's that?" She pointed to an image of a pink elephant dancing in a tutu in the sidebar of the site.

"That's a placeholder," Sparrow said, "I'm going to add a widget there where people can sign up for our newsletter."

"This isn't live is it?" Maggie looked horrified.

"No. Of course not. It won't go live until it's finalized."

"But the existing website is still up, right?"

"Yes, Luddite, it won't come down until I switch it out for the new site."

"Forgive me. Technology is not my sweet spot."

Sparrow glanced back at Carol and rolled her eyes.

"I saw that," Maggie said, "Let's talk Trip Tips, since we seem to be having an impromptu staff meeting. How's that going? Any more negative reviews lately?"

"Nope," with a few clicks of her mouse, Sparrow found the Cormorant Inn page on the Trip Tips website. "All is well. We even got a couple of positive reviews yesterday."

"Fantastic. And when people check out are you asking them to leave a review?"

"Yes ma'am. See? This one from yesterday is from the Arnolds."

Maggie leaned toward the screen, "Oooo, five stars!" she fairly squealed, "God bless you, Ron and Karen."

The front door to the inn swung open, and all three women looked up from the computer screen. Elliott Simon walked through the door, smiling at them. "Good morning, ladies. Something seems to have your attention."

"We got a five star review on Trip Tips, thanks to Sparrow's awesome front desk work. She charms the pants off our guests and they leave happy."

"Really?" Elliott raised his eyebrows, "Exactly what kind of an inn is this?"

Maggie blushed furiously, realizing what she'd said. Carol, being the more experienced flirt, rescued her friend, "Come and stay with us sometime, Mr. Simon, and you'll find out for yourself."

Now it was Elliott's turn to blush.

Maggie stood up out of her chair, "Ignore her," she said to Elliott. "How can we help you?"

Elliott held aloft a cake box, "Libby baked this late yesterday and asked me to bring it by."

"Thank you," Maggie reached over the counter and took the box from him, "Tonight's dessert."

Before Maggie knew what was happening, Carol smoothly took the box from her hands, "I'll put this in the kitchen for Greg." She made eye contact with Sparrow as she turned to go, "Come with me. I need to show you something in the kitchen."

But Sparrow was hunkered down in front of her computer, "I'm just going to finish this page…ow!"

Carol had kicked her ankle. "Sparrow," she said, eyes wide with meaning, "come and see this thing."

Sparrow stood up, straightening her red tunic, "Excuse me. I have a thing to see in the kitchen, apparently."

When both women were gone, Maggie suddenly noticed the quiet in the lobby. She could hear the clock behind her ticking and the sound of her breath. "So," she said, "What's up, Elliott?" *Smooth,* she thought.

"Well, in addition to being a cake delivery boy, I wanted to fill you in on the conversation I had with Michael Keith."

"Wow, that was fast. When did you talk to him?"

"This morning. So I was wondering if you'd like to go have a bite to eat and I'll give you my impressions."

"That would be fantastic." She glanced down at the desk, "But you know what? Now is not a good time. I'm in the middle of a bunch of paperwork and stuff for the inn, and Carol has the GST filing to do and I should probably help with that." She paused, feeling her heart hammering in her chest, "Never a dull moment!" Even to herself, her chipperness sounded ridiculous.

Elliott stood up a little straighter and tapped his hands on the counter. "Sure. Another time then." He backed up a pace. "Why don't you call me at the bakery when you've got a minute and I'll fill you in then?"

"Sounds good." Maggie smiled at him and watched as he turned and pulled open the door to leave. She wasn't too preoccupied to notice how great his butt looked in his jeans.

The door closed with its pleasing thunk and before Maggie knew what was happening Carol had grabbed her upper arms from behind and was practically shouting in her right ear, "Are you fucking kidding me? That handsome, handsome man just asked you out and you blew him off." She spun Maggie around to face her and gripped her shoulders tightly, glaring into her friend's eyes.

"He did not ask me out," Maggie tried to squirm away but Carol's grip was too tight, "We decided yesterday to do a little digging into the accidents and stuff here at the inn and he was just going to tell me about a conversation he had with Michael Keith. He did *not* ask me out."

Carol continued glaring at her friend and then looked over her shoulder at Sparrow, who was standing in the kitchen doorway, taking a bite out of an apple. Carol jerked her head at the girl in a 'Tell her' motion.

Sparrow nodded and spoke around her apple, "He totally likes you, Mags. He just asked you out."

Maggie looked back and forth from one woman to the other, defiance in her eyes at first and then realization dawning, "Shit."

"Get out there," Carol propelled her friend around from behind the desk and toward the front door, "Go! Go!"

Maggie dug her heels in and tried to grab onto the wide, wooden bannister that led to the suites upstairs. "No! Are you kidding? I'll look like an idiot, running after him."

"If you don't go out there now and tell him you've changed your mind, I'm going to waltz out there and tell him I'll have lunch with him." Carol paused, then adding for emphasis, "And it won't just be lunch, either."

Maggie knew Carol well enough after thirty years of friendship to know that she would do exactly what she said, without hesitation. Maggie lifted her shoulders up, turned, and pulled open the front door.

She could see Elliott's truck idling in the short term lot. She trotted across the gravel, her heart in her mouth, terrified and, if she was totally honest with herself, also exhilarated. Elliott was twisted in his seat, about to back up. She tapped on the window.

He startled slightly and turned to face her. She made an apologetic face at him through the glass and lifted her hand in a slight wave. He put the truck in park and pushed a button on the armrest. The window slid down with an electric noise.

"Hey," she said.

"Hey," he said back. She could see in his eyes that he was slightly hurt.

"Sorry about that." She fidgeted and shoved her hands in her back pockets and then took them out again, "I, uh, I'd love to take you up on your offer and hear about what Michael Keith said."

"Really?"

"Really. I really would. I'll say it again. I *really* would." She smiled at him again, her exhilaration morphing into self-consciousness and embarrassment while he sat quietly, watching her. If he didn't agree soon she'd have to run screaming back into the inn. She glanced away, thinking, *breathe.*

"What about your tax filing?"

She looked back and though his tone sounded a little dark, his eyes were smiling. She grinned at him, realizing he was teasing her. "I think maybe Carol can handle that on her own."

"Oh, good. Because…" he leaned back in his seat slightly so she could see the passenger seat beside him where a large wicker basket with a handle sat. It appeared to be full of wrapped packages of food and Maggie could see the top of a wine bottle sticking out of one corner of the basket. It was sitting on a folded blue tartan blanket.

"You brought a picnic."

"I did."

She met his eyes again and held them for a few seconds. "I'll get my jacket."

Twelve

THE TRUCKED BUMPED AND BOUNCED down a narrow rutted track only wide enough for one vehicle, its wheels following the grooves in the forest floor. Elliott leaned forward in his seat, peering through the windshield. The track wound on, curving slightly at times. Maggie noticed a stirring behind her bellybutton, a feeling she hadn't had in a very long time. She enjoyed Elliott's quiet as he concentrated on keeping his truck on the track and not bumping it against one of the large and imposing spruce trees that crowded the path, their branches scraping against the windows and the side of the truck.

Elliott put his foot on the brake and slowed the truck to a stop. He looked over at Maggie, "I think Libby gave me the wrong directions. I don't think this is where we're supposed to be."

Maggie smiled at him, "We're almost there. Keep going."

"You know about this place?"

"Of course I know about this place. I was born on this island, remember?"

"Right. So keep going?"

"Keep going."

The truck edged forward and picked up a tiny bit of speed. After two or three quiet minutes, Maggie pointed to the left. "There. See? You can park there."

Carved out of the forest was a space big enough for two cars, if they were friendly. Elliott pulled in and turned off the truck. "I was thinking we were going to have to reverse all the way down that track to the road." He lifted the basket off Maggie's lap and they hopped out of the car. Holding the blanket in one arm, Maggie opened the back door for Ruby, who had been invited along as well. The brown dog began sniffing the forest floor immediately, her tail aloft.

"Where to now?" Elliott asked, "Libby said there would be a trail."

Maggie pointed to their left. Elliott squinted and shrugged, "I'll take your word for it. Lead on."

The path forced them to walk single file, but Maggie didn't mind. She knew it was only a five minute walk to where they were headed.

"How far is it?" Elliott asked.

"About an hour," she answered without looking back. When he didn't say anything for several moments she finally turned and winked at him.

He grinned, "Thank God for that. My arm would have fallen off after an hour of carrying this basket."

Ruby crashed around in the forest on either side of them, crossing the trail in front of or behind them at regular intervals, her nose down, her eyes alight with pleasure. Soon Maggie could see the spot where the forest thinned out and then stopped. She stepped out onto the mossy rocks and to one side, so that Elliott could stand beside her and take in the view.

"Wow!" he said.

She didn't answer, letting him soak in what he was seeing.

They were on a bluff, a rocky headland covered in moss and pine needles. Below them the sea sparkled and glinted, silent. Several hundred yards offshore there was a tiny island, perhaps the size of a grocery store parking lot, with a small dock sticking out into the water. Maggie watched as Elliott looked left and then right. She liked the way his eyes seemed to be appreciating what he was seeing. Finally he turned and met her eyes, "Nice."

"Not bad, hey? C'mon up here. We can spread the blanket out."

They walked up a slight incline in the smooth rock face to a plateau where there was a flat space the size of an average living room, as though specifically designed for picnics. Off to one side was a wooden bench with iron arms and legs, bolted into the rock just in front of a twisted, red Arbutus tree. Elliott wandered over to it and read the plaque fixed on the top rail of its back. Maggie knew what it said.

An ever fixed mark. 12 September 1975

She opened the blanket and shook it, letting it fall gently toward the rocks, and then tugged at its corners to spread it out to its full width and length. Elliott joined her and set the basket down. Elliott seemed shy as he gestured for Maggie to sit and then did so himself. The day had warmed up and they both removed their jackets. Ruby came thundering out of the underbrush, her nails clicking on the rocks, and careened over to the blanket, sticking her nose in the basket.

"Hey!" Maggie chided her, "Out."

Ruby looked at Maggie, making sure she meant it, and then trotted off in the direction opposite from where she'd come, pretending not to care that she wasn't invited to the picnic.

"First things first," Elliott said. He dug around in the basket until he came up with two stainless steel cups that were shaped like wine glasses without stems. He handed these to Maggie and then pulled the wine bottle out of the basket as well, disrupting a small round of cheese. He unscrewed the top of the wine bottle and motioned to Maggie to hold her cup out. She did so and he poured generously, then switched to the second cup. Bottle returned to the basket, Maggie handed him one of the cups and they touched glasses, toasting.

"To new friends," he said.

"New friends."

Maggie sipped her wine and was suddenly awash with giddiness.

She realized this was the first date she'd been on in at least…well, she had to think about it. Had it really been that long? She looked over at Elliott, who was poking around inside the basket, examining the contents. He looked up when he felt Maggie's gaze on him.

"Is it too early to break out the cheese and crackers?"

"Not at all," she said. "I'm starved."

With the sun warming their faces and the occasional seagull floating by, they munched on brie and crackers. There was also homemade antipasto that Maggie recognized as being Edith Fleming's from the Farmer's Market, a loaf of Libby's French bread, herbed butter, a tin of olives, a jar of pickled asparagus, also from the market, cloth napkins, forks, knives and a bottle of sparkling water.

"She thinks of everything."

"Who?"

"Libby. She packed the basket." Elliott looked up at her and explained further. "She called me just as I was leaving the Keith's and instructed me to come to her house and pick it up and then go and get you so I could tell you my news."

Some of the shine went out of the day for Maggie, "Does your sister have a side gig as a matchmaker?"

At Maggie's tone, Elliott's head snapped up from buttering a chunk of bread he'd torn off the loaf. Maggie turned her face away and closed her eyes, pretending to be soaking up the sun.

"Hey," Elliott said, knife suspended in the air.

"Yes?" Maggie kept her eyes closed.

"Look at me, please."

Face hot with what she hoped was sun, Maggie turned and looked at Elliott. She could see that his eyes were concerned, "She did it because she could tell I had a great time yesterday at our lunch, and she also knows I'm shy about asking women out. Especially beautiful women like you."

Maggie held his gaze for a second and then smiled, "You're laying it on pretty thick."

"No, I'm not. You are beautiful. And the best part is you don't know it."

"I meant the butter. You're laying it on the bread a bit thick. You can tell me how beautiful I am all day long." She grinned.

Over olives, bread, cheese and wine Elliott shared the conversation he'd had with Keith, beginning with his encounter with the tightly clothed teenager in the lobby.

"Meredith," Maggie explained.

"Is she a Keith?"

"Yep. Born and bred. She's Trent's daughter from his first marriage."

Elliott shared his impressions of Michael; his hard shell, the slight air of bragging when he spoke of the two properties he and his brother owned, and the charm he turned on when guests were present.

"That's Michael all right." Maggie nibbled on a piece of bread with a gooey piece of brie on it. "He's all charm when it's good for business. But when he doesn't need anything from you? Yeesh." She shivered as though she was cold.

As Elliott took a sip of wine, he looked out over the water, thinking. "I couldn't come out and ask him if he or his brothers had sabotaged your inn, of course. So I don't quite know what I expected to accomplish by going there. But maybe it was just worth getting the lay of the land, seeing him up close and personal. I dunno," he shrugged a little, "maybe it was silly to think I could help."

"I don't think it was silly."

He squinted at Maggie, the sun and the sea bright in his eyes. "Do you think they are the type of people who would deliberately try to affect your business?"

Maggie thought about this for a moment, closing her eyes and turning her face up toward the sun again. When she spoke her voice was serious and quieter than usual, "Here's what I know about the Keiths. It boils down to two things. First of all, they've never really made themselves a part of the island community. Living in a place like this, you need your neighbors. The island is, for all of us who live here, our home and our livelihood. It's like," she held her hands up, trying to find the right description, "we're all caretakers of this place. We all play a role in keeping it safe and beautiful and in taking care of it and of each other. Does that make sense?"

"It does."

"And because this is an island, as residents we all get an immediate sense of what that looks like. For example, when someone falls ill and needs help, or when the community pulls together to achieve something, like building the community center or arguing with BC Ferries about the increased fees and decreased sailings. That kind of stuff."

She took a bite of a cracker and continued, "So, we're in this together, I guess is the best way to say it. We've all got a hand on an oar and we row together." She looked at Elliott, willing him to understand. As someone born and raised in a city she wasn't sure he would.

But he said, "Got it. It's how I think we should all feel about the whole planet."

She smiled, realizing he understood, so she continued. "The Keiths keep themselves separate from the rest of the island community. That's the big difference with them. They are on the island, but they are not of it. They never, ever come to a community meeting. They've never participated in any of the fundraising drives we've had for various charities. A few years ago two of the constables on the island and the volunteer firemen did a fundraising thing for cancer. Ernest Allen's nine-year-old granddaughter had cancer."

"Oh, no."

"She's okay now, thank God. But one of the effects of her chemo was that she lost all her hair. So Earnest decided to shave his head in solidarity with her – it was so sweet – and then all his firemen buddies and the constables got involved. They organized a fundraiser for Tara – that's his granddaughter – and her family, because her mom, Earnest's daughter, had to quit her job to take care of Tara while all this was going on. They organized a fund raiser and people raised money by getting pledges to shave their heads."

She liked that Elliott's eyes were crinkling while he watched her talk.

She continued, "Pretty much everyone on the island joined in. We had a pledge drive and then on Tara's birthday in June, she and her mom and dad came over to the island and we threw a big party. And we all shaved our heads."

"Really?" Elliott glanced at Maggie's thick braid.

"Really. It was so great. Those of us with longer hair, like me, first got a trim so we could give the hair to one of those places that makes wigs for cancer patients. And then they brought out the clippers and we all went bald." She laughed at the memory. "For the rest of the summer, everywhere you went on the island, you'd see bald and then, as it began to grow back in, fuzzy heads."

"It sounds amazing."

"It was. Women, men, kids even did it. It was spectacular. We raised almost sixty thousand dollars for Tara and her family."

"Holy cow."

"Right? And Tara has been cancer-free for six years now, I think."

"What a great story."

"It's one of my all-time favorite memories of living here. And I have a *lot* of great memories. But my point is – and you can probably guess where I'm going with this…"

Elliott jumped in, "The Keiths didn't participate."

Maggie touched her nose with the tip of one index finger. "You got it in one."

"What's the second thing?"

Maggie squinted at him.

"You said you knew two things about the Keiths."

"Oh, right. The second thing is a much shorter story and it's much more personal. When my mum died, six months after my father, I had the funeral here on the island, naturally. The whole community came out." Her face had gone somber. She looked out toward the horizon, not seeing anything. "And Michael and Trent Keith approached me about selling my inn to them." She turned at looked at Elliott, "At the reception."

"No."

She nodded slightly, her eyes still mostly seeing the scene from that day, "We were at the community center, which is named after my dad, by the way, and those two…*brothers* came up to me and asked me if I had thought of selling the inn now that," she held her fingers up, making air quotes, "there was nothing left on the island for me." Her hands flopped down in her lap.

"That's despicable. What did you do?"

"I was so shocked I couldn't move or speak or even think. Luckily Carol happened to be standing behind me talking to someone and she overheard what they said. Well," Maggie smiled a bit at this memory, "Carol can be a bit of a challenge as a friend sometimes, but one thing she never, ever fails at is loyalty. She launched herself at Trent, punching and kicking him, screaming like a banshee. Frank Nelson came running from the other side of the hall and tried to pull her off, but when he saw the look on my face he *instantly*," she snapped her fingers, "intuited that they had done something wrong. He grabbed a couple of other guys, and they threw the Keiths out. Walked them right out of the hall and into the parking lot and told them not to come back or they'd be spending the night inside the jail cell."

"Wow."

"They threatened to sue, of course, for police harassment but it was an empty threat. I think they knew it would be their word against the whole island, and all of us would back up Frank and the other fellows who helped out."

"Jeez. So much drama in such a peaceful place."

"Yep." Maggie stretched her legs out from their bent position. "Good times."

Elliott thought about what she'd said for a moment, and then spoke, "From this, I gather you think it might be possible for the Keiths to do something dirty to you and the inn."

Maggie plucked a long blade of grass out from a crack in the rocks beside the blanket and twirled it in her fingers. "I do. I think they're land hungry and they obviously have no tact or manners. And the three brothers have raised their kids to be just like them." A light went on in Maggie's eyes and she looked up sharply from watching the feathered head of the grass spin in a looping circle.

"What?" Elliott could see that something had occurred to her.

"Bill, the third brother," she said, still thinking. "He just divorced his second wife, and he and his son, Jason, have come back to live on the island. For several years Bill and his wife were the reigning king and queen of real estate on Salt Spring Island. But about six months ago, he and Jason moved back here. I guess the ex-wife got the business over there in the divorce. Bill bought a place over on the north side of Juliet."

"What made you think of them just now?"

"Two weeks ago I was at the farmer's market, and I saw Jason at one of the tables. He's probably twenty-two now, and he was chatting to one of the girls at the table. They must have gone to high school together. I can't remember her name. Anyway," she continued, thinking out loud, "I hadn't seen Jason since he was about ten. He was such a sweet kid. Kind and gentle. He used to love when he'd see me around because I'd always let him pet Jolene, our dog before Ruby. He'd get right down on the ground with her if I was talking to his mum, and let her kiss his face, and he'd rub her tummy. So when I saw him at the market I hardly recognized him. He's all," she searched for the word, "hard. Like his dad and his uncles. His face is hard and cold. His eyes are scary, actually. It made me nervous for this girl he was chatting up. If she was my daughter I wouldn't let her within ten miles of that boy." She drifted off, remembering.

Elliott waited a few minutes, letting her think, and then prompted her, "Is that it?"

"No. No, that isn't it. Here's the weird part: I didn't think he recognized me. I bought my produce from the girl and was about to leave, and then Jason said my name. 'Maggie Archer.' Like that. Both my names. So I said, 'Hello, Jason Keith,' mimicking him, 'You're all grown up. Nice to see you.'" She paused again, thinking, "And then it got really weird. He said, 'Maggie Archer, we've got our eye on you.' I must've looked at the girl and then back to him because he said, 'No, not her and me. Me and my dad. We're gunning for your property, just so you know.'"

"You're joking."

"No, I'm not and I can't believe I forgot about that until now. I went back to the inn that day and one of the toilets was plugged and there was some other crisis I'm forgetting now, so the whole conversation went right out of my head."

"What do you think he meant?"

"Good question. Did he mean that he and Bill want to buy my place? Or do they want to sell it to someone else? I don't know if Bill is selling real estate here or not."

He looked across the blanket at her from where he was sitting, rolling the last bit of wine around in his stainless steel cup. "Maybe we should find out."

She smiled at him, "Maybe we should," and wondered again why he was helping her. She knew, of course, the reasons he'd given her – he needed something to do, a project, while he was on the island and Frank Nelson didn't want him to leave – but she wondered if that was all. She let herself wonder if he did actually think she was beautiful. The thought made her blush. She broke eye contact with him and wiped some imaginary crumbs from her lap.

"Let's talk about something else," she said.

"What should we talk about?"

"Who's your favorite musician?"

"Oh, good one. Classical or modern? Dead or alive?"

"Doesn't matter. Any or all of the above."

And so they fell into a rhythm of alternating asking random questions like this, and answering them. What was your favorite book as a kid? When did you first learn that Santa Claus isn't real? Who was your favorite relative growing up who wasn't in your family of origin? Share a piece of trivia you know that is random and strange. What was your worst birthday ever?

"Easy," Elliott answered to that one, "one year, when my ex-wife and I had been married about eighteen months, she threw me a big surprise party and invited all my friends. She had it catered and she had booked one of the rooms at our club."

"Ooo, fancy," Maggie murmured but smiled at him.

He continued, "My birthday is in late September so the weather was still really nice. We could go outside to the patio and there were tables set up. She hired a band and people danced on the patio. She even strung up those really cheesy colored paper lantern ball things. You know the ones I mean?"

Maggie nodded.

"And they actually looked great. They made it all look really nice." He paused for a moment remembering.

"I said worst birthday," Maggie reminded him.

He leaned over toward her holding out the jar of pickled asparagus. She chose one and just as she was about to bite into he said, "Everyone got food poisoning."

"No!"

"Yes. Ten people ended up in the hospital and the rest of us were laid up for days. It. Was. Awful."

Maggie covered her mouth in horror, the asparagus forgotten. But Elliott started to laugh and when he did, she did as well.

He choked out more details, laughing, tears running down his cheeks, "The band got sick, too. They almost sued us."

"Oh, no." Maggie held her sides and rocked back and forth a bit, her cheeks hurting.

"My best friend, Miles, went to work the next day because he thought he was okay and he ended up throwing up on the bus."

"Stop!"

"On a little old lady."

"No!"

"Oh man, it was gnarly." Elliott wiped his eyes and tried to catch his breath.

Little hiccups of laughter escaped from Maggie as she did the same. "Don't ever invite me to your birthday party."

"Don't worry. I've never had a party since."

Something about laughing so ferociously was deeply intimate. Maggie felt a deep release inside her when her laughter started to subside. The feeling made her a little bold. "Why did you get divorced?" she asked.

Their eyes met and she could see him considering what to say. In the pause before his words she wondered if he would tell her the truth, or at least a first date (or was this the second date?) version of it.

"We made a mistake. We never should have gotten married." He sighed and flicked a pine needle from the blanket. "I thought it was what you were supposed to do, you know; grow up, get a job, get married, buy a house, have kids. But when I did some of that it didn't feel real. It felt like I was pretending to be a grown-up, not actually being one. I knew it was a mistake once the wedding train started moving, but I thought that all of it – the ceremony, the commitment, the *china,*" he smiled at her, making fun of himself, "would make it seem real. But it didn't. And then we were married and we were buying a house and…" He trailed off, and looked at Maggie, no explanation needed.

"I'm sorry," she said.

"Lesson learned, I guess. I hope I have a better sense of who I am now. It was a pretty expensive mistake though."

Maggie scrunched up her nose, "Ick."

"Ick indeed," he said, "So expensive, in fact, that I am now living above my sister's bakery in what is technically her office, while I wait to go to a job in Vancouver that I really doubt I'm going to like."

"What's the job?"

"It's an environmental engineering job with a firm downtown. It's a great opportunity, as my dad would say, and I'm not exactly in a position to turn it down. Hell, if Libby offered me a job as a dishwasher I should probably take it. But," he looked out at the water and took a deep breath, "I miss the parks already."

"Will you be inside all the time?"

"Yup."

"Suit and tie?"

"Yup."

"Cubicle?"

"I think I might get something that resembles an office."

"A cubicle with higher walls?"

"Something like that."

Maggie wasn't sure what to say. He seemed like a man who was lost and it was all she could do not to wrap him in her arms, take him home, tuck him up in front of the fire and bake him cookies.

He broke into her thoughts, "What about you?"

She tried going back to the lighter tone of their random questions. "Worst birthday ever? Let's see…"

"No. Have you ever been married?"

"I haven't." She could have happily left it at that, but knew that Elliott deserved more, given what he'd shared with her. So after a couple of seconds she continued. "I'm not sure I'm entirely cut out for marriage. Living here on the island is all I've ever known and the inn is my life. The staff are like my children, even when they're older than me. Some part of me thinks the right partnership would be nice, and some part of me thinks marriage looks like a lot of work. And I'm already overworked."

"It might be nice to have someone to share the workload at the inn."

"You're right. It might. But at the same time, who would want to take on a broken down old inn and the woman who is chained to it?"

"I imagine there are quite a few men on this island who would take you up on that offer in a heartbeat."

"Possibly," she smiled, thinking this over, "but here's the thing about growing up in a place like this. Almost all the men my age are the fellows I went to high school with. I know them better than their parents know them, probably. Too much information about someone is not sexy. And the ones who have stayed and made a life here are, shall we say, 'eccentric'."

"Like you?"

She laughed quietly, "Probably."

Thirteen

As Maggie entered the lodge, she was greeted by Carol, Sparrow and Greg, all lined up with their backs against the reception counter, looking at her, expectation in their eyes. Ruby barged past her through the front door and trotted into the kitchen to her water bowl. Maggie looked down the row of faces and smiled a wide grin at them all.

"Hello staff."

"Hello boss," they all chorused.

"Anything to tell us?" Carol, naturally, was the first one to start probing.

"Not a thing. Get back to work, you miscreants," she tried to sound like a tyrant.

"As if!" Carol snorted. "Did we see a kiss out there by the handsome knight's carriage?"

Maggie made demure motions as though playing with a long skirt, and looked up from underneath her eyelashes. "It's possible that he kissed my cheek."

"Your cheek?" Carol was horrified, "What is this? 1850? I've had entire relationships that didn't last as long as your lunch date."

"He was being a gentleman. Now seriously. Enough. Get back to work."

"No way, man," Sparrow stepped forward and grabbed Maggie by the elbow. "You're going to tell us everything."

Greg rolled his eyes, "This was fun, ladies, but I'll leave you to it." He patted Maggie's shoulder as he passed her on his way to the kitchen, "Good for you, Mags. You need to get laid."

Maggie gasped and took a swipe at him, but he was too quick. Sparrow led her around the desk and plopped her into a chair and wheeled her into the far corner of the front desk so she couldn't escape. Carol took the second chair and Sparrow hopped up on the desk, crossing her legs under her.

"Spill," Sparrow said.

Even to herself, Maggie thought she must appear to be all shiny and glowing. She felt ridiculous and couldn't wipe the grin off her face. "It was good," she said. "Really nice."

"That's it?"

"Well… I'm not used to sharing this kind of information. What do you want me to say?"

"I don't know about Sparrow," Carol leaned back in her chair and crossed her long legs, "but I want you to say that he tore your clothes off and made mad, passionate love to you all afternoon. And that you loved it." She raised her eyebrows, expectant, "Please tell me that's what happened."

"That is *not* what happened. You know me, Carol. I am not that woman. Not that there's anything wrong with freedom of sexual expression," she held her hands up, surrendering, "but I am just not that way. And I don't think Elliott is either."

"He's a man, Mags. Of course he's that way."

"Well, that wasn't what this afternoon was about. I know I sound like Rebecca of Sunnybrook Farm, but it was nice. We went to Pete's Park and sat on the bluff and ate our lunch and drank some wine and talked. It was lovely." She smiled again at the memory.

"It sounds as boring as shite."

"Carol, stop." Sparrow swatted her shoulder from above, "Maggie, I think it sounds perfect. What's he like?"

The three ladies spent the early part of the evening rehashing every detail of Maggie's date. It was the first date Sparrow had ever known her boss to have gone on. Greg brought them plates of dinner from the kitchen loaded with roasted lamb, roasted potatoes, asparagus and squash. They set the plates in their laps, or on the desktop, and laughed at Elliott's worst birthday story.

Over coffee after dinner, Maggie worked up the courage to say the thing she'd been avoiding since she arrived home. The thing that felt most intimate and therefore most dangerous about her time with Elliott. "I almost fell asleep."

Sparrow and Carol both froze and looked over at her.

"What?" Carol asked, confused.

"I almost fell asleep. Twice. Once when we were lying on the rocks and I had put my head back to look at the sky. And then again in the truck on the way home."

Her audience was quiet for a moment, processing this revelation and then, appropriately, Sparrow spoke up, "Your soul knows him. It feels safe with him."

Maggie looked at her young employee who was ancient in so many ways. "I think you're right," she said finally.

"Uh, oh," Carol said.

Maggie met her eyes, "What do you mean?"

"On second thought," Carol said, "I shouldn't say 'uh, oh'. I should have said 'Hooray!'"

Maggie frowned, cautious. "Why?"

"You need some excitement in your life, Mags. Some complication. You work too much and play too little. I don't exactly know what 'your soul knows him' means." She made air quotes as she said this and rolled her eyes in Sparrow's direction. "But I can see that he lights you up. That, my friend, is a good thing."

Maggie groaned. "I'm elated and terrified at the same time. But I don't need this complication. Especially not at this moment with a dead body on our hands and someone possibly trying to sabotage the inn." Her eyes widened as she looked at Sparrow and Carol.

"This is terrible. He's leaving the island in a day or two. What if I really like him?"

Carol grinned, enjoying her friend's torment. "Strap in, honey. This could be a wild ride." She looked at Sparrow. "And we've got a ringside seat."

Maggie tried to focus on paperwork and admin details after that, but she couldn't concentrate. Carol finally sent her home after she spent 20 minutes searching for the 'right' pen only to drop it in Carol's coffee cup.

"Get out of here, would you please? You're going to end up dumping a glass of water on the computer or something."

It took some convincing, but Maggie was glad now that she was wrapped up in the fleece blanket on her couch with Ruby lying on her feet, snoring. The television was on, but she wasn't seeing the screen. She cradled a glass of wine in her hand and stared out the window at the layered darkness. She could just see the darker masses of the trees pressed against the blue-black sky. The waves lapping at the rocks and shore below her cabin were so familiar to her that she almost couldn't hear them.

She woke with a start, her neck stiff from being tilted at an odd angle on the couch. She had been dreaming of her parents, something that happened less frequently now. They had been calling to her, yelling at her frantically from a long way away. She had kept straining, trying to hear them, but in the dream Ruby was beside her barking, and the barking was drowning out her parents voices. "Quiet, Ruby! Quiet!" she kept yelling at the dream-dog but as soon as her parents called to her again, Ruby's bark was all she could hear.

The dog was barking for real, she now realized as she woke.

Dazed and fuzzy-headed she looked around and saw that Ruby was at the front door of the house, standing on the tile floor, her legs and tail stiff. Her nose pressed against the door frame between barks.

"Ruby," she said, throwing the blanket off of herself and lowering her legs to the floor, putting her feet in her sheepskin slippers, "Come on, now. Enough."

She walked toward the kitchen, planning to ignore the dog and get a glass of water before heading to her bed. But as Maggie's head cleared from the dream she saw that the normally obedient and usually placid Ruby was almost frantic. She turned on the kitchen light and could see that the ruff on Ruby's neck was standing straight up, as it did when she met a dog she felt threatened by or unsure of. As Maggie observed this, the dog turned her body half way around, looking pointedly at Maggie, and then turned back and continued barking at the door.

"Something's wrong, isn't it, girl?" A chill began to travel along Maggie's skin, up her legs and then her arms, and finally making her scalp tingle. "What is it Rubes?"

The door to Maggie's home was one of her favorite parts of the house. It was designed in the craftsman style that her father adored, and was solid oak, stained a deep, rich, rust brown. Across the top of the door it had two layers of window panes, set in rows of three each across the width of the door. Maggie squeezed past Ruby and leaned against the door, peering through one of the lower window panes.

Though her house was set apart from the rest of the resort and she couldn't see the inn or any of the freestanding cabins that surrounded it, as she looked out into the night she saw an orange glow, flickering and moving in the direction of the inn.

"Fire," she whispered.

Fourteen

Ruby objected strenuously to being left in the house. Maggie could still hear her, barking frantically and howling. But Maggie couldn't risk the dog being loose in the chaos she knew would ensue.

She ran as fast as her slippered feet would carry her along the tree-lined path that led from her house to the inn. She'd been traveling that path every day since she was in her mother's womb. She knew every tree branch, every root, every rock. Though it was the kind of pitch black that city dwellers never experience, Maggie flew through the trees without even seeing the ground below her or the trees beside her. And still, it was like a dream she often had of trying to get somewhere, knowing she was late, and her legs were leaden, hardly moving. The harder she tried and the more frustrated she got with her lack of progress, the slower she moved. It was like that now.

Normally she could walk between the inn and her home in five or six minutes. At a jog, when she was in a hurry, she could do it in three and a half. Tonight she reached the inn's parking lot in less than two minutes, though to her it felt like two hours.

A quick scan of the front of the inn told her the fire was not there. She ran to her left, across the gravel lot, rocks and stones bludgeoning her feet. The orange glow was coming from the area to the left of the inn as she faced it. Sprinting up onto the treed area beside the lodge building, she slipped on a thick bed of pine needles and went down on one knee. She was up again almost before she'd realized she'd fallen, racing down the length of the lodge, now able to hear the crackle of flames.

To her left were four cabins. She mentally reviewed the guest list in her head and thought that only one was occupied tonight. Still running, she followed the noise and light and discovered that the fire was further into the woods than she had originally thought.

Quickly turning, she ran back the way she'd come, up onto a flagstone walkway and threw herself at a door tucked under the great room of the lodge, where the land dipped down to the water.

She pounded on the door with both fists, "Carol! Carol! Open up. Fire." She grabbed the door knob and turned and the door flew open just as her friend, staggered into the hallway of the suite, a red Chinese silk robe held around her.

"What the fuck, Mags?" Her eyes were barely open and her mascara was smeared. Her blond hair was sticking out from her head at odd angles.

Maggie's breath was coming ragged and in bursts, "Fire. Carol, one of the cabins is on fire."

"Oh Jesus, no. Greg!" Carol yelled and disappeared from Maggie's sight.

"Wait! Carol!" Maggie took the six feet into Carol's kitchen in three giant bounds and grabbed the phone out of its cradle off the kitchen counter. Carol reappeared in the hallway that led to the bathroom, "Is anyone registered in the cabins here on this side?"

"Oh jeez. Let me think." As Maggie dialed 911, she could see the wheels spinning in Carol's head.

Greg appeared in the bedroom doorway, blinking in the light, naked and confused.

The line rang, once, twice, "Put some clothes on, Greg. One of the cabins is on fire."

"Right," the chef said, as though she'd just asked him to pour her a cup of coffee. He turned and disappeared back into Carol's bedroom.

"Fire, police or ambulance?" the female voice on the telephone said in Maggie's ear.

"Fire," she said. "Cormorant Inn. 687 Wellington Street. Juliet Island."

Carol was still muttering to herself. "The Arnold's?" she looked at Maggie for confirmation.

"They checked out on Sunday."

"What day is it?"

"Monday. Well, Tuesday morning."

"Tuesday. Tuesday." Carol looked as though she might faint.

The 911 operator came back on the line, "Confirm address please: 687 Wellington Street, Juliet Island, Southern Gulf Islands."

"That's correct." Maggie heard a crash from Carol's bedroom and a loud 'fuck' from Greg.

Since she had arrived at Carol's apartment, perhaps ninety seconds had elapsed. Maggie felt as though three years might have gone by. She was talking to the 911 operator and talking and listening to Carol and Greg, but in her vision all she could see were orange flames, and her ears could only hear the roar and crackle of a wood fire the size of a house.

Carol's eyes, which had been whirling around the room while she thought came back and locked on Maggie's, "I can't remember if anyone's registered in those cabins. There's the Perez family in the Otter cabin on the other side. And everyone else is in the lodge rooms."

Maggie's field of vision shrank to just what was immediately in front of her while she too tried to visualize the guest registry. She could see Carol was frozen and awaiting further instruction. "Go get dressed."

The red robe disappeared down the hall again.

"Trucks are on the way, ma'am. Please stay on the line." Maggie set the phone down, still engaged, on the kitchen counter and grabbed Greg by the shirt front, dragging him out the front door of Carol's suite.

As any islander anywhere will tell you, fire tops the list of things to be afraid of. In the summer, each of British Columbia's Southern Gulf Islands are like a tinder box. Most years, open fires are banned from late May through late September. The islands are covered in decades old pine and spruce trees. The undergrowth in forested areas is covered in a carpet of dry needles and leaves; a pyromaniac's dream. The homes and other buildings are mostly built of wood, which is so plentiful in this part of the world.

Once outside, Maggie and Greg dragged the garden hose from the inn down the hill to see if it would reach the flames. It did, and the water flowed, but it was like spitting on a forest fire. It had almost no effect.

Carol pulled on jeans, a t-shirt and a pair of canvas sneakers and came stumbling through the orange darkness.

"Let's check the cabins," Maggie said, "I still can't remember if anyone's in the ones on this side. You check Starfish and Spinnaker. I'll check Orca and Salmon."

Carol nodded and took off down a cedar chip path. She had to take a roundabout route to the two cabins to avoid the smoke and flames.

Maggie ran in the opposite direction toward Orca cabin. In the distance, she could faintly hear Ruby barking. And beyond that, much to Maggie's relief, the sound of fire engine sirens. Her slippers were nearly useless as protection from the sticks and stones on the path and she had to almost shuffle along so they wouldn't fall off. Maggie cursed herself for not taking one minute to grab a pair of running shoes or hiking boots. Finally she made it to the cabin and bolted up the three stairs to the porch. The lights were off and she quickly glanced down to see if there were any signs of occupation beside the front door. People often left their muddy or sandy shoes and boots outside. She couldn't see anything, but it was pitch dark, so she pounded on the door.

"Hello!" she called. "Anyone there?"

She tried the doorknob but the cabin was locked, as they always were in-between guests. She didn't have her master key with her. She pounded again and then stepped over to peek through the front window. What she could see in the darkness of the cabin looked clean and tidy. Maggie scrunched up her eyes, trying to spot any of the personal detritus that guests invariably leave lying around; shoes on the floor, clothes on the sofa. There seemed to be nothing.

The sirens were louder now. Behind her, Maggie could still hear the crackle of the fire, and now also voices yelling. Her heart in her throat, Maggie banged on the door one more time and then, nearly convinced the cabin was empty, she turned to run down the steps and head toward Salmon cabin.

This one was down a little slope and close to the back of the cabin that was on fire. As she ran around the back of the cabin, the snapping and roar of the fire reached her once again. Shielding her eyes from the flames, she ran around the side of Salmon cabin and up onto its porch. Right away she saw a pair of hiking boots on their sides beside the front door. The realization rushed in on her as she remembered there was in fact a guest registered in this cabin. A photographer from Saskatoon who was on his own.

"Shaun!" she called, frantically pounding on the door. "Shaun Sanna! It's Maggie! There's a fire! Can you hear me?"

She pounded as loudly as she could. There was no response from within. Maggie stepped to her right, nearly tripping over the boots, and peered in through the front window. She pounded her fist on the glass, continuing to call Shaun's name. She could see a rain jacket thrown over the back of one of the dining room chairs. In the little galley kitchen she could see a computer bag on the counter, along with what looked like a tripod and other camera equipment.

She turned and looked out from the front porch. The cabin that was on fire was about twenty feet from the porch she stood on. She could feel the heat coming off of it, the way you can feel the heat from a fireplace or wood stove. It was like a wall that kept pushing closer toward her.

Maggie turned back and began pounding on the door again, frantic now. She could still hear the sirens, which meant the trucks hadn't reached the inn yet. Behind her something in the engulfed cabin crashed, sending a firework spray of sparks up into the night sky. Maggie jumped at the sound, her nerves raw and flayed. She turned and looked back once more at the flames. She couldn't be sure, but she thought they were creeping across the dry forest floor toward her.

"Goddammit," she whispered through gritted teeth, *"how could anyone sleep through this?"*

The sirens were louder and closer, but Maggie didn't think she could wait for them. If the fire got any closer to this cabin, it could become fully engulfed in seconds.

Grabbing one of Shaun's boots, she slid it over her right hand. Closing her eyes and shielding them, with her right arm she punched the boot against the living room window. It bounced back, the glass holding strong.

"You're going to have to do better than that Archer."

She took a deep breath and swung again, this time really meaning it.

And it worked.

Fifteen

"YOU COULD HAVE BEEN KILLED! Or at the very least lost an arm."

One of the volunteer firemen was bandaging Maggie's arm. "I know. But I had to get in."

He looked at her with concern in his eyes. His name was Tad Caruso. His mother had taught Maggie math in high school. "How were you planning to crawl through a window frame filled with shards of broken glass?"

"I hadn't really thought that far ahead. Ouch! That stings."

"Hold still."

The cavalry in the form of the island's volunteer fire department had arrived just as Maggie had leapt out of the way of the broken glass that rained down on the porch where she stood. A small piece had caught her on the arm, and Tad was right, she had been lucky it hadn't been any larger. Two of the firemen pulled her away from the window. One dragged her away from the cabin, up to the inn's porch, while the other kicked the door to the cabin down. Shaun Sanna's clothes and toiletries were there, but he was not.

Meanwhile, several other firemen connected hoses from a tanker truck and began working hard to get the fire under control. Maggie stood on the inn's porch, watching, transfixed, while aglow with amber light, the firemen worked. In just under an hour she felt something shift and she realized later that it was at that moment the firemen felt they had the fire under control.

"What time is it?" she looked to her left, finding Greg and Carol standing there, which almost surprised her, so lost had she been in fear and adrenaline.

In the gradually lightening sky, Maggie could see that Greg was dressed in a black t-shirt under a dark blue zip-up hoodie and a pair of what looked like pink sweatpants that stopped mid-calf. His bare feet were slipped into his neon green kitchen Crocks. Carol, between Maggie and Greg, had one of the inn's yellow rain slickers on overtop a huge pair of grey sweatpants tucked into dark green rubber boots. Both their faces were smudged with soot and Carol's hair was still standing on end like Medusa's snakes.

Seeing them, Maggie started to laugh, more with hysteria than mirth, "Wow. You guys are a pretty sight. Greg, are those Carol's sweats?"

He looked down and seemed to notice his wardrobe for the first time, "Um, no," he lied. "They're mine. Don't you like them?" He held one leg out, flashing his bare calf. "I wanted Hello Kitty but they didn't have my size."

They still had an inn to run. Soon the guests would be hungry. Many of those from the rooms in the main lodge had drifted down to the deck to watch the fire being put out, awakened by the sirens and the light of the flames. Many of them made a point of coming to Maggie and giving her a hug, empathizing with her, and offering words of comfort and support.

Shaun Sanna appeared with a quizzical expression on his face, which doubled when Maggie threw herself at him and gave him a big hug.

"What the...?"

"I'm so glad you're okay. Where were you?" Maggie was breathless with relief and shock.

"I um…" Shaun tucked his hands in his jeans pockets and hesitated. "I was uh…"

A woman appeared from behind him, hugging a thick green cardigan around her chest. Maggie thought her name was Andrea. She was staying in one of the rooms in the main lodge. "He was with me," she said matter-of-factly.

As the morning dawned, and the fire was reduced to a smoldering pile of black ash, Maggie herded everyone into the lodge, giving instructions for coffee to be made and the usual breakfast buffet to be laid out. Carol and Greg were instructed to go back to Carol's suite and either trade clothes – they had clearly grabbed each other's in the rush to get dressed – or find something new to wear.

"And comb your hair," Maggie said to Carol, taking a swipe at the tufted mess on her friend's head. She had not yet processed the fact that her assistant manager/best friend and her chef were sleeping together. That conversation would have to wait for another moment.

Sparrow arrived for her shift, having heard the news on the island grapevine. She burst into tears upon seeing Maggie and had to be consoled for several minutes. But once the emotional storm had passed, she insisted Maggie take a seat at one of the dining tables while she took over orchestrating the breakfast. Silver rings flashing and bracelets jangling, she stepped up to the task with Maggie watching, marveling at the support that surrounded her.

Shortly thereafter, Libby and Elliott arrived, both their faces creased with concern, both their arms full of wide, shallow bakery boxes.

"Mags!" Libby cried and set her stack of boxes on the kitchen counter, enveloping Maggie in a hug. Maggie looked over Libby's shoulder at Elliott, whose face she was touched to see was lined with worry. "Thank God no one was hurt."

"That is for sure." Maggie wiped a couple of tears away from her cheeks. "Everyone is safe and...oh!! Ruby! She's still in the cabin. I need to go get her."

"I'll go," Elliott said, "Do I need a key?"

"No, it's unlocked. Thank you."

He disappeared down the front hallway, while Libby began opening the boxes and layering croissants, danishes, donuts and muffins on platters. "Some of this stuff is day old, but I don't think anyone will complain."

"Thank you, Libby. You are a life saver."

Activity, voices and noise swirled around Maggie, leaving her weak with gratitude. She sat, exhausted and close to tears, while guests, staff and friends alike ate and then organized the clean-up. She wasn't hungry, but Libby forced a chocolate croissant on her and made sure she ate it. Sparrow made her a latté.

Ruby burst into the room, tail wagging, nails clicking on the hardwood floor, her face smiling, greeting all the guests and pinging round the room like a pinball, from one guest to another. She was not usually allowed in the breakfast room and was thrilled at the exception being made today. She made the most of it, begging treats from everyone. Elliott came in behind Ruby and saw that the chair beside Maggie was momentarily free. He sat down and pulled it a little closer to her.

He reached out and took one of her hands. "How are you?"

"Good. I'm good, thanks Elliott. It's all going to be okay."

His lips curled in a slight smile, "I mean really, Maggie. How are you?"

She started to cry. He grabbed a paper napkin from the table and handed it to her and wrapped his right arm around her shoulders. She sniffled and wiped her eyes, her back straight. With his right hand he squeezed her shoulder slightly, and she felt the gesture for what it was, an invitation to let go.

Since her parents had passed away, Maggie had relied on no

one but herself. She was the rock around which all the guests and staff at the inn swirled. She answered dozens of questions a day, made numerous decisions, large and small, coordinated, organized, counseled and advised. The regular guests who returned each year shared their problems and concerns with her, sometimes even the new guests did, as well. She had the natural host's gift for listening, and as a result, people shared their problems.

But rarely did she share her concerns with anyone. Carol, her best friend and assistant manager, was a little too broken and a little too self-absorbed to be a good listener. She tried, but the conversation always rather quickly turned back to herself. Maggie appreciated her effort but knew that being a soft place to land for her friend would never be one of Carol's strengths.

And so, without her parents' counsel, Maggie had learned to forge on alone. She rarely thought about needing someone to talk to, someone to cry with, someone who would listen to her, without interrupting, without judging, for as long as she needed to talk. The inn and its guests and staff filled her up, gave her a sense of purpose, filled her days with joy and laughter and camaraderie. She had decided, once she was through with most of the grieving over her mother and father's passing, that if Ruby was the closest thing she had to someone who would really listen to her, then that would have to be enough. This disappointed her, but she also believed in the importance of being grateful for what she had, and not bitter about what she didn't have.

So when she felt the little squeeze on her shoulder, the invitation from Elliott for her to lean into him, to let down her burdens for just a moment, she hesitated. She was so used to the weight of everything that she wasn't sure who she would be without it. It flashed through her mind to pretend she didn't understand what he was offering her. To wipe her eyes and nose and take a deep breath and carry on.

But when she looked at him in that moment and their eyes met, it was like he saw that thought as clearly as if it had been painted across her forehead. And he wasn't having any of it. He squeezed her shoulder again, this time with a tiny bit more force.

Maggie's face dissolved, and she buried it in Elliott's shoulder. He pulled her closer, wrapping both arms around her, rubbing her back, his chin nestled in beside her ear.

"I'm right here," he said, quietly whispering in her ear. "I'm right here."

Sixteen

While Maggie wept into Elliott's chest, the activity in the inn continued. Ruby came, concerned, and sat between her mistress's feet, occasionally taking a swipe at Maggie's hand with her tongue. But otherwise the guests and staff gave Maggie and Elliott the space they needed, creating a little bubble around them. Orbiting around them like planets around a paired sun.

Maggie let her body do what it needed to do, and when the tears began to ease up, she sniffled a bit and then raised her head, looking at Elliott.

"You're doing great," he said. "It's all okay."

It wasn't really all okay, but she appreciated the sentiment. Maggie's breath began to return to normal, but interrupted occasionally with little shuddering gasps.

"Do you need anything?" Elliott whispered to her.

Maggie shook her head, just grateful to have him there with her. The ferocity of her gratitude surprised her. For someone so independent, she was stunned by how much it meant to her that Elliott was there with her.

She heard a slight commotion at the front door of the inn and turned to find the volunteer firemen, her friends and members of her community, walking toward her, faces blackened with soot but their expressions satisfied with the outcome of a situation that could have been much worse. They had taken their jackets, suspendered pants, and boots off and left them on the front porch, so as they came past the reception desk and into the great room and dining room they looked like a group of overgrown children who had escaped their beds in the middle of the night. Some were wearing the jeans they had put on under their firefighting pants, but many were in pajama bottoms. All were in their stocking feet.

The crowd in the dining room burst into spontaneous applause as they appeared, cheering and clapping, one or two wolf whistles thrown in for good measure. The men beamed and waved and clapped each other on the back.

There were nine of them, all local to the island, all known to Maggie and the staff at the inn. Three of them sat down at Maggie's table. The others grabbed an empty table and carried it over to set it down next to her. They grabbed chairs and then began to head toward the coffee urns but Sparrow stopped them, motioning for them to sit down so she could serve them.

Constable Frank Nelson was the first to speak, "Well, Maggie, you were very lucky."

"Thank you all so much for everything." She looked from one face to the next, making sure she met each man's eyes. Young Brandon Every was there, and she realized she didn't know he was a firefighter. Gerry Stewart nodded to Elliott and winked at Maggie, while Earnest Allen, who ran the gas station, grabbed a platter of baked goods and set it down in the middle of the table. The men fell on it like greedy starlings. Libby took a break from bussing tables for the guests and sat beside her brother, Elliott.

Frank was obviously the leader, and he did most of the talking. "Do you want the bad news first, or the good news?"

Maggie took a deep breath, "The bad news."

"The cabin is a write off. And everything in it."

She sat with this for a moment, letting it sink in. "And the good news?"

"Well, the good news is, no lives were lost and that was the only building that burned. If this had been late August, the story could have been much worse."

"Right," Maggie nodded.

"It's true, Maggie." Gerry spoke up, flecks of donut icing on his chin, "You could have lost the whole thing." He gestured around him with one hand, "The lodge. The whole kit and caboodle."

She took another deep breath, "You're right Gerry. And Frank." She looked from one to the other, "We are very lucky." Her eyes pricked with tears again.

"Was that a guest cabin?" Brandon spoke up for the first time.

She heard Libby's voice from behind her and felt a hand on her shoulder, "It was your parents' cabin, wasn't it Mags?"

Maggie took a deep breath and nodded but wasn't able to speak.

Libby helped her out. "I think you've been keeping furniture you weren't using in there, and Christmas decorations and lights. Old tools and stuff. Right?"

A few more tears spilled out of Maggie'e eyes and she swiped at them with her napkin, nodding. "It was the cabin they first built on the land, when there was nothing else here. It was one room and they lived in it for three years while they built the lodge." She blew her nose, her breath becoming a little ragged again. She felt Elliott's hand rub her back.

Frank Nelson leaned forward and patted her knee, his professional mask slipping a bit. Maggie smiled weakly at him. "Young lady, your parents would be happy that you and all the guests are safe. That's what they would care about."

"You're right, Frank. I know. It's just going to take me awhile to absorb it all."

"I know. Listen. We need to tell you something else while we're at it." He glanced at Gerry and then back to Maggie.

Seeing their grave looks, Maggie tried to joke, "Yikes. There's more bad news?"

"There is, I'm afraid," Gerry spoke now, leaning forward, resting his elbows on the table, "It looks like there's a possibility that an accelerant was used to start the fire."

Seventeen

Ruby didn't like being relegated to the backseat. She kept pressing her nose forward between the driver's and passenger's seats, and Maggie kept having to tell her "no" and push her back.

"Sorry about this," Maggie said, "she's used to sitting here in this seat while I drive."

"No problem," Elliott smiled at her, "I like it that she wants to be part of the team."

It was just after noon and Elliott was driving Maggie (and Ruby) across the island. He was relieved to have something to do in the aftermath of the fire and the chaos that was unfolding at the inn. After Maggie's initial burst of emotion, which had made him feel very protective of her and, if he was totally honest with himself, much closer to this woman he'd only known for three days, he had been at a loss about what to do to help. The fire crew got suited up once again, after they'd been fed and watered sufficiently, and went back down to the cabin to investigate a little further. They asked Maggie to stay away until they gave her the 'all-clear,' and she agreed, though she wasn't happy about it.

She and Elliott both drifted around the great room and the dining room, picking up coffee cups and abandoned plates, returning them to the kitchen. Libby went back to the bakery, promising to return later with more goodies. Maggie was still wearing her clothes from yesterday, which smelled of smoke. She noticed that she had somehow torn a hole in the calf of her jeans.

When she'd dropped and broken her third plate inside of ten minutes, Carol took her hand. "Look, you need some sleep. And to get out of those clothes. Go home. Have a shower and a nap. And don't come back until you're rested."

Greg watched from behind the kitchen counter, his hoodie replaced by his chef's coat and his hair back in its artfully tussled style. When Maggie objected, saying she wanted to stay, he stepped in, taking her by the arm and guiding her over to Elliott. "Dude, walk her down to her house. If she won't go, carry her."

"Roger that." Elliott took Maggie's arm from Greg and began to steer her toward the front door. He was pleased that Greg had charged him with Maggie's care, and not just because it gave him something to do.

As they walked, Maggie called instructions out to Carol, "Find the file on the insurance will you, please? It should be in the third drawer of the filing cabinet. And call Taylor and ask if she'll come in early to help clean this place up."

"Will do."

"Make sure Sparrow keeps a list of anyone who calls to see if they can help. We might need them."

"She's already on it."

"And start making a list of anything we might have been keeping in that cabin."

"Already on that, too. Would you please go away and let us handle things for five minutes?"

As Elliott pushed the front door open and guided the inn's owner through it, Maggie looked back at Carol, "By the way, when did you and Greg start hooking up?"

"Get out," Carol said, with mock seriousness. She winked at her friend as she said it.

Maggie insisted that Elliott stay with her while she showered and changed. "I want to *do* something. I can't just sit here and think about what's happening. I'm afraid for my guests now. If the fire was deliberately set, whoever's behind this is pretty damn serious. What if someone gets hurt?"

"That fear is perfectly reasonable. I think you should rest. You won't be able to help anyone if you're a sleep-deprived zombie."

"*Dude*," Maggie said, mustering some lightheartedness and mimicking Greg, "there's no way I could sleep now. I'm completely wired with fear and anxiety."

"You've been up nearly all night. You must be exhausted." He was talking to her through the bathroom door.

"I am, but I also feel like I've had nineteen espressos. I need to move around before I'll be able to sleep."

He heard the water in the tub start, and then the shift in sound as it switched to the shower head. The sound of the shower curtain moving reached him and he stepped away from the door, knowing Maggie wouldn't be able to hear him any longer.

He was rattled too, he realized. And not just because fire is terrifying. He went and stood at one of the living room windows and looked out toward the ocean, where waves lapped over the obsidian rocks. How long had he known Maggie, he wondered to himself. Less than seventy-two hours he calculated. He had been counting down the hours until he would move to the mainland, perhaps with as much dread as excitement, and now, much to his surprise, he found thoughts and feelings about Maggie interfering with his plans.

He was really worried about this woman, despite how capable she was. The shower droned on, leaving him to think. He watched the seawater undulating. A gull floated above the churning tide and then disappeared down the shore. In a rush of vulnerability that made him decidedly uncomfortable, he recognized that he cared about what happened to Maggie.

Going for lunch and then the picnic with her had been a distraction – granted, a very pleasant one. But those times together had, for him, been partly a way to kill time before he left the island. What better way to do that than with a smart, independent, pretty woman? Now though, he was wading into unexpected territory.

In the aftermath of the fire, when he and Libby first arrived at the inn, the clench of worry that gripped his heart had shocked him. As he and his sister worked their way through the crowd, he had looked for Maggie's face, and upon seeing it, had felt faint with relief. It mattered very much to him that she was safe.

"Shit," he said to himself quietly.

The ocean didn't reply.

He turned from the window, distracting himself from these complicated feelings. Along the mantelpiece above the fireplace were photos of Maggie with her parents and a succession of Labrador Retrievers. He could see from the photos that Maggie had inherited her mother's eyes and chestnut hair and her father's upright posture and slightly crooked nose. He sat on the wheat colored couch, Ruby snoring gently beside him, and thought about who this woman was and how her home reflected her. It was not showy at all. 'Comfortable' was the adjective he would have used. The home was mostly windows; they filled almost every wall and in the room where he sat they soared from the floor to about ten feet, and then above that was another triangular set, fitted into the peaked roof. There were a couple of paintings depicting animals hanging on the few walls that weren't covered in windows. In one, a pair of wolves sat in twilight, stars just appearing in the sky, the animals' fur glistening with snowflakes. In another, a grizzly bear waded through a river, an unlucky salmon caught in its jaws. Both paintings depicted the animals looking straight at the viewer, not with hostility but with a mix of curiosity and intelligence, as though they were saying, "I see you."

He reflected that this suited Maggie's personality exactly. What he knew of her so far was that she was direct, with a quiet power that lurked beneath the surface. He wondered if she was even aware of it. When she listened to him talk, she looked straight at him and listened with her whole body. He first noticed it when they had lunch together on the pub deck on Sunday. He found it both arousing and unsettling. He wasn't sure anyone had ever listened to him in that way before. Certainly his wife hadn't.

And now she sat, absorbed in her own thoughts, in the passenger seat of his truck. Her hair was still wet, but she had braided it anyway. He noticed she held it up to her nose every once in a while and sniffed it.

She did that now and looked over at him, "It smells."

"Your hair?"

She shuddered. "I can still smell the smoke."

They were on their way to visit Francis Best, an old friend of her father's and pretty much the original realtor on the island. He had sold Maggie's parents their lot and had made a small fortune selling and re-selling many of the other properties on the island.

"He's like royalty," Maggie explained. "Everyone on Juliet knows him and respects him. He's such a good guy and has so much integrity. That got him into trouble, actually, several times."

"How?" Elliott glanced over at her.

"He has a tendency to tell the truth rather than say the tactful thing, sometimes. He's usually right but he just never learned to hold his tongue in instances where it might be better to say less than more."

They rode the rest of the way in silence, Maggie pointing out which turns to take, until they arrived at Francis Best's property. Elliott could see very little of it from where they parked on the road. A cedar hedge, at least fifteen feet high, bordered the road. It was only when they opened a wooden door built into the hedge that Elliott got the full impact of the piece of property. When they closed the door behind them, Elliott felt as though he'd stepped through a looking glass into Wonderland. Ahead of him stood a Craftsman-style home, painted yellow, window panes glinting in the sun, an air of lightness and grace about it. Surrounding it was a lawn as neat and tidy as any golf course he'd ever seen. Beyond the house was a beach and a small bay. He could hear the water lapping at the sand. Maggie stood still and let him absorb it all. When he looked down at her finally, after taking it all in, she smiled, "It's something isn't it?"

Elliott could only nod. It was gorgeous.

"Come," she said, taking his hand. Their palms fitted together, they walked along the fine gravel path that led toward the house. Ruby tacked back and forth in front of them, nose down, tail erect. Elliott was enjoying the feeling of Maggie's hand in his. They skirted the house – Maggie seemed to know where they were going – and another vista opened up before them on the far side of the house. A glass greenhouse sat beside an area surrounded by an eight-foot wire fence, which Elliott assumed was a garden. The fence would serve to keep the island's tiny breed of deer away from the vegetables. He could see someone moving around in the greenhouse. Maggie let go of his hand, much to his dismay, and pulled open the door calling out, "Francis?"

A man appeared as if from nowhere several yards away. He was wearing blue denim overalls over a long sleeved t-shirt and had a small trowel in one hand.

The greenhouse was filled with rows of tables, all covered in various sizes of pots, all growing something green. From the ceiling in places hung baskets as well, some dripping with trailing greenery. It was humid in the greenhouse, naturally, and Elliott found it stuffy after the clean air and bright sunshine outside. But the smells of soil and foliage were pleasing and he imagined how peaceful it must be to work in here.

The man in overalls came down the center aisle to meet them. Setting his trowel down on a table, he pulled Maggie into an embrace. "How are you, my dear? It's been too long."

"I'm okay, thanks, Francis."

Elliott's mother would have called Francis 'stout'. He was

probably five foot ten, but he looked shorter because he was thick all over. Not quite fat, just solid. His hair was grey but still speckled with brown throughout, and his face, as Elliott watched him over Maggie's shoulder, was the perfect Santa Clause face. So perfect for that role, it was like he was from central casting. He had no white beard or mustache, but his crinkly eyes were obviously used to smiling and laughing. His nose was slightly bulbous, but not unattractively so, and his eyebrows were mostly white, thick but carefully groomed.

The man held her at arms-length, absorbing her features, his eyes sparkling at her. Then his expression shifted. He had seen something in her face, "What is it? What's happened?"

"Haven't you heard?"

"Heard what? I've been out here since almost before dawn."

"Mom and Dad's cabin caught fire last night and burned down."

"Good heavens, my dear! Are you alright? What on earth happened?"

"We don't know. That's why we're here, Francis. I want to ask you some questions."

"Me?" The old man looked up from Maggie's face and for the first time seemed to see Elliott there. He looked back to Maggie, still holding her shoulders, "My dear. I'll tell you what I can. Whatever you need. First, tell me, who is this handsome stranger you've brought to see me? Second question; may I keep him?"

Maggie introduced Elliott to Francis, explaining briefly that they were trying to find out if the string of accidents at the inn were, in fact, accidental, or if there was someone out to do harm.

"Intrigue," Francis said, when Maggie finished, "I love it. It's like a John LeCarré novel. Well then, let's do this properly. Come inside for tea. And bring your handsome friend." He winked at Elliott.

The inside of the house was just as beautiful as the outside, masterfully decorated in a way that exuded comfort and warmth and coziness, without being twee. Francis led them through a back door into a mudroom lined with padded benches and a stone floor that Elliott imagined cost more than a year of his Parks Canada salary. Ruby pushed past them, trotting into the kitchen and making a beeline for one of the kitchen cupboards. Francis waved Maggie and Elliott over to a pair of couches that sat off to one side of the kitchen's island, while he found the tin Ruby remembered and gave her a treat; a long, green stick that she brought into the sitting area and proceeded to chew on the area rug. Francis fussed around the kitchen putting on the kettle and pulling china cups out of a glass-fronted cupboard.

The walls, at least in the kitchen and sitting areas, were a soft yellow color that only enhanced the sunshine streaming through the plentiful windows. As Elliott sat down on a floral sofa, he could see beyond the kitchen to a wide wooden staircase that led upstairs. Beside this there was a wide hallway that led from the front door. Paintings hung here and there, mostly watercolors of seascapes and west coast scenes. To Elliott's left was a river rock fireplace, much like the one at the Cormorant Inn, although on a much smaller scale, flanked by floor-to-ceiling bookshelves with doored cupboards on the bottom level. Scattered around the shelves were photos of what Elliott assumed were Francis' friends and family. In pride of place, at the center of one shelf, was an eight-by-ten photo in an ornate but not gaudy silver frame of Francis and, Elliott assumed, his husband. Maggie had said on the way over that his name was Nathan. Where Francis was thick and burly, Nathan, at least in the photo, appeared to be all lines and angles. His eyes were identical to Francis' though; clear, bright, jolly elf eyes. The whole room screamed money but without being rude about it. The ceilings above seemed higher than normal, but Elliott wasn't sure if that was true or if it was just an impression given by the tall windows everywhere.

While Elliot became familiar with his surroundings, Maggie made small talk, "Where's Nathan?"

"Oh, he's gone to the mainland for some terribly important business meeting. I don't know. I stopped listening when he said 'Board of Directors'."

"I thought he was retired."

"He is. Technically. But he likes to keep his hand in. He needs a reason to get out of bed in the morning and keeping his eye on the markets and on his investments seems to make him happy. It all goes over my head." Francis set a tray down on the coffee table between the two couches and explained to Elliott, "My husband is the city mouse. I'm the country mouse. Can you tell?" He did a little pose in his overalls, putting one hand on his hip.

The kettle began to whistle, and Francis hustled back around the kitchen island and finished making the pot of tea. When he returned to the sitting area he set the pot down on the tray. He went to a set of cupboards that flanked the fireplace to Elliott and Maggie's left and returned to the couch with a navy blue towel in his hands. He flipped it open and laid it out on the couch facing Maggie and Elliott, and then turned and sat down, "If I get dirt on this sofa, Nathan will never speak to me again." He smiled at his guests, "Now, shall I be mother?" He leaned forward and chose a large white ceramic mug from among the two more delicate tea cups on the tray, "I brought a manly mug for our manly man," he winked again at Elliott.

"Francis, stop flirting with Elliott!" Maggie pretended to be harsh but smiled when she said it.

"Oh, poo. Let an old queen have some fun. You don't mind, do you, son?"

"It's a nice change of pace, Francis." Elliott reached for the mug Francis was handing him, "Maggie hardly flirts with me at all."

Francis barked a little laugh and looked at Maggie, winking, "There. See? I know how to keep a man happy."

Tea poured, and everyone settled in with whatever combination of milk and sugar they needed, and a shortbread biscuit that the absent Nathan apparently made from his mother's recipe. Francis looked at Maggie, concern lining his face, his 'friendly fairy' mask dropping. "My darling. You look like shit. Tell me everything."

Maggie began with the fire, telling Francis how Ruby had woken her up in the wee hours that morning, barking hysterically. At her name the dog stopped chewing briefly, her mouth open in mid-chew. When she didn't hear any further instruction, she went back to the task of devouring the treat. Maggie explained that the volunteer firemen thought that an accelerant had been used to start the fire.

Francis gasped, "Oh, my dear. Diabolical."

Then Maggie worked her way backwards, beginning with the sinking of the fishing boat she'd been in on Saturday and moving from there to the other things that had been happening at the inn. When she finished, she paused and took a bite of her cookie, "I'm starting to think I'm going crazy, Francis."

"I think that day has long passed, chérie." He tapped his cookie over his tea cup like a cigarette and smiled fondly at his friend, "But tell me this, how do you think I can help?"

"What we're trying to do," when she said 'we' Maggie looked beside her at Elliott and he felt his heart swell a bit, "is figure out if anyone is deliberately trying to sabotage the inn. The number of things that have happened are too numerous to be a coincidence. And now, the fire," Maggie shivered, "means that whatever's going on is getting more serious."

Francis' brow furrowed, "Didn't I hear about a man from the inn drowning the other day?"

"Yes." Maggie put her tea cup down on the coffee table. "I'm sure that's not related to what we're looking into. But it hasn't helped the inn's reputation. Francis..." she faltered, looking for words, "if things don't get better, if I can't figure out what's going on, I'm going to lose the inn."

"Oh, honey." Francis looked at her with genuine concern in his eyes, "We are not going to let that happen. But I still don't get it – what can *I* do for you?"

Maggie settled back onto the sofa. She had left her boots in the mud room, and now she pulled her legs up under her, setting cross-legged. "What we're doing is looking at people who might want to take the inn away from me."

"Yes. With you so far."

"Elliott spoke to Michael Keith yesterday."

Francis looked directly at Elliott, "I'm sorry you had to go through that. A family of snakes if I ever saw one."

Maggie continued, "I also vaguely remembered a story about another family on the island who hated Mum and Dad. But I don't know any of the details. I was young when I first heard the story. It was one of those dinner party conversations my parents had with another couple when I was five or six. And you know how it is when you're a kid, you don't have any context for what's going on, and I wasn't all that interested anyway. I was bored and asked to be excused from the table."

Francis chuckled, "I still get that way."

"So I wondered, since you knew Mum and Dad then, and you sold them the property the inn is on, if you might know about this family or what happened back then."

"Do you know the name of the people?"

"I just have a vague sense that it was something like 'Peters' or 'Palmer'. I'm sure it started with a 'P'."

Elliott could see Francis thinking, his fingers tapping lightly on the bottom of his rose-patterned tea cup. The only sounds in the room were Ruby's vigorous chewing and the tick of the grandmother clock that stood against a wall opposite Elliott. He was admiring it's fine wooden casing and the unusual design of its pendulum when Francis' eyes flew open, and he burst forth, saying, "Petrov!"

Eighteen

ELLIOTT KNEW THEY WERE IN for a good long yarn, when after his exclamation, Francis stood up and went to the stove, lighting the fire under the kettle again so that he could freshen the teapot. He stood at the island, his hands placed palms down, slightly wider than his shoulders, on the granite countertop looking over Maggie and Elliott's heads at the stone fireplace without seeing it.

"Good God. George Petrov," he murmured to himself, "I haven't thought about you in years."

Elliott could see that Maggie was relaxed in Francis' presence. Her shoulders had dropped away from her ears and she seemed less fidgety. Without thinking, Elliott reached over and rubbed her left knee. She turned from watching Francis and looked at him, and he could see that the faintest bit of hope had returned to her eyes. She put her hand over his and squeezed his fingers slightly, which made Elliott ridiculously happy.

Francis returned to the sitting area with the teapot, still muttering under his breath. Maggie moved her hand back to her lap and Elliott reluctantly did the same. Francis made sure everyone had what tea and biscuits they needed and then, his own cup refreshed, he sat back on his towel-covered love seat and took a deep breath.

"My dear," he said, "this goes back to the days before you were born."

Elliott could tell the man was going to relish telling his story.

Francis and Nathan moved to Juliet Island in the early 1960s, "Almost before electricity, honey," Francis said and grinned at her. "There was nothing here. And I mean *nothing*. The roads were all gravel and the ferry ran twice a week, if we were lucky. That was how I got into gardening." He waved a hand toward the backyard, "I had to! Otherwise we would have had very little to eat."

He was exaggerating slightly, he admitted. There had been one small grocery store attached to the hardware store, and that was where people bought canned goods and flour and other staples, not to mention their shingles and roofing nails. "But if you didn't want to pay nine dollars for a head of lettuce, you grew it yourself."

The island, he went on to explain, was mostly occupied by farmers. People who had left society behind long ago and lived in splendid isolation on Juliet Island, rarely traveling back to the mainland. But, he further explained, that generation of islanders was getting on in years, and many of them were selling up and moving to places where they would have easier access to doctors and hospitals. Francis saw an opportunity and got his real estate license. Nathan was working in the city at the time, commuting to the island on the weekends, "And I needed something to do. Gardening couldn't fill all my hours, especially in the winter. And in those days, of course, we had no TV, no internet. It was pretty quiet here by myself."

Francis surprised himself with a natural flair for selling and became the island's best-known and most well-liked realtor within a very short period of time. He waved his hand across in front of his eyes quoting, "'For the Best in Juliet Island real estate, call Francis Best'. Oh, honey," he looked at Maggie, "I thought I was the cat's patoot. I wore suits and ties," he laughed at the memory, "And a fedora! It was amazing."

Business was booming. It was the 60s and many from Vancouver, and other parts of the country, were looking for a way to drop out and get back to the land.

"Most of them didn't last," Francis explained, "they tried it for a year or two but the septic fields and the dark wet winters made short work of many folks. Which was great for me," his eyes lit up, "because I could end up getting a sales commission on the same piece of property several times over. It was like printing money." He sighed, "I'm not a greedy man, but holy hell, we made a *lot* of money for a couple of decades there." He drifted off, remembering his glory days, and then looked back to Maggie and Elliott, "Anyway. Where was I? Oh yes, property. Specifically, the lot where your delightful inn now resides."

The waterfront land where the inn is located had originally been owned by a wealthy British ex-general named Edgar Combs. He owned a farm inland, as well, where he raised and bred Jersey cows and made cheese. The waterfront lot where the Cormorant Inn would eventually be built was special to him. It was where he had brought his children to play and he said it reminded him of the coastal town in the south of England where he'd grown up, looking out at the English channel.

When it came time for him and his wife to move to Victoria and live out their days in the comfort of a home with central heating instead of a wood stove, he hired Francis to help him sell the farm and the waterfront property. The farm had been snatched up immediately by a family from Penticton looking to escape the heat of the summers there, and the deep snows of the winter.

"And your mum and dad, of course, were interested in the waterfront piece of property." Francis put down his tea cup and continued his story, a dreamy look in his eyes, "Your dad had a vision, God bless him. There was no tourism on the island back then. This place was the back of beyond and no one came here unless they lived here. But somehow your dad knew the Gulf Islands would become a tourist destination one day. I don't know how he could see it, but he could. It was very clear to him. And he knew that an inn or a B&B built on that land overlooking the water would be idyllic. He was right of course, but everyone at the time thought he was nuts."

"Even my mum?"

"Especially your mum," Francis laughed. "But she loved your father fiercely and if that was what he wanted to do, then she planned to support him. He could do no wrong in her eyes. They were," he paused, thinking back, "unlike any other couple I'd ever met. Two such strong personalities but they fit together like a hand in a glove."

Out of the corner of his eye, Elliott noticed Maggie wipe a tear from her cheek.

Francis continued explaining. There had been another man interested in Edgar Combs' waterfront land. George Petrov.

"A rude man. Totally full of himself." Francis shook his head at the memory, "But he had more money than anyone I've ever met, before or since, and he was determined to own that land. He had plans to build a big, grand house on it and live there like a king in his feudal kingdom. Petrov had a manner, though, of rubbing everyone the wrong way. He was totally oblivious to social etiquette and manners and people's feelings. The only social skill he had was bullying, poor fellow."

Petrov had approached Francis about buying Combs' land and Combs had considered the offer carefully. "Your dad put in a bid, too, of course, but it was far below Petrov's. Your parents were penniless dreamers, not moguls like Petrov. I thought for sure the land would go to Petrov. But then he made an error that cost him the whole thing."

Petrov, according to Francis, had been convinced Combs would sell him the land. He had gone to the lot before the sale went through, and had used small wooden stakes and string to mark out where his grand house would be, looking out over the water, declaring his mastery over nature and the people of Juliet Island.

"What he hadn't counted on was that Combs came to the island from Victoria one weekend for a last look at his farm and his oceanfront view." Francis paused, "He was dying. He'd been diagnosed with lung cancer – he'd been a three-packs-a-day guy since the war – and he wanted to say goodbye to this place that had been so good to him and that he loved so much." Their host paused again, this time for dramatic effect, "He found Petrov's stakes in his property."

"What happened?" Elliott was on the edge of his seat.

Francis held one hand out toward Maggie, smiling. "The Archer's got the property. The rest is history."

"Wow," Maggie breathed.

"Yep. Combs was enraged that Petrov had the audacity to mark out how he would use the land before he'd even purchased it. Combs couldn't stand rudeness, and Petrov was rudeness personified. I was surprised that the deal had actually gone as far as it did. I think the only reason it did was that I was mediating between them. They were like chalk and cheese, those two. One, the old British Sergeant Major who was all about honor and discipline and," Francis searched for a term, "doing things the 'right' way. And the other, a bully right to his core, with money that came from no-one-knows-where." Francis clapped his hands together gently, "That was it. Combs sold your dad the property for about a quarter of what Petrov would have paid for it."

"Wow," Maggie said again.

"Wow, indeed, my girl." Francis, who had edged forward on his seat with the excitement of his story, now leaned back again, relaxing, "I haven't thought of that drama for decades."

"So," Maggie said, thinking out loud, "You think that if there was anyone who had it out for dad and the inn, it would be Petrov?"

"I do. Your dad had so few enemies, he was practically a saint.

And even this," Francis waggled one hand around in a circle, searching for a word, "*incident* wasn't his fault. It was totally Petrov who fucked that up. But," Francis now held up a stubby index finger, pointing at the ceiling, "Petrov was not the kind of guy to admit he had done wrong or to take responsibility for his actions."

"What happened to Petrov?" Elliott asked, and noticed Maggie nodding from her seat.

"He hung around Juliet Island for a while, bad-mouthing Maggie's dad to anyone who would listen. And then after a year or two he got tired of no one paying him any attention and took his sour grapes and moved to Pender Island. I think he started one of the first marinas over there."

"Where is he now?" Maggie and Elliott spoke in unison.

"Look at you two, all in sync." Francis batted his eyelashes at them and then got serious again, "He died. I heard he passed away in, oh, I dunno, 1994 or something."

"What?" Maggie sounded puzzled, "Wait. Why did you tell us this story then? If Petrov is dead how could he be the one sabotaging the inn?"

Francis answered her question with a question, "When did you say the accidents and weird things at the inn started happening?"

"About six months ago."

"That's what I thought. About six months ago someone approached me, thinking I was still in real estate, asking me if I knew if the Cormorant Inn was up for sale."

"No," Maggie leaned forward over her crossed knees. "Who?"

Francis looked back and forth from Elliott to Maggie, and then held one hand up beside his mouth, as though he was sharing a secret, and stage-whispered, "Inna Petrov. George's only child."

Nineteen

THE TIDE WAS MIDWAY THROUGH coming back in, and as a result the beach was slightly wider than usual. Ruby ran to and fro, zig-zagging across the dark, wet sand just beside the waves calmly slopping up on the beach. She ran with her nose down, as usual, sniffing every rock and clam shell, occasionally picking something up in her mouth to taste it before spitting it out. Her feet kicked up little pops of sand wherever she went, her nails digging into the beach.

Maggie wanted to bring Ruby out for a run before they got into the truck. "She needs to move after all the treats Francis gave her," she said as they navigated the wooden staircase at the end the road that bordered Francis' property.

The beach was a perfect crescent shape, ending at both tips in a small rocky bluff. Elliott held Maggie's hand as they walked down to one end of the beach and then turned and retraced their steps. On their left they could see Francis and Nathan's home, its entire front filled with windows that looked out onto this bay. The beach and bay were solely Francis and Nathan's domain. There was a second house on the opposite side of the road from theirs, which also looked out onto the beach. But when he walked them to the gate in the cedar hedge, Francis explained to Elliott that he and Nathan had bought that property years ago and now used the home on it as their guest house.

"Nathan's mother used to come and spend the summers with

us. Thank God she had her own place to stay. That woman's voice could peel the paint off walls." Francis rolled his eyes dramatically.

Francis hugged Maggie, assuring her it would all be okay, and told her to call him if she needed anything. He and Elliott had shaken hands, and Francis had held on for a few seconds longer than a standard handshake. He looked into Elliott's eyes, his own eyes serious instead of twinkly for the first time. "Be good to her," he said, nodding toward Maggie. "Understood?"

Thus, the beach was entirely deserted as Maggie and Elliott walked, and for this Elliott was grateful. It was peaceful and calm and, he suspected, just what Maggie needed after a traumatizing night and almost no sleep. They walked and talked, mulling over what Francis had told them. Maggie thought that she remembered hearing some of the information when she was a child, but had never heard the full story, or any of the names involved. Not that she would have remembered if she had.

"I was much more interested in Nancy Drew and the Famous Five than my parents' grown up stories."

Ruby approached with a thick stick about three feet long in her mouth and dropped it at Maggie's feet. Maggie looked at her dog and then up at Elliott. "If I throw it in the water for her, she's going to be wet when she gets in your truck."

As an answer, he bent down, picked up the stick, and threw it for the dog. Ruby bounded away, leaping into the water and swimming out to sea. "My truck has smelled of far worse things than wet dog," he said, and pulled Maggie into him.

She wrapped her arms very pleasingly around his torso and they stood there quietly, not speaking, listening to the waves and watching Ruby. Elliott could feel her heart beating against his chest. She had her face pressed into his neck and he realized she was right; her hair did still smell of smoke.

Ruby returned, dropping the stick at their feet and letting out one sharp bark, breaking them out of the moment. Maggie bent down this time and picked up the soggy stick, and threw it into the waves. Her hand was wet as Elliott took it. They continued walking down toward the tip of the beach they hadn't visited yet.

"So?" he asked, "What now?"

Maggie kicked at a rock that was partially buried in the sand, "Now we go and talk to Inna Petrov."

"Really? Right now?"

"No time like the present."

"Aren't you tired?"

"I'm exhausted. But I'm also weirdly wired. I have a zillion questions in my head and none of them have answers. It's like a hive of bees in there. I couldn't sleep even if I tried."

Ruby returned again, dropping the stick and then shaking from head to foot, letting sea water fly all around her, the tags on her collar rattling. Elliott threw the stick for her once more.

"Do you know where Inna lives?"

"I think so. I know the street Francis described, over on Lost Lake, and I'm pretty sure we can find the house if it's like he described."

"I'm happy to go with you if you still want company." He was surprised at the uncertainty he heard in his own voice. *You fool,* he thought, *you're afraid of rejection.*

But she didn't reject him. She turned and faced him, putting her hands lightly on his waist, "I want your company," she said, looking straight into his eyes, a slight smile on her lips.

He kissed her then, and she greeted his kiss warmly. She pulled herself closer to him, wrapping her arms all the way around him and leaning into him with the full length of her body. They stayed that way for some time, kissing and nuzzling one another. Elliot wanted to be closer to her but he wasn't sure how to accomplish that except by climbing inside her clothes with her, which wasn't an entirely unappealing prospect. Then he stopped thinking altogether. His mind drifted away while he felt the softness of her cheeks and lips and the way her hands pushed gently at his back. He wasn't sure how long they stayed this way, but at some point he became aware that Ruby had been barking at them for a while. Maggie finally began to laugh when the dog pushed her nose against their legs and pawed at their feet. She looked down at her dog, saying with mock anger, "Ruby! Can't you see I'm enjoying myself?"

Elliott grinned, delighted at this description.

Twenty

MAGGIE FELT LIKE SHE COULDN'T stop smiling. The grin pasted across her face was threatening to make her cheeks hurt but she couldn't stop. She stole a glance at Elliott across the truck cab every now and then and felt like giggling like a schoolgirl. Even though she'd only had about two hours of sleep, she felt wide awake and energized.

How long had it been since a man had kissed her? she wondered. She counted back and decided it had been at least five years. So long that she'd forgotten how great it felt. Her whole body felt alive now in a way it hadn't since before her parents got sick.

And he was so tall! She loved that, it made her feel feminine. She'd always been the tallest girl in her class at school and had felt like a lumbering giant most of the time, especially in middle school. In high school the boys had caught up, but even so, she had been head and shoulders taller than some of them. With Elliott she had to lean her head back and reach up to kiss him. It was divine.

The truck began to slow down and then stopped. She looked through the windshield and saw they were at the end of a road that had no exit. A wall of pine trees faced her.

Elliott looked over at her and grinned, "I thought you were navigating."

Maggie smiled back at him, "Sorry. I'm a little distracted."

"Should I turn around?"

"Yes, please."

Eventually, with Maggie a little more focused, they made their way to Green Lane, which was where Francis said they would find Inna's house. "A charmless little box," Francis had said, "Light blue, I think. A brown mini-van parked out front with a caved-in rear bumper."

"There it is," Maggie said, peering through her window. "That must be it."

Francis had been right. It was charmless, especially from the road. Beyond the house she could see Lost Lake, so perhaps the esthetically pleasing part of the house faced the lake.

They left Ruby in the truck and mounted the wooden steps to the home, which was indeed completely square, like an oversized moving box. A raw length of two by four was nailed into the siding beside the stairs to serve as a handrail. A wheelchair ramp sloped down to the driveway from the porch as well, it's surface covered in some sort of black non-slip fabric that was curling and tearing at the edges. A wheelchair sat parked in the corner of the porch.

Maggie rapped on the glass of the screen door. She could smell cigarette smoke from where she stood.

"Who's there?" A voice called out from the house.

"Maggie Archer to see Inna Petrov." Maggie felt like she was leaving a voicemail message.

A woman appeared behind the glass. She had a faded pink housecoat that she was holding closed with one hand. Sticking out below the hem Maggie could see plaid pajama bottoms. The woman's feet were bare and her toenails were painted a dark red that was almost black. Her hair appeared to be long and blonde, though it was pulled untidily into a mass on the back of her head, so it was hard to tell. She had a cigarette in the hand that wasn't holding the robe and a sour expression on her face. "Who?" she said, peering through the glass and looking Maggie and Elliott up and down.

"Maggie Archer. I own the Cormorant Inn. I think our fathers knew one another, and I wondered if I could talk to you for a moment."

The woman was silent, but she stayed, staring out though the glass.

"Who is it?" Another voice, this one gravelly and followed by a cough came from the recesses of the house.

The woman who Maggie assumed was Inna said, without turning her head, "She says her name's Maggie Archer. She knew Dad."

"I didn't know your father…" Maggie started to explain. But the second voice came again, "Let her in, then. Don't leave guests standing on the porch."

Maggie stepped out of the way while Inna pushed the door open. She motioned for Maggie and Elliott to move past her. They stepped into an entryway that was so small it was almost like an elevator. Maggie and Elliott stood squeezed together, Inna facing them. At one side there was a doorless closet filled to overflowing with coats, hats, shoes and boots that spilled onto the floor around them.

"Come," Inna moved past them into what appeared to be the main room of the house. The floor was linoleum and creaked under Maggie's boots. At the far end of the room were two large picture windows beside one another, each about eight feet wide and five feet high. They looked out onto Lost Lake and were the best feature of what was a truly awful residence. Francis had called it charmless, but he obviously had never been inside. If he had he wouldn't have been so generous in his description.

There was enough furniture in the room to fill a space three times the size. In fact, as Maggie and Elliott entered the room they ended up pressed into the back of a love seat, which was about the only place to stand. Inna weaved through a maze of upholstered chairs, reclining chairs and couches before she landed in one that was obviously hers. An ashtray sat on the arm, and without looking at it, she steadied it with a reflexive, obviously habitual motion as she sat down. Two bookcases sat facing one another from opposite sides of the room, layers of magazines and newspapers filling each shelf. Scattered around the room in small pots were plants in various stages of demise. A fern, whose leaves were all brown and crisp looking, sat forlornly in the seat of a baby's high chair in the far corner of the room beside a television that flickered with blue light.

Maggie felt as though she was viewing all this through a thick fog. She fought an urge to rub her eyes to clear them of the cigarette smoke.

"Who did you say you were?" A woman who resembled Inna around the downturned mouth and squinty eyes sat in a brown reclining chair beside Inna's, both big toes pointing through holes in her blue socks. She, too, was wearing a bathrobe, though hers was the color of a blue lupine. Her hair was entirely white and wrapped over the top of her head in a long braid.

"I'm Maggie Archer and this is my friend Elliott Simon. Are you Mrs. Petrov?"

"Yes. Do I know you?"

"No ma'am, I don't think you do. But I believe my father, Reginald Archer, knew your husband."

The older woman sat back a little, thinking, her fingers worrying the free end of the belt on her robe.

Inna was staring at the television, though the sound was muted. She spoke to her mother without turning her head, "The Archers who stole that land on the bluff from Dad."

The effect of her daughter's information on the older woman was instantaneous and violent. Mrs. Petrov heaved herself forward, the footrest of the chair folding down into its closed position with a snap and the chair creaking and groaning. She scooted herself forward on the seat of the chair when it was parallel with the floor and pointed a long, yellowed finger at Maggie, "You!" She started to cough, her cheeks puffing up and her mouth forming a precise round 'O'. Maggie waited. When the paroxysm slowed, the woman said it again, "You! How can you be in my house? How is this possible? Get out. Get out!" She started to cough again and fell back against the chair, her chest heaving.

Throughout this display, Inna continued watching the silent shapes float around on the TV screen, seemingly oblivious.

Maggie tried to explain her presence when the coughing began to slow again, "Mrs. Petrov, I just want to ask you a few questions. I don't want to upset you…"

Seized again by coughing, the old woman couldn't speak. With wild eyes and a claw-like hand she began to grab at the arm of her daughter's chair, motioning for Inna to get up and escort the visitors out of the house.

"It's okay, Mama. Just listen to them."

The woman's flailing and coughing began to worsen. Maggie was terrified they would induce a heart attack if they stayed any longer. "It's okay. We'll go." She touched Elliott's arm and they side-stepped their way to the entryway and then out the front door. They started down the steps when Maggie heard the front door open behind her. She turned and Inna was there, still smoking, still holding her bathrobe closed with one hand.

"What is your question?" she whispered. "Maybe I can help."

Maggie was surprised at the offer, but didn't pass it up, "We were just speaking to Francis Best. He mentioned that you recently asked him about my inn. I wanted to know why and also find out how your mother felt about my father. But," Maggie gestured toward the living room, "I think I have the answer to the second question, at least."

Inna snorted, "She's not a woman who can ever let anything go."

"I see that."

"As for why I was asking about the inn…" Inna looked away over the scrubby patch of land that could be considered her front yard. She took another drag of her cigarette and eventually turned back to look at Maggie. She gave her shoulders a slight shrug. "Curiosity, I suppose. Mama and I moved back to this island from

Salt Spring six months ago. Mama never liked that island. Too busy, she said. But Papa liked it there. Anyway, we bumped into Francis at the market one day a few months ago and I just wondered." She shrugged again. "I wondered what was going on with the place that had caused so much anger in my papa."

Maggie wasn't sure she believed the woman. Her manner was guarded, as though she was hiding something, but without knowing her, Maggie couldn't tell if that was unusual.

"There was a fire last night at your hotel, yes?" Inna took a pull on her cigarette and then blew smoke sideways, away from the house.

"Yes," Maggie wasn't surprised Inna knew this. The island grapevine never failed to keep the population informed of current events.

"You're wondering if we had anything to do with it. Because of the bad blood between our families."

Maggie's head jerked back a little. She was stunned and embarrassed that her motives were so transparent. "Well…" she hesitated again.

"It's okay," Inna said, waving the hand with the cigarette, "if our positions were reversed I'd wonder the same thing. But I can tell you we didn't." She gestured toward the living room beyond the glass of the screened door, "Mama can't do anything on her own these days, and I'm her caregiver. I'm never more than ten feet away from her. We were here last night. All night. Watching those stupid reality TV shows she likes." She made finger quotes around 'reality'. "The only place we ever go is to the community center so she can play bridge with her cronies. It drives her mental that the building is named after your father but, if she didn't go there she'd be housebound."

They heard some coughing from inside the house and then Mrs. Petrov's gravelly voice, "Inna!"

"I'd better go or she'll get worked up again. Is that what you came for?"

Maggie nodded and said thank you. The screen door bashed into the frame after Inna went back inside.

As Maggie and Elliott walked back to his truck, Ruby watched them from the driver's seat. "Impressive detective work, Mags," Elliott said. It was the first time he'd called her by her family nickname.

"I didn't do anything." She opened the passenger door and shooed Ruby into the back seat.

"Genius," Elliott said, climbing into his seat, "you got the information you needed. Pure genius."

"Did you believe her?"

He paused while he was putting his seatbelt on. "Not entirely. Did you?"

Maggie thought for a few minutes, replaying the previous moments in her mind's eye. "They're close, obviously. Mother and daughter. Or, at least, they're bound to one another it seems. I dunno." She chewed on a hangnail, gazing through the windshield but not seeing the trees just beyond it. "I expect that Inna would say pretty much anything to protect her mum. Don't you?" She turned in her seat to look at Elliott.

He thought for a moment and then nodded. "That was my impression, too."

In the back seat Ruby huffed out a long sigh.

"Where to now, boss?" Elliott finally asked.

He smiled at her while he finished putting his seatbelt on and she noticed, not for the first time, that when he looked directly at her like that, she felt as though she was surrounded by light.

Elliott backed out of the Petrov's driveway and onto Green Lane. He turned left and they drove for a few minutes in silence until Elliott realized he didn't know where they were going. He pulled just off the narrow road into the top of a driveway and put the truck in park. Maggie looked over at him, questions in her eyes.

"What?" she said and then yawned a huge, jaw cracking yawn, covering her mouth with both hands, "Excuse me. I think last night is catching up with me."

"I think I should take you home so you can have a nap."

"No," she said, in a slightly whiny voice, "I want to carry on. Let's go to the community center and see if they can confirm that Inna and her mum are inseparable." Maggie yawned again, her body shuddering slightly with the effort.

Elliott put the truck into drive again and pulled out. They approached a T intersection and he turned right.

"Ooops," Maggie said, "the community center's the other way. I guess you're still learning your way around the island."

"Nope. I'm not lost this time. I know exactly where I'm going. I'm taking you home, young lady. You need a nap or you're going to drop. The community center can wait until tomorrow."

Maggie looked over at him and screwed up her face in objection, but she knew he was right. She was having trouble staying awake.

The drive to the inn was only five minutes, but she was drifting off when they turned onto Wellington Street. She pulled her head up off the seat back and said through another yawn, "Go past the main driveway."

Elliott did as she bid.

"Slow down," she said, "See that spruce tree with the reflector?"

"Yes."

"Turn in there."

Elliott slowed down so that he could maneuver the truck onto a track that was almost invisible from the road. They bumped along, the truck squeezing through evergreen trees like someone working their way through a crowded room. The track opened up a bit and he saw that they were at Maggie's back door.

"Ta da," she said, smiling. "Now you know the secret entryway to my superhero hideout. I normally just take the road down from the inn's parking lot, but this way those busybodies at the inn won't know I'm home."

Elliott turned off the truck and unclipped his seatbelt. He pointed at her, "Stay there."

She did as he asked and watched as he walked around the front of the truck and came to her door. He opened it and offered her his hand, pulling her out and into his arms.

They kissed again. Ruby leapt into the front seat and jumped down onto the ground, nearly knocking the couple over, but that didn't stop them. Maggie snuggled right into Elliott's chest, her arms wrapped tightly around his neck. She could hear his breathing and the quiet thump of his heart. She could have stayed there all day, but after some time, he pulled away and lifted a hand so that he could caress her cheek with one thumb.

"You better get inside and get some sleep."

"Okay," she said, reluctance in her voice.

"I'll call you later."

"Okay."

He kissed her once more, briefly, and then pointed her toward her front door. Her feet carried her up the path and through the front door. She turned and waved before closing it behind her.

Kicking off her boots, and letting her jacket fall onto the entryway floor, she staggered toward the bedroom and fell face first onto her bed. Ruby jumped up onto the bed beside her but Maggie didn't notice. She was already asleep.

Twenty-One

THE BAKERY SMELLED AS ALL bakeries should, of yeast and flour, sweetness and home. The bell above the door rang as Elliott pushed through it. He nodded to Amber, who was helping a customer, placing still warm loaves of bread into paper bags. The fluorescent-haired clerk smiled at him as he walked around her behind the counter toward the kitchen, and if he'd known the lascivious thoughts she had about her boss's handsome brother he would have blushed.

Libby was in her usual spot at the kitchen's island, papers spread out in front of her, a pen in one hand.

"Hey, you're not up to your elbows in icing sugar," he said, moving to the large double-doored fridge.

"Checking my list. Making sure I'm remembering all the speciality orders for this week." She looked up at him, her glasses glinting, "What's up with you?"

"Just here for refueling." He pulled a plastic container from one of the shelves and grabbed a tomato, a glass jar of homemade mayonnaise, roast beef, and a brick of Havarti cheese, closing the fridge door with his foot.

"How's Maggie doing? Any more news about the fire?"

"None that I'm aware of." Elliott started to grab a loaf of bread off a cooling rack but Libby swatted his wrist with her pen.

"Don't touch that. Those are for customers." She pulled a brown paper bag off a different shelf, "Here use this one. It's already been started."

Elliott pulled a half loaf of French country bread out of the bag, grabbed the long bread knife from the magnetized holder on the wall, and began cutting himself several thick slices of bread.

"Where is she?" Libby held her hand out and her brother cut her two slices of bread as well.

"She was falling asleep on her feet so I took her home to have a nap."

"Good man."

They ate standing at the island, washing their roast beef and cheese sandwiches down with beer from the fridge. Elliott shared what he knew from their bit of investigation.

"I wouldn't trust those Petrovs as far as I could throw them," Libby offered when Elliott was done. "But I also do tend to believe that Inna couldn't leave her mother for more than a few minutes at a time. The old woman is plenty sick from what I hear."

"I think tomorrow, when Maggie's feeling better, we'll go to the community center and see what they have to say. It sounds like that's the only place they go regularly. The staff there, or the other visitors, might know a bit more about them."

Libby chewed, staring off into space. Elliott waited for her to form her thoughts.

She turned back to look at him after a few moments, "You know who it occurs to me might be a help in all this?"

"Who?"

"Grace Miller and Eleanor Jones."

"Who are they?"

"Builders. They own the building company on the island with the best reputation for quality and fair practices. They build large, custom design homes. If anyone knows about dirty deeds going on with the island's developers, or people who were interested in ruining Maggie's business, it might be them."

Elliott thought for a few seconds. "Okay, I'll add that to the list of places Maggie and I should visit."

Now it was Libby's turn to think. "She might appreciate if you talk to Grace and Eleanor now, while she's resting. The sooner the answers are found, the sooner she'll be able to stop worrying. And," Libby said, raising an eyebrow at her brother, "it might put you even deeper in her good graces."

Elliott grinned. "You don't need to say any more. Draw me a map. Where do I find the famous Grace and Eleanor?"

He could hear the construction site before he saw it. His truck ground slowly over a gravel drive that wound through trees, reminding him of the secret driveway at Maggie's house. He heard a band saw, primarily, and as he got closer, the sound of hammers and electronic nail guns.

As he came to the edge of the woods, the building site was impressive; lush, green meadows like something out of an English period drama spread out in every direction around the bones of a house that rose up majestically toward the clear blue sky. The house appeared as though it would be three stories high when finished. Men in jeans and tool belts crawled over and around it, like ants at an abandoned picnic. The whir and whine of activity was in stark contrast to the peaceful surroundings. Sawhorses were set up here and there, creating temporary work tables. Piles of two-by-fours and other materials lay along the border of the gravel drive. Elliott parked his truck and got out, scanning the area for any sign of a woman. He spotted one, finally, coming out of the house and down the temporary steps that led from what would be the front door. She was carrying a set of what he assumed must be the architectural or engineering plans for the house; long sheets of paper rolled into a tube. She saw Elliott looking at her and handed the papers to the man walking beside her. He peeled off and went around the side of the house, while the woman strode across the driveway toward Elliott.

"Can I help you?"

She was tiny. Elliott wondered if she topped five feet. Her hair was white blonde and seemed naturally so, although he knew he was a terrible judge of those sorts of things, and it was cut into what he thought women called a 'pixie cut.' Short all over, it was wispy and fine and looked like the down that new babies often have on their heads. While she was physically small, her energy was not. She marched directly over to Elliott, head held high, shoulders back, and he could see her examining him, wondering why he was there. She stopped directly in front of him, put her hands on her tiny hips, and looked directly into Elliott's eyes, her expression not challenging, but not super warm either.

Libby had instructed her brother to drop her name. Grace and Eleanor were, apparently, very good customers of The Bakeri. Elliott held out his right hand, "I'm Elliott Simon, Libby's brother."

The woman took his hand and they shook, Elliott making sure he didn't crush her tiny bird-like hand. "Grace Miller," she said, and then, "Libby from The Bakeri?"

"Yes. In fact," he turned and opened the passenger door of his truck and pulled out two large, flat bakery boxes, "she sent these over for your crew."

Elliott held the two boxes flat on his palms and Grace lifted up the corner of one and peeked in. Then she looked up at Elliott. "Oh, my," she said. "Your sister is making friends for life." She began to walk away and motioned with her head for Elliott to follow.

She led him over to a piece of plywood that had been set up on two sawhorses. There were three carafes there as well, one labelled 'Decaf,' paper cups and plastic lids, small bowls filled with cream containers and sugar packets. Grace patted the makeshift table and Elliott set the boxes down, moving them so they were side-by-side. He and Grace lifted the lids off, revealing the slices of lemon loaf and banana bread, cinnamon buns, croissants, and other goodies that filled each box. Grace put the first two fingers of each hand in the corner of her mouth and let out a whistle so shrill and loud it startled him. All the activity on the site stopped instantly and every eye turned and looked at Grace.

She held one arm aloft and made a sweeping motion, "Coffee break, guys," she yelled.

Within seconds, the table was surrounded by men dressed in an almost identical uniform of t-shirt, jeans, steel-toed boots and tool belt. They were obviously very pleased about the proffered treats, a couple going as far as slapping Elliott on the back in thanks.

While they were helping themselves and pouring coffee, Grace caught Elliott's eye and motioned for him to follow her again. They crunched along the driveway around to the side of the house where there were two picnic benches set up. Grace climbed up to sit on the tabletop of one of the benches, resting her tiny feet on the seat. Elliott followed suit and wondered if she'd had to buy her steel-toed boots in a children's shop, they were so small. From where they sat, they could see the crowd around the makeshift buffet table, smiling and chewing, baked goods disappearing down their throats in one or two bites.

"You made my crew happy," the woman said, "so now you're in my good graces. I assume you're not just here to dispense treats. What can I do for you?"

She was stunningly beautiful. Hers was one of those faces that was so symmetrical, the skin so unblemished and perfect; she was like a doll that had come to life. Her eyes were clear blue, like a Caribbean sea, and it was readily apparent that there was a tremendous amount of intelligence behind them. Elliott found himself lost for a second. He mentally shook himself and focused on the task at hand.

"I've come to ask you some questions about development on the island."

"Okay. Ask away."

Elliott explained that he and Maggie were trying to find out if someone was deliberately sabotaging the Cormorant Inn. He shared some of the accidents that had been happening and outlined the information they'd gathered so far, or lack of it, and the people they'd talked to, including Michael Keith and Inna Petrov. "Libby suggested I come and talk to you. She said you and your business partner know a lot about development on the island and might have some insight into who could be trying to get Maggie to sell."

"I heard about the fire last night. Was anyone hurt?"

While Elliott shared the events of the fire, Grace listened politely. Behind her eyes he could see her thinking. It was almost like a tangible force, as though her thoughts were generating steam or noise around them. When he'd finished she was quiet for a moment.

"So you think someone's doing these things deliberately?"

"We're not positive, but Maggie has a sense that there's more going on than just bad luck at the inn. The incident with the boat, especially, seemed unlikely to have been just an accident. And now the firemen are saying they suspect an accelerant was used on the cabin last night."

"Jeez. That's not good." Grace raised her eyebrows and then lowered them. She was quiet again, and turned her head to look at the half-built house in front of her. "You see this place?" She gestured with one had toward the wooden structure, "Some Hollywood type is having this built. An actor with too much hair and big pectoral muscles. He's about as smart as my right boot," she lifted her foot off the bench seat and then put it back down again, "but he makes up for it by being a belligerent asshole." She turned and smiled at Elliott, letting him in on the joke. "And he's got more money than God. He bought this piece of land sight unseen and hired Ellie and me – that's my partner, Eleanor – the same way. He's never been to the island. Skypes with us occasionally to see how things are going, but mostly just writes us big checks."

Elliott wondered briefly what this had to do with the issue

he'd come to her with, but he let her talk, figuring that with those intelligent eyes she knew what she was doing.

She continued, "Juliet Island has become something of a trendy place for the rich and famous these days. I've built two other houses for Hollywood guys just in the last year; one a waterfront place made of glass, overlooking Eber Sound, and the other a stone building modeled – I kid you not – on Windsor Castle. It's got a round turret and everything."

A tall man approached the bench where Elliott and Grace sat. He was at least as tall as Elliott, but much bulkier everywhere. Thick like a bulldog, where Elliott was lean like a racehorse. The man's t-shirt looked exhausted from the strain of holding itself together over his biceps. His hammer's blue grip banged against his right leg as he walked. He held a paper coffee cup in one hand and a paper plate in the other. As he got closer, Elliott could see the plate had a couple of muffins balanced on it. "Boss," the man said, addressing Grace, "you'd better take these before everything is gone. Otherwise you'll miss out."

He handed the plate to Grace, lifted his coffee cup in a 'cheers' gesture to Elliott and then turned and began to walk away.

"Thanks, Bernie," Grace said, "you're a doll."

The man, without looking back, raised his cup again over his shoulder.

Grace offered the plate to Elliott, who declined, his sandwich from Libby's kitchen still filling him up pleasantly. Grace took a muffin for herself and laid the plate on the bench beside her. She began to pick at the muffin, putting tiny chunks in her mouth and chewing thoughtfully.

"So, on the one hand," she continued from where she had left off, "it's a great thing that Juliet is going through this little boom. It keeps guys like Bernie employed, not to mention Eleanor and me. But," she paused, "there is also a downside. And that is the cutthroat stuff that starts to happen when lots of money is involved." She put the muffin down on the plate beside her, less than a quarter of the top nibbled away, and wiped the crumbs off her lap, "I've had other builders come to my sites while Eleanor and I were away and try to hire my entire crew right out from under me. Luckily for me I hire good guys and they told those fuckers to get lost, but it would have been disastrous if they hadn't."

Elliott couldn't know how the crew felt about Eleanor, or course, but given how Bernie had just treated Grace – with obvious affection and thoughtfulness – Elliott suspected that her crew's loyalty probably had a lot to do with her leadership and generosity, and not just the crew's goodwill. When the men had swarmed the table for their coffee break he noticed an air of relaxation and contentment. It was one he recognized from when he was leading small crews of men in the parks. You could always tell when a group was discontented, even if no one spoke, and his impression of Grace's work site was that this was a very happy group.

She spoke again, over his thoughts, "I've also had wood and supplies stolen from our sites. We've had to hire a security guard with a dog to patrol each site at night. For a place where most people don't lock their front doors, it's disappointing to be dealing with that kind of stuff on this island."

Elliott made a quiet sound to indicate he was listening. He didn't want to comment and stop the flow of information.

"So," Grace slapped her palms on her thighs, "all that is to say that it isn't inconceivable to me that someone would be trying some dirty deeds to get Maggie off that piece of land. It is, without a doubt, one of the loveliest and most picturesque parcels on the island. Waterfront, beaches, those small bluffs that just add to the visual appeal, good water source, south facing; it has it all really." She looked at Elliott for the first time in awhile, "But anyone on this island who knows Maggie, even by reputation, knows she will never sell. That place is her home. It's not just a business to her."

Elliott nodded, and his thoughts drifted to Maggie, remembering her arms around him and the way she laid one foot over his when they kissed.

"Uh, oh," Grace said.

Elliott snapped to and looked over at the house, thinking an accident was about to happen. He saw nothing out of place and looked back at Grace to find her watching him, curiosity and mirth in her eyes. "What?" he said.

"I always knew that one day someone amazing would come along and snap Maggie Archer up. I would have tried to win her myself, but she doesn't play for my team."

Elliott felt heat rising up his throat to his face.

"She's a good woman," Grace continued, "and you might just be worthy of her."

Elliott began to stammer, "I'm not… That is, we don't… I'm, uh, I'm leaving for the mainland in a few days, as soon as Constable Nelson gives me the green light. I'm just helping Maggie out until then."

Grace raised her eyebrows, pierced him with her blue gaze and then smiled, widely and without guile. "Whatever you say, handsome."

Twenty-Two

THE INN WAS QUIET TUESDAY evening. There were a few guests in the great room, reading or chatting. A fire had been lit in the enormous stone fireplace that cast a pleasant orange glow over the room. The room was as large as the main floor of a decent-sized house. Scattered around it were many couches, comfy chairs, end tables and coffee tables. The room was windowed on three sides with two large French doors at the far end that led out to the wide wooden deck that overlooked the sea.

Maggie sat around the corner from the great room at the front desk, going over the Trip Tips reviews.

She had slept for three hours, and woken disoriented, the sun on its way down. Hungry, she and Ruby wandered up to the lodge and let Greg feed them both. Now she was wide awake, despite the late hour, and knew it would be ages before she would be able to sleep again.

Behind her, she could hear Greg singing quietly to himself as he cleaned the kitchen and prepped some sort of roast for the next night's supper.

She stretched and yawned, leaning back in her chair. Under the reception desk Ruby's tail thumped on the floor at the movement. Maggie folded forward and reached under the desk to rub the dog's haunch.

"Who's a good girl, Ruby?" she said quietly to her dog. "Is she a good dog?"

Ruby made a small moan of pleasure and laid her head back down on her bed, her tail still twitching slightly.

"Hello?" the voice came from above.

Maggie sat up, careful not to bang her head on the bottom of the desk.

June Brier was there, looking anxiously out from beneath shadowed eyes.

"Mrs. Brier," Maggie said, straightening her sweater, "can I help you?"

The grieving widow was disheveled, to say the least, in stark contrast to how she'd looked the day before. Grief was obviously taking its toll. In addition to her shadowed eyes, her blond hair, normally without a hair out of place, was squashed on one side of her head and almost matted on the other. She was wearing a pink bathrobe over what Maggie glimpsed to be an old Pink Floyd concert t-shirt. From where she sat, Maggie couldn't see what she had on her legs.

Sparrow had been assigned the task of checking in on Mrs. Brier at mealtimes to see if she was hungry. So far the woman had refused all offers except one, when she asked for some dry toast. It was clear she had hardly eaten anything since she arrived at the inn on Sunday. If possible her cheekbones and chin were even more prominent. This was a very different woman from the contemptuous one Maggie had encountered the day before. In less than forty-eight hours June Brier seemed to have disintegrated. Gone was the social mask of control. Gone were the easy-breezy California surfer chick clothes. The tight 'LA Face' (as Melissa had called it) was still there, but the makeup that turned it into a work of art was long gone, along with the false eyelashes.

"The kitchen's probably closed, isn't it?" June looked over Maggie's shoulder through the door that led to the kitchen.

"It is," Maggie answered, and then, taking pity on the woman, "but the chef is still here and I'm sure he could whip something up for you. What would you like?"

"Oh, I don't know. I don't want to be any trouble."

"It's no trouble, Mrs. Brier. What can we get you?"

June started to turn away from the desk, "That's okay. I think I have a granola bar in my purse."

Maggie's natural instinct for taking care of her guests overtook her, despite June's obviously false attempt at self-reliance. Maggie scooted around the desk and intercepted her. She put her arm around June's shoulder and turned her around.

"Come on, now," she said, adopting the gentle tone she used with kids when they were afraid to pet Ruby. "You clearly need something to eat. And Chef Greg is right here. What can we make you? Some scrambled eggs? Some toast? A bowl of soup? There's some lovely butternut squash and apple soup left over from lunch."

Maggie guided June around the desk to the staff side and sat her in the second task chair. It wasn't the most comfortable or comforting place, but Maggie sensed that if she sat June down anywhere out of sight, the woman would disappear.

June sagged into the chair and leaned on one of the arms. She picked at one end of the belt on her robe while Maggie waited for her to make a decision about what to eat.

"Maybe some soup," June finally said.

"Great." Maggie stepped into the kitchen doorway. She interrupted Greg's whistling, "Could you please warm up some soup for Mrs. Brier."

"Aye-aye, Captain," the chef said, and pulled a small pot out from under the counter.

Maggie settled into her own chair and smiled at June. "Is there anything else you'd like? Can I get you a glass of wine?"

"No thanks. I've had a couple of those sleeping pills the doctor prescribed so I'd better not."

Maggie was astounded that the woman was awake if she'd taken two tablets. She did look a little glassy-eyed, now that Maggie looked closer.

"Arthur was a good guy," June said in a way that indicated this idea had been on her mind for a long time.

"He was always very polite and friendly to us," Maggie agreed.

"He took good care of me. And he was home sometimes. Not like my other husbands who I had to practically chain to the house to get them to spend time with me."

It was obvious that June needed to vent some feelings. Maggie sensed it didn't matter what she said in response, so she just listened, nodding and feeling sorry for the lonely and bereaved woman in front of her. She wondered if June had any girlfriends at home who might provide her with some solace. She suspected not if June was sitting in the lobby of a far-away inn after midnight, pouring out her heart to a relative stranger.

June was rambling and Maggie had a bit of trouble following the thread of the conversation, but after a few minutes she realized she didn't have to. Just being present was enough.

"What issit about men that they turn us into fools?" Her words were starting to slur slightly. Maggie wondered when June had taken those sleeping pills because they seemed to be kicking in. She was about to answer but June carried on, not needing input.

"I tellya. My next husband is going to have to be quite something to compare to Arthur."

Greg appeared with a tray in his hands. He handed it to Maggie who set it on the desk.

"Come on, June. Let's get some food into you. Try this soup." Maggie handed her guest the bowl, making sure June was holding onto it properly before she let go. She then handed June a spoon and the woman took a few tentative sips.

"Hot," she said.

"Give it a few minutes to cool down."

"It's never enough, is it?"

Maggie looked at her guest quizzically. "What's never enough?"

"The time. The time they spend with you. Is it? It's never enough."

"Eat some soup, June."

The grieving widow did as she was told, blowing sloppily on spoonfuls of soup and then lifting them to her plump lips.

After a few mouthfuls, June began to have trouble with her aim. Twice she missed her mouth and jabbed her chin with the spoon, soup spilling onto her robe. Maggie realized she must have taken the sleeping pills just before coming downstairs. They were obviously beginning to have an effect. She reached forward and took the bowl out of June's hands.

"Greg?" she called into the kitchen.

The chef appeared in the doorway. "Yes, boss?"

"Help me get Mrs. Brier up to her room."

Greg threw his tea towel over one shoulder and stepped over beside June's chair. The widow's chin was nodding toward her chest now, and her eyes were closing. One of her hands fell off the chair's armrest into her lap and lay there like a strand of spaghetti.

Greg and Maggie positioned themselves on either side of her and each pulled an arm over their shoulder.

"One. Two." Maggie said.

On three they both stood, pulling June up with them. As they moved around the desk toward the stairs, June's feet made an attempt to shuffle along, but mostly Maggie and Greg were carrying her.

Getting their guest up the stairs was a struggle. At one point June began to wake up. She tried to turn and head back down the staircase, which undoubtedly would have been a disaster. Maggie and Greg kept a tight hold on her but wrestling and carrying a grown woman up a flight of stairs is harder than it sounds.

"Wheresa soup?" June mumbled, "Imma cuckoo." She tried to push Greg away, her movements sloppy and loose.

Greg grunted and tried to take hold around June's waist. The bathrobe was not helping; it made it hard to get a good grip on her.

"Maggie," Greg pushed June's hand out of his face, "Have you got her?"

Maggie was crouching down, trying to keep June's right arm over her shoulders. "Come on, June. Let's get you to bed."

The woman was still mumbling. Maggie only caught the odd word or two and none of it seemed to make sense. An opiate-induced rant.

Suddenly June's head lifted up and she tried to maneuver it so she could look at Greg. "Yer cutey," she said. "Howza planner? Imma cuckoo, didja know?" June chuckled to herself as Maggie and Greg lifted her up another step.

The mumbling continued while Maggie and Greg got June all the way up the staircase and down the hall to her room. Maggie propped their guest up against Greg while she fished in the pockets of the bathrobe for a room key. She came up empty so tried the knob and found it wasn't locked. Maggie said a silent prayer, grateful that the Cormorant Inn hadn't moved into the 21st century by installing card locks.

They basically dragged June across the threshold toward her bed. The room was even messier than it had been the day before. The maids had been instructed not to disturb the widow and it showed. The bed was a tangled mess of sheets, pillows and duvet. When they laid June down on it, Maggie's hand bumped into something hard buried under a knot of sheets. She pulled out a blue canvas sneaker and through threw it on the floor.

"Get her legs up," Maggie instructed.

Greg grabbed June's ankles and hoisted them onto the bed.

The mumbling stopped, having been replaced by snoring. Maggie found a pillow and placed it under June's head.

"Maybe roll her over onto her side in case she throws up," Greg said, the voice of experience with mood-altering substances.

"Right," Maggie said and did as instructed.

June mumbled something Maggie didn't understand and then commenced breathing heavily when she was balanced on her side.

"Poor lady," Maggie said, breathing a little heavily herself from the exertion, and looking down at the sleeping guest.

Greg, ever on the lookout for a good buzz, looked over her head toward his boss. "Think she'll share whatever it is she's on?"

Twenty-Three

MAGGIE'S KNAPSACK BRUSHED AGAINST A low hanging branch as she ducked under the enormous tree that had partially collapsed and was hanging over the wooden boardwalk. The forest around her was dense with green: green light; green foliage; green moss and lichen. And where it wasn't green it was thick with evergreen and deciduous tree trunks. The quiet was absolute. All she could hear, apart from her own breathing, was Elliott's footsteps on the boardwalk behind her.

When she arrived at the inn that morning, she was refreshed from an exceptionally long sleep, if not entirely at peace. Carol met her at the back door that led into the kitchen with a navy blue knapsack held by one strap in her left hand, and a reusable coffee mug in her right. Maggie assumed Carol was leaving the lodge with this gear in her hands, and stepped back to let her friend pass.

"Where are you going?"

"Nowhere. But you're going on a date."

"What?" Maggie had a lot on her mind, which churned even as she slept, going over the reasons and the people who might possibly be out to ruin her business, so she didn't catch onto Carol's meaning.

"Take this," Carol handed her the knapsack, "and put it on." She had waited, her 'headmistress face' in place, as she liked to call the stern look she adopted whenever she wanted immediate obedience from someone.

Maggie decided to humor her friend, and looped the straps

over her shoulders. "There. Happy?" She made a move toward the kitchen door, reaching around Carol with one hand.

Carol side-stepped, blocking her. "Oh, no. Now take this," she handed Maggie the coffee mug and then grasped her by the shoulders and turned her around. They walked, Carol guiding Maggie from behind, along the porch to the front of the inn. A sharp left and they continued across the width of the inn until they reached the wide front steps that led down in to the small drop-off parking lot. Elliott was there, Maggie could see, leaning up against his truck, his hands in his jeans pockets, one ankle crossed over the other. Maggie's stomach did a little flip at the sight of him. When she smiled at him, he smiled back, and his eyes had looked lit from within.

As the Maggie-Carol train clumped down the four steps, Carol said, "This nice man is keenly aware that you've had a rough few days and he would like to take you on a date." They stopped in front of Elliott.

Maggie looked back and forth from the handsome man in front of her to her determined friend who was now beside her. She was tempted. He was looking at her the way a hungry man looks at a buffet. Finally she spoke, "Elliott I'd love to. You know I would," she reached out and touched his arm, "But there is so much to do here and I'm sure I have phone calls to return and paperwork to do about the fire. Right Carol?"

"We've got it handled," Carol said, brooking no argument "and by 'we' I mean Sparrow. That girl, despite all the talk about 'energy' and 'chakras,' not to mention the Stevie Nicks wardrobe, could put professional organizers to shame. She's got it all in hand and she can fill you in at dinner tonight. Right, Elliott?"

Maggie interrupted before Elliott could speak, "What? Dinner? Where?"

Carol put her arms behind Maggie again and pushed her toward Elliott. Before she knew what was happening, he guided her around to the passenger side of the truck, opened the door and practically lifted her into the seat. He closed the door gently and then climbed in behind the wheel, grinning at her, "Buckle up."

From the time Maggie was about ten years old, she had been the one taking care of others. She had inherited her parents' hospitality gene and was a natural-born hostess. The comments left most often in the guest book at the inn, and in recent years on online review sites, spoke consistently of how cared-for and nurtured guests felt at the Cormorant Inn. Words like 'homey', 'comforting' and 'embracing' were used. Maggie knew how to take care of others. She had been born and bred to do so, and it made her happier than almost anything to find a guest who felt so comfortable, and so at peace at the inn, that he or she had fallen asleep on one of the couches in front of the fire in the great room. She didn't know what city life was like, having never lived in one, but from how her guests reacted to the peace, quiet and soothing rhythms of the inn, she assumed it was nothing like life on Juliet Island. She always wanted, as had her parents, each guest to have a magical experience at the inn, and to feel as though they had been renewed. She achieved this nearly 100% of the time.

What she was less-accomplished at was taking care of herself. She frequently forgot to eat. Some days would go by when all she would take time for was an apple until Greg brought her a plate from the kitchen at supper time and set it down in front of her on the reception desk. He'd often sit with her and chat while she ate, knowing she'd forget about the meal unless he distracted her from the computer screen or the pile of papers in front of her. She usually ran on less than six hours of sleep and hadn't had a holiday away from the island in more than five years. She worked seven days a week, and though it fulfilled her and she couldn't imagine a life without such purpose and passion, at times she was willing to admit to herself that she might be headed for a serious burnout. Her parents had had each other to lean on. She did not have them any longer, or anyone else.

As a result of being a professional nurturer, and being damn good at that job, she was somewhat uncomfortable as she and Elliott walked along the raised wooden walkway through the rain forest. It was clear that he and Carol had conspired to take care of her today, and as much as she needed that, the newness of it was uncomfortable. She talked to herself silently as they walked, reassuring herself that it was okay to accept help and that if Elliott had gone to the trouble of arranging this morning for her, she could at least be gracious about it and embrace what he was offering.

The forest gave way and the boardwalk ended. The couple emerged into the weak May sunshine onto grey, mossy rocks. The ocean lay straight ahead and they could hear where it met the rocks below in a foamy collision.

"I don't see it," Elliott said.

"It's right down there," Maggie looked down, pointing, where the edge of the forest met the rocky shore. "Let me go get changed," she said, "and then we can make our way down. Do you have your suit on?"

He smiled at her, "Yep. Under my jeans. All I have to do is strip off."

She walked into the forest, over fallen trees and ferns, until she felt she was protected from sight by the curtain of trunks and leaves. She fished around in the knapsack Carol had given her, past a towel and two containers with sandwiches, until, at the very bottom, she found her old one-piece Speedo swim suit with the racing back. "Sexy," she muttered to herself, full of irony.

As quickly as she could, Maggie pulled off her clothes and stepped into the suit. She shoved her jeans, t-shirt, underwear and jacket into the knapsack and reemerged from the tree line wearing her bathing suit and running shoes. Elliott was standing where she'd left him, his clothes in a small pile at his feet. He was wearing black swimming trunks that almost reached his knees. They stood looking at one another. She wondered what he saw and tried not to think about her pasty skin and the gross mole on her right leg.

He was muscled, which she had expected, but not overly so. Toned, she supposed would be the best word to describe him. She could see the vestiges of a farmer's tan, probably left over from his last summer in the parks. His chest had what she considered the perfect amount of hair on it. Enough that he looked like a man. Not so much that he looked like an area rug.

It had been so long since she'd seen a man her age, one she was on a date with, no less, without his shirt on that for a moment she felt utterly paralyzed. All thought left her head and she stood rooted like the trees behind her.

Elliott kindly saved her, "So? How do we get down there?"

She woke up and smiled at him, "Follow me." Dropping her knapsack near his clothes, she kicked off her shoes and gingerly picked her way over the rocks toward the ocean. They came to a cleft in the rocks, like a crevasse. "Watch your step here. We just climb down between these…" She trailed off and made her way into the crevasse, being careful of her soft, bare feet on the boulders. The sound of the ocean beside them muted as they climbed down. Very soon she could feel the heat coming off the pool below them. She reached the water's edge. Maggie was holding on with one hand to the rocks that were now beside her and reaching over her head with the other hand to steady herself. She carefully climbed into the hot pool, feeling her way along until the bottom dropped away and she could float farther out. Elliott followed her, and she turned to watch his face. She saw the surprise and pleasure as the warm water enveloped his legs and then his torso as he picked his way into the pool. He floated out toward her, a look of wonder on his face.

"It really is hot," he said.

She smiled at him, enjoying his amazement.

"Just like a hot tub."

He paddled around, feeling the hot water on his body, leaning back sometimes and letting himself float.

Maggie treaded water and watched him.

He turned back to her after a few minutes, "When Carol said 'natural hot spring' I took that with a grain of salt, but this is incredible!"

"Isn't it nice?" Maggie let her own head fall back into the water and closed her eyes.

They were silent for quite a while, floating. Occasionally their feet or hands would graze one another, and Maggie found herself reveling in those tiny moments. She tried to imagine that her worries and the strain of the past few weeks and months were being pulled out of her into the warm water. She pictured them floating away, into the sea that they could hear but not see, surrounded as they were by walls of granite. She felt her body relax some, the tension in her neck eased and her shoulders felt slightly more pliable.

When she almost became so relaxed that she felt like she might fall asleep, she righted herself and swam over to where the hot water met the dark grey walls of the pool. She searched around with her hands and feet until she found what she was looking for; a little shelf where, when she sat on it, just the tops of her shoulders and her head cleared the waterline.

"Is there room for me?" Elliott paddled over and sat beside her. He looked at her, taking her in, "You look much more relaxed now."

"I feel so much better. Thank you."

"It was Carol's idea."

"Well, thank you to you both. This was just what I needed."

Under the water he found her hand and took it in his own. They sat, holding hands, listening to the ocean beyond the rock walls and watching the blue sky above them. It was like they were sitting in the bottom of a tea cup, the grey walls reaching up high above their heads.

"Why is there no one else here?" Elliott's voice was almost a whisper, not wanting to shatter the quiet.

Maggie answered quietly, "It's a local secret. The islanders actively try to keep non-locals from knowing about it. It doesn't work, of course, and each year more and more people find out about it. But we do our best to keep our mouths shut. In the colder months you might find a few people here on any given day. We lucked out, although it is May, and there's less call for hot springs as the summer approaches."

He pulled her hand up out of the water and kissed her dripping palm. Releasing it, he leaned over and began to kiss her. She thought she felt relaxed before, but now she floated in a cloud of ease and stillness. Her hands touched his sides, under the water, and then moved around to his back. She felt him shift slightly on the rocky shelf they were sitting on and in one smooth movement he pulled her onto his lap, so that she was sitting sideways. She wrapped her arms around his neck and he held her tightly around her waist. He tasted not unpleasantly of the minerals from the water. She loved the feeling of their chests being pressed tightly together. He rubbed and caressed her back with his wide, strong hands.

At one point he began kissing her neck, sending shivers down her whole body. His mouth moved onto her shoulder and then, with one hand, he began to slip the strap of her bathing suit over her shoulder and down her arm.

Breathless and almost entirely mesmerized by his touch, a part of her brain that was still conscious startled and she pulled away, floating back from him, treading water in the deepest part of the pool.

He looked at her, concern lining his face, "I'm sorry. Was that too much?"

Her whole body was flooded with feeling and emotion. She wasn't sure she'd be able to form a coherent sentence. "No, not at all. Well, yes, sort of."

Elliott's face fell almost imperceptibly.

She rushed in, babbling, not wanting him to feel bad, "It was amazing. Lovely, really, Elliott." She smiled at him and tried to rouse a smile from him, almost succeeding. "I just…I, um," she struggled, searching for ways to describe all that she was feeling and all the conflicting messages from her heart and brain, "This is so great. So beautiful, Elliott, and so thoughtful. And you're amazing. I'm just feeling… a bit overwhelmed."

"You've had a lot to deal with the last few days."

Maggie nodded, still treading water. "Hey," she said, "why don't we go sit in the sun for a while. Carol packed some snacks."

She felt lame and it was awkward between them for a few minutes after they got dressed. Carol had packed a tartan picnic blanket that had been Maggie's mother's. They spread it on the rocks above the hot pool and sat down to look out over the ocean and the other islands in front of them. She pulled a bag of chips and two cans of pop from her backpack and handed one to Elliott.

They sat quietly for a few moments, crunching on potato chips. A wasp buzzed around them, attracted by the sweet smell of the sodas. Maggie stretched her legs out in front of her and tried to relax.

She started to ask Elliott a question and he spoke at the same time.

"Oh, sorry," she said, "you go."

"No, you go first," he said, popping a chip in his mouth. "What were you going to say?"

"Tell me about your new job. Are you looking forward to it?"

Elliott waggled his head a bit, hesitating. "I think I am. The firm is a really good one and I feel very fortunate to get the job. The money will be good, which is nice. It's funny," he stared out at the water, "now that my marriage is over, I'll be earning the kind of money that my ex-wife wanted me to."

"Life can be funny that way," Maggie said.

"It can."

"Is the job downtown?" she asked.

"Yes. Right downtown. Burrard and Dunsmuir. I'll be able to walk to work from the place I'm renting in Yaletown, so that's good." He sounded as though he was talking himself into the positive aspects of this job.

"What did you like about the Parks Canada work?"

"Only everything," he said and smiled at her. "Being outdoors almost all the time. The adventures. The fact that every day was different. The autonomy. The animals. The quiet." He sighed a huge sigh and ate another chip.

"I'm sorry you had to leave that job. It sounds perfect for you."

"It really was. I was an idiot to let my wife talk me into quitting. A total idiot." He shook his head ruefully. "But I was trying to be a grown-up and I thought that's what it would take to do that and to save my marriage. I tried to step up and do what I thought was the responsible thing." He shrugged.

Having never been married, Maggie didn't know what to say. She wondered though, if asking one's spouse to be something they're not was the right way to go about things.

The tension Maggie felt had eased a bit and now she was enjoying the quiet, watching the water. She felt peaceful, which was a welcome feeling. Elliot flicked a bug off his knee and Maggie looked over at him. The sun was hitting his damp hair and making it glow around the edges. Her stomach did a little flip, which caught her off guard. The more she knew about him, the more she liked him. He was kind and thoughtful. Honest and respectful. And smart, which she always found particularly attractive. Maggie felt anxious suddenly, about everything she was feeling toward Elliott.

Surely it was unwise to feel such things about someone who could be leaving the island in a matter of days, if not hours.

She stood up, "Maybe we should be getting back."

Elliott looked up at her, slightly startled. "Okay, sure." He stood as well and, concluding what he'd been saying about his city job, said casually, "It will be good to get out of limbo. I've been rudderless for a while and I'm looking forward to getting on with my life."

He stepped off the blanket and Maggie lifted it off the ground and shook it. She noticed a little jolt of hurt run through her. Elliott kept talking but she wasn't hearing him. The feeling of hurt surprised her with its intensity. She chastised herself internally and wondered what had caused such a reaction. She nodded at Elliott, smiling slightly, though she was still thinking and not listening.

It was his use of the word 'limbo' she realized after a moment. It made her think that he felt that what was happening between them wasn't real.

Together they folded the blanket and she tucked it under her arm. When they had their backpacks on and the picnic basket in hand, she turned and led them back to the path that would take them to Elliott's truck. With her back to him, she felt tears prick her eyes.

Twenty-Four

"Could you pull in here for a second?"

"Sure."

The truck slowed and pulled off onto a widened area of the graveled shoulder that looked as though it had once been intended to be the start of a driveway. A sagging barbed wire fence with wooden posts, cracked and bleached by the sun, bordered a field beyond the road. In the far distance Maggie could see four or five sheep with black faces going about their sheep business.

"I just want to say a few things before we get back to the inn." She turned and leaned her back against the inside of the passenger door, crooking her left leg up so her knee pushed into the center of the truck. Elliott shut the engine off and turned to look at her. She tried to guess what he was thinking or feeling but couldn't come up with much. Her own feelings were so muddled and almost overwhelming that she had a full plate just dealing with herself.

"Thank you so much for this morning. It was," she searched for a word until she found the one that suited best, "healing."

"I'm glad," he said.

"And thank you so much for your help over the past few days. I don't know that we've actually discovered anything but I feel better for having at least looked for answers."

"Good."

"I'm sorry I um…got a bit nervous there in the hot spring."

"Don't be sorry." He looked pained and she was sorry she had phrased it that way.

"Well, I guess, what I mean is, I feel like I spoiled what could have otherwise been a spectacularly romantic time."

Elliott started to speak but she stopped him with a small movement of her hand.

"Please, let me get this out." A few tears leaked from the corners of her eyes and she wiped them away quickly, "I really like you, Elliott. You're the first guy I've been drawn to in…well, almost forever. I think you're smart and funny and kind." She smiled weakly at him and took a deep breath, "But I think I need to pull back. You're leaving Juliet very soon. Maybe even this week, if Frank Nelson gives you the green light. You've got a job waiting for you in Vancouver. I'm sure you're wanting to rebuild your life after the really tough time you've been through. And I'm just not the kind of woman who can," she took a deep breath to calm herself, "who cannot care about someone I sleep with. I tried when I was younger, when all the girls around me were having their experimental years and it just made me miserable. It was awful. I hated myself. And I ended up hating the men I casually slept with."

Elliott tried to edge into her speech, "I didn't…"

"I know! I know. You're not pushing me. That's not what I'm saying. I guess what I'm doing is addressing how I feel. I feel really, *really* safe around you, Elliott. Like I could easily lean on you and rely on you and need you. But I can't let myself do that. Do you understand?" She squinted at him through the tears threatening to spill over from her eyes and thought she saw him nod. "If I begin to, or…if I *continue* to feel the way I feel about you, then when you leave I will be an even bigger mess than I am now. My life needs me to be really strong now. I can't fall apart. I can't risk a broken heart. I need to figure out what's going on with the inn. And I need to save it from failing, which it's on the verge of doing. So, could we just be friends? Would that be okay? And, as much as I'd like you to continue, could you not kiss me anymore?"

Her throat hurt from holding in the cry that wanted to come, but she refused to seem weak and vulnerable in this moment. She wanted to give the appearance of strength, even if she didn't feel it. Crying, she thought, would confuse Elliott. It would send a mixed message.

He sat looking at her, quietly. She wondered if his brown eyes looked a little glassy, as though he might be close to tears as well, but when he spoke his voice was calm. "Maggie Archer, I will be happy to be your friend. You are a remarkable woman and I am lucky to know you. Thank you for being so honest with me."

"Thank you," Maggie whispered, "thank you for understanding."

"No, it's no trouble." She thought his expression seemed somewhat closed off now and suggested to herself that she should be grateful for that. "You're right. I do have a life waiting for me in the city. And I do look forward to getting my shit together after several years of it slowly falling apart." He grimaced at her, "I'm sorry if I pushed you too far, too fast."

"Don't be!" She reached out and put both hands on his right knee and looked up into his eyes, almost pleading, "Please don't be. I've loved every second of these last few days. Aside from almost drowning, and the fire, it's been the best time I've had in a long time." She grinned at him, trying to break the tension, and he smiled at her.

She sat upright and blew out a big breath, collecting herself. Elliott looked through the windshield, a faraway gaze in his eyes.

He turned to her, "Do you still want me to come with you to the Libertas dinner tonight?"

"Tell me what that's about. I had no idea that was part of today's agenda."

Elliott explained that it had been Grace the builder's idea. At the end of their chat at the building site she had asked him if he and Maggie had spoken to the Libertas family.

"Who?" he'd queried.

"Jack and Petal Libertas. Their daughter, Sparrow, works at the inn."

He agreed that he'd met Sparrow but had asked Grace what Sparrow's parents could have to do with the mystery of the accidents at the Cormorant Inn.

"Jack and Petal Libertas," Grace had explained, "are the unofficial king and queen of Juliet Island. So while Reg Archer, Maggie's dad, was the defacto mayor, Jack and Petal are our benevolent rulers. Two of the nicest people you'll ever meet. Total hippies, as you might have guessed from Sparrow's name, not to mention her outlook on life. They made their first fortune growing and selling pot. And they are now wealthy beyond your wildest dreams. They own and run the Gulf Islands' first vineyard, plus they own several organic vineyards and wine-making operations in the Okanagan. Not to mention a dozen other businesses. They know everyone and everything that moves on this island, including all the planned developments and, more importantly, rivalries between the developers. If anyone has heard a whisper about someone wanting to force Maggie out, it will be them. Nothing moves on this island without them hearing about it."

In the truck, Maggie listened to Elliott explain Grace's theory, the occasional hiccup escaping her chest.

"So," he concluded, "when I left Grace I dropped by the inn after going to the community center…"

Maggie interrupted, "You did? What did they say?"

"Didn't I tell you?"

Maggie shook her head.

"Sorry. I guess I forgot." He looked a little sheepish, "Tell me if it was the wrong thing to do, making some inquires for you."

"It wasn't. I'm pleased you did. One less thing for me on a very full plate."

"Good," Elliott nodded. "Well, after I talked to Grace, I called the inn to see if you were awake and Carol said you hadn't appeared again. So I thought I'd just pop over there quickly and see what they had to say about Inna and her mother."

"And?"

"And I talked to a nice woman named Rose."

"Rose Tennant?"

"I'm not sure. Older lady. Really curly hair dyed bright brassy red. Calls everyone 'Sugar'."

Maggie chuckled softly, "Yes, that's Rose."

"Well, Sugar," Elliott said, mimicking Rose's tone, "she said that Inna and Vera, her mother, do drop by the center twice a week so Vera can play bridge. She said that Inna doesn't leave the room, just sits in a chair against a wall and reads. Sometimes she falls asleep. And Rose doubts that she is ever out of her mother's line of sight. I guess Vera is pretty demanding, although Rose didn't come out and say that exactly."

Maggie thought about this for a second, and was about to speak when Elliott continued.

"But, they haven't been to the game for a couple of weeks. Rose assumed it was because Vera's health wasn't good enough."

Maggie's eyes grew wide. "Really?"

Elliott nodded, "Yep."

"Oh, my." Maggie looked out the windshield, following the sheep with her eyes, but not seeing them. "So that would mean they don't have any witnesses for where they were the night of the fire."

"Yep," Elliott said again. "Which brings us to the Libertas family."

She turned and looked at Elliott again, her eyes wanting to soak him in. "What's the deal with this dinner I'm hearing about?"

"I mentioned what Grace said about Sparrow's family to Carol when I dropped by the inn after going to the community center, and she immediately picked up the phone and secured us an invitation for dinner tonight."

"Huh," Maggie said, mostly to herself, "I should have thought of them. Grace is exactly right."

They were quiet for a few moments, both thinking their separate but similar thoughts.

Elliott finally broke the silence, "Would you like me to take you or would you rather go alone?"

"I'd like you to take me." Maggie smiled at him, "I always attend every function on my own and it will be a treat to have a," she hesitated and then smiled, "friend with me."

The remainder of the drive back to the lodge was quiet. Maggie was lost in her thoughts and was also trying not to cry. She knew that when she was alone she would allow herself to let go of the tears that she was holding in. Her mouth had told Elliott that she didn't want to get closer to him, but her heart had other wishes. She was pushing away the awareness at the edge of her consciousness that was telling her it was too late. She already loved him. The pain and the grief that would come with fully accepting this would have to wait.

Elliott pulled the truck into the drop-off parking lot beside Frank Nelson's patrol car. Maggie could see Frank coming down the steps of the inn toward them. "What now?" she muttered under her breath.

Frank went straight to Elliott while Maggie walked around the truck. When she reached the two men they were shaking hands.

Frank turned to Maggie, "Hey Maggie, good news. The coroner in Victoria has determined that Mr. Brier's death was an accident, so we're closing the file."

"That is good, Frank. Any idea how he got in the water?"

"Not really. There was a fair sized 'contusion', as the doctors say, on his head but they haven't been able to determine if it happened peri – or postmortem. I don't imagine that he walked out into the ocean, so either he fell out of a boat or fell off one of the bluffs."

"You didn't find a boat adrift, did you?"

"No, but that's not to say there isn't one. It's a big ocean out there and the currents can take stuff miles away. Brandon's been looking into reports of missing boats on the island and there are a couple from two different marinas that we haven't been able to find."

Maggie thought about this for a moment, "Well, there we are then. An unfortunate accident. I'm so sorry for Mr. Brier. And his wife." Maggie thought of June, here in the inn, grieving and unable to leave the place where her husband died.

"I was just saying to Mr. Simon," Frank interrupted Maggie's thoughts, "that he's free to go. Case closed."

"Thank you, Constable."

"You're welcome. Safe travels." Frank nodded at Maggie and moved away toward his vehicle.

Maggie felt Elliott's eyes on her and looked up. "There we are then," she said brightly, hiding her disappointment, "you can get on with your life."

Elliott took one of her hands in his and squeezed it gently. He didn't say anything.

Twenty-Five

Maggie had said that dinner would be fairly casual at the Libertas house. "Jack and Petal don't really stand on ceremony. They're the ultimate hippies." But Elliott thought the least he could do was present himself in a clean shirt and jeans.

He had found two button-down oxford shirts in the bottom of his suitcase and chose the light blue one, which was the less wrinkled of the two. Showered and freshly shaven, wearing only a towel wrapped around his waist, he stepped out of the bathroom and found Libby crouched down in front of the filing cabinet.

She looked up, "How were the hot springs?"

"How did you hear about that?"

"Brother, you'll figure it out eventually, but nothing happens on this island without everyone knowing about it."

He sat down on the couch and began to clean his fingernails with a small pair of clippers. He was feeling raw and vulnerable from the afternoon's events, not that he would have ever used any of those words to describe himself, so when he replied to Libby his tone was a bit harsher than he intended, "Does the whole island know that Maggie and I are now officially 'just friends'?"

Libby heard the edge in her brother's voice. She kept looking through the hanging files in the cabinet drawer so as not to spook him by approaching him directly, and said, casually over her shoulder, "What do you mean?"

Elliott kept his head down, focused on his fingernails, "Nothing. We just had a talk this afternoon about…stuff."

Libby's knees were starting to ache but she stayed where she was, and still didn't turn her head to look at Elliott, "What kind of stuff?"

"Friend stuff, I guess," he avoided the truth, "Oh, and Frank Nelson just gave me the go ahead to leave. I can move to the city now."

Now that they seemed on surer ground, Libby stood up, her knees cracking, "Hey, that's great." She closed the cabinet drawer with her foot and carried a few sheets of paper over to the desk where Elliott's suitcase was. She put the papers down on one corner and then moved a coffee mug that was filled with pens and pencils over to stand on the paper, providing a paperweight. She turned and leaned her behind on the desk, "Have you called your buddy at the architecture firm?"

"Environmental engineering."

"Whatever. Have you called him?"

"Not yet." Elliott looked at his watch, "It's too late now. I'll call him in the morning."

"Well, congratulations. I know you were keen to move on and get the next phase of your life started, so I'm happy for you."

"Thanks." He looked at her glumly.

"Wow. Calm down, E. Your excitement is overwhelming me."

"Ha ha."

"Dude, this is what you wanted."

"I know."

"So, what's the deal? You look like you just lost your best friend."

Libby didn't realize it but she'd come closer to the truth than Elliott would allow. He stood up, a smile pasted on his face. "You're right. It's great." He walked back toward the bathroom, clippers in hand.

Elliot buttoned the cuffs of his shirt as he walked down the stairs from his temporary home. He heard voices as he opened the back door and entered the Bakeri's kitchen. Glancing at his watch he saw that it was after 5:30 p.m. and the shop should be closed. Libby's voice reached him and she had her stern, big sister tone on.

"I'm sorry gentlemen, you'll have to come back later. He's not here."

Elliott walked past the large island in the middle of the kitchen and then through the doorway into the front of the shop. He found Libby standing behind the cash register, facing two men across the counter. One he recognized as Michael Keith, from their brief conversation two days earlier. The other man he hadn't seen before, but given his resemblance to Michael, Elliott assumed this was one of his brothers.

"Well, look who it is," Michael said as Elliott went to stand beside his sister, who startled slightly.

"Oh, there you are," she said, "I thought you'd left."

"What's up?" Elliott could feel the tension in the room. Beside him, Libby's posture was stiff and waves of hostility rolled off her, which was highly unusual. Elliott's curiosity was roused.

"You know Michael Keith," she said, gesturing. "Have you met his charming brother, Trent? They were just asking about you."

"Fuck you, Simon," Trent said, looking at Libby and calling her by her last name in a juvenile, high-school-football kind of way. He looked back to Elliott, "I understand you were sneaking around our property the other day, asking questions about real estate on the island."

Elliott knew Libby could take care of herself. She was as fiercely independent as any woman he'd ever known, and smarter than almost anyone he'd ever met. But she was still his sister. Trent's hurled expletive made Elliott want to jump across the counter and strangle the man. He took a quiet breath before he answered. "What did you just say to my sister?"

"Answer me," Trent said. "What were you doing sneaking around our lodge?"

"I'll answer you when and if I feel like it." Elliott kept his eyes drilling into Trent's. "Apologize to my sister."

"Or what?" Trent sneered.

"Okay, guys, this is ridiculous. Put away your rulers." Libby put one hand gently on Elliott's arm, trying to calm him down. "It's okay, E. I don't take offense at Trent. Everyone on the island knows he's a raging asshole." She looked directly at Trent when she said this.

"See?" Trent pointed at Libby. "She gives as good as she gets. Now are you going to answer me or not?"

Trent was right; Libby could dish it out as well as anyone. But that didn't give this prick the right to come into her store and insult her. He took another breath and waited. Outside a car drove past the window in the parking lot. Elliott hadn't taken his gaze off Trent. The silence stretched out. Elliott was a large and fit man, but there were two of the Keiths. Despite this, after a few moments, whatever Trent saw in Elliott's eyes made him concede.

He glanced at Libby. "Sorry. That was uncalled for."

Libby nodded.

Trent looked back to Elliott and raised his eyebrows.

"First," Elliott said, "I wasn't 'sneaking around'. I made myself known to the girl in the lobby as soon as I got to the lodge and then I followed her directions to find Michael."

Elliott was going to continue, but Trent interrupted him, which Elliott assumed was probably fairly standard behavior. "But you said you were looking to buy a place and that you were doing 'research,'" Trent made air quotes with his index fingers, "about island real estate. But that was all bullshit, wasn't it? You're working for Maggie Archer."

Elliott debated about dignifying this with an answer, and then settled on, "I am not working for Maggie Archer."

Michael started to speak but Trent, clearly the alpha in the sibling relationship, shushed his brother with a small motion of his hand.

"Working with her then," Trent said. "Trying to find out why that shit-box she calls an Inn is failing. I'll tell you why it's failing and save you the trouble. It's failing because the Archers couldn't manage their way out of a wet paper bag. They're kiss-ass hosts, and all, but they can't figure out how to make a buck. Never could. The parents were hopeless and the daughter is worse."

Elliott thought for a second, his eyes moving from Trent to Michael and then back again. "Let me ask you this, Pop Tart," he finally said, "so what?"

Trent looked puzzled. "What do you mean 'so what'?"

"I mean, what do you care? So what if Maggie's business isn't doing well. And so what if I'm trying to help her. What's it to you guys?"

Trent didn't have an answer for this. He started to speak but then snapped his jaw closed. He glared at Libby, like what was happening was somehow her fault. Rallying, he said, "We care because we don't want you coming to our inns and bothering our guests."

"I didn't bother your guests."

"Good. Keep it that way. That's all we're concerned about." Trent tapped his brother on the shoulder and they turned to go.

When the door had closed behind them, Libby walked out from behind the counter and locked it. She turned the Open sign around so the Closed side faced out, saying, "Is it just me or was that weird?"

Elliott nodded, thinking. "It was weird. The fact that both of them had to come all the way over here to threaten me to stay away from them is odd."

Libby was quiet for a few seconds, watching the Keiths back their truck out of its parking space. When the vehicle exited onto the road, she turned to face her brother, "Did you really call Trent 'Pop Tart'?"

Elliott grinned at her. "Don't mess with me, man. I'm fierce with the insults."

Twenty-Six

MAGGIE COULD TELL THAT ELLIOTT was having trouble stifling his laughter. The man who stood before them had a pan flute in his hands, and at the end of each stanza of poetry he was reciting, he would play a few notes on the flute. The flute looked like a child's toy in his hands; the man had to be at least six and a half feet tall. He had hands the size of dinner plates and his bare feet that poked out from beneath his ragged jean hems looked like they belonged to a Cornish giant. His face was partially obscured by a cloudy mane of salt-and-pepper hair, and he had a generous beard and mustache that rivaled those of Santa Claus. His shirt was more like a tunic; it fell to his hips, seemed beaded in places, and long drawstrings dangled from the collar. All in all he was a spectacular sight; huge, colorful and musical. Maggie knew that Uncle Sunshine, as the Libertas family called him, could be a lot to wrap your mind around at first meeting, but she had seen enough of Elliott to believe that he would take it in stride.

The poetry reading (with flute accompaniment) was apparently a Libertas tradition and tonight it had been Sunshine's turn. Poems were not graded or compared, but there was a tacit understanding that original poetry, conceived and birthed by the person reciting it, was appreciated with slightly more enthusiasm than recited poetry by another author.

When Sunshine's recitation of 'Ode to the Barnacle' was finished, he produced an odd set of notes from his flute that had Maggie wondering if he was a beginner flautist or a jazz flautist.

The group around the dinner table clapped and whistled. Sunshine bowed and then took his seat to Elliott's right. Maggie, seated across from Elliott, caught his eye and had to look quickly away, for fear she would burst out laughing at his bemused expression. Sunshine thumped him on the back and offered to let Elliott handle his flute.

"Made it myself," he said proudly, "when I was in Ecuador last fall."

Elliott made appreciative noises and Maggie could feel him not looking at her as well.

The Libertas family had welcomed Maggie and Elliott with a warmth and kindness that threatened to bring Maggie to tears for the umpteenth time that day. When they had walked up the porch steps to the front door, two small children had burst forth before they could knock, followed by Sparrow's mum, Petal Libertas. She had hugged Maggie in a generous and nurturing embrace, as was her style, and had then done the same to Elliott, much to his amusement, which Maggie saw in his eyes.

The children barreled into the house and were introduced while they roared past as Petal's granddaughters, April and Jelly (short for Joanie).

"We're a full table tonight, which is such a blessing," Petal said as she took Maggie's arm and led her through to the kitchen where the family was gathered. Maggie and Elliott were introduced to Sparrow's brother, Bear, and his wife, Susan (parents of the two small creatures from the front entrance who were now climbing their father as though he was a tree). Jack Libertas detached himself from the stove briefly to shake Elliott's hand and kiss Maggie on the cheek. Uncle Sunshine, who was not actually related to the family, waved at them from a sofa in the sitting area where he and Sparrow seemed to be in deep discussion.

When Maggie and Elliott were both settled on a barstool at the kitchen's island, a glass of wine in front of each of them, Maggie began to relax. The drive over had been slightly awkward. She felt emotional and therefore a bit tense, determined to put on a breezy show for Elliott; all friendship and no entanglement. It wasn't easy but the swirl of noise and activity around them now made it much easier.

While Jack worked at the stove, Maggie and Petal caught up on island gossip. While she chatted, she wondered what Elliott thought of the Libertas home. It was easily the grandest on the island, rivaling even Francis and Nathan's home. Done in the craftsman style that Maggie was particularly fond of, the house was proportioned beautifully, with large rooms and lots of windows. It was decorated tastefully but without pretense; Petal was more about comfort than style. Most of the art was either her own or locally produced. The Libertas family made a point of supporting island artists and craftspeople. It was probably not apparent to Elliott, but the house, while beautiful, had also been built with environmental standards that would make David Suzuki swoon. Solar panels on the roof provided power and heat, while rainwater was collected from the metal roof into huge tanks to then be used on the gardens in the dry summers. The black water from the kitchens and bathrooms was also reused, and almost all the fixtures had been sourced from outfits like Habitat for Humanity, which recycled materials for reuse.

This attention to environmental impact was part of the Libertas family philosophy, and one that they applied in every area of their lives and businesses. And yet, they were never pretentious or heavy-handed when they shared information about reducing a home or a business's impact on the environment. As Grace had said to Elliott the day before, you could not hope to meet a nicer, more generous and kind family.

Maggie glanced at Elliott when Petal went to check a pot on the stove, her long, colorful maxi-dress swirling behind her. He looked content and at ease, which pleased her. He noticed her gaze and met her eyes. They both smiled and then Elliott surprised her by raising his glass of wine to her. "To friends," he said. They clinked glasses gently, a little private moment passing between them.

Petal turned back from the stove just then, and put the tea towel she was holding on the kitchen counter, "If you two aren't just the cutest thing ever," she said. She closed her eyes briefly and put one hand to her heart, "Oh, my." She opened her eyes again and focused on her guests. Maggie felt like she was in a spotlight.

Petal was forty-five but looked at least ten years younger. Her wavy, auburn hair was casually piled on her head tonight, with strands falling down over her shoulders here and there. Her blue eyes, which could be fierce when she was provoked, were now soft and wide open. The bracelets on both her arms jangled quietly as she put her hands on the island and seemed to be soaking Maggie and Elliott into her soul.

"Oh, my," she said again, breathing deeply, "you two. Your energies are dancing together in the most beautiful way. It's breathtaking." She closed her eyes again and breathed, "I see only good things for you as a couple. This pairing will support you both to find fulfillment and happiness. Oh! It's a good one." Her eyes popped open again, shining. "The angels are laughing." She clapped her hands together with delight, like a small child.

Maggie was stunned and for a moment didn't know what to say. She felt Elliott tense up beside her and rushed in to save them any further embarrassment, "Elliott and I are just friends, Petal. We're not a couple."

Petal's face fell briefly, but then lit up again. She laughed, a bright, tinkling laugh that Maggie had always imagined was the way fairies would sound when they laughed. "That's what you think."

Maggie took a sip of wine to hide her embarrassment.

Jack requested Petal's help with the lamb and she turned away from them. Maggie glanced over at Elliott and mouthed 'Sorry' to him. He shrugged and grimaced at her, clearly a bit unnerved by

Petal's pronouncement. Sparrow arrived at the counter and saved them, "Mom fancies herself a bit of a psychic, don't you Mom?"

"Not a psychic, dear. An energy reader."

With her mother's back turned, Sparrow was able to roll her eyes at Elliott and Maggie. "Right. And what was that thing you said to me last year about a surprising new form of creative expression coming into my life?" She made air quotes around the end of her sentence.

Petal and Sparrow began gently arguing about whatever the prediction had been and much to Maggie's relief, the moment passed.

The meal proved chaotic, with April and Jelly running the show after Uncle Sunshine had completed his performance. The two girls, ages seven and four, were wound up like frenzied, spinning tops as a result of having both Sunshine and two strangers to show off for. They told stories, interrupting one another all through the meal, competing for everyone's attention and virtually ignoring their food. They also continually left the table to go and find something or do something that was vitally important, at least to them. Bear was apparently the stricter parent; asking the girls to eat with their mouths closed and not kick the table legs. Susan seemed surrounded by her own bubble of serenity, unable to see or hear the chaos around her. Sparrow spent much of the meal with one or the other of her nieces in her lap, which she clearly enjoyed, cuddling them and burying her face in their hair. Jack and Petal slotted comfortably into the role of indulgent grandparents, siding with the children during arguments with Bear over uneaten squash and a refusal on Jelly's part to eat her peas because they had touched her meat.

Maggie felt swept along as though on a raft in a wild, roaring, white water river. Her ears rang with the volume in the dining room, a decibel level she felt even her inn didn't reach on nights when hosting wedding receptions. Through it all Elliott looked amused. He glanced at Maggie often, grinning and animated. April had taken a strong liking to him and when she wasn't chastising her younger sister for ruining a story she was telling, or jumping down from her chair to go and fetch her latest drawing to show the adults, she was shamelessly batting her eyelashes at Elliott, who was seated on her right. Maggie felt a deeply embarrassing stab of jealousy at the attention her dinner 'friend' focused on April, and combatted it by asking Sunshine about his time in Ecuador.

"By God, that was a good meal, if I do say so myself." Jack sank down in his armchair in the living room, a cigar in one hand and a glass of cognac in the other, and stretched his long legs out in front of him, crossing them at the ankles. He looked as deeply satisfied as the cat who ate the cream.

The children were herded upstairs for baths and bedtime stories, although not without loud and vociferous protestations. It took both parents to get them up the stairs and they were only finally convinced to obey when Sparrow bribed them by saying she would invent a story to tell them, but only if they bathed and got ready for bed on their best behavior. She was sitting now on the long grey sofa, waiting to be summoned, her feet in her mother's lap. Sunshine had excused himself after the meal to go for a walk and "say goodnight to the stars" as he put it. Thus it was five adults who sat in front of the fire in the living room in relative peace, only the occasional shriek and splash coming from upstairs.

"Dearest Maggie," Jack said, after a few puffs of his cigar, "Sparrow says you're having some trouble at the inn. What can I do to help?"

Jack's kindness and the fact that such a busy and powerful man would take the time to concern himself with her woes touched Maggie at her core. She wished for a brief moment that the Libertas family would adopt her and let her move into their beautiful home and hide out in one of the upstairs bedrooms that overlooked their vineyard. Giving herself a slight shake and reminding herself how she valued her independence, she glanced at Elliott, who was seated beside her in an upholstered chair that was the twin of the one she was in. She was exhausted, she suddenly realized, and the thought of explaining everything to Jack almost made her want to cry. The long sleep she'd had the night before had been much needed, but all the emotion of the day, plus the worry about the inn, had worn her down. As she met Elliott's eyes, something happened in their gaze. She saw his eyes taking her in, noticed him noticing the weariness she imagined surrounded her own eyes, the droop in her eyelids, the shadows below. It was just a glance, a tiny moment, but she felt more seen, more understood, than perhaps she ever had. It stunned her. She froze with surprise, relief and then longing, for what was probably an instant, but felt much longer.

Then Elliott stepped in, rescuing her once again, as he had done in Tyee Bay. "I think I can answer some of that, Jack. Maggie's pretty worn out by everything that's happened."

Elliott explained to Jack and Petal about the accidents that had been occurring at the inn and the unexplained fire. "Immediately afterwards, Frank Nelson said it looked like an accelerant had been used to start the fire."

"It was," Jack said, looking at Elliott and then Maggie.

"What?" Maggie spoke up, sitting up a little straighter in her chair. "Who told you that?"

"Bear is part of the volunteer fire department. He wasn't at the fire the other night because he and Susan were traveling back from the Okanagan. But he stopped by the fire hall today and the men filled him in. They had a closer look once the site cooled and the fire was definitely set on purpose. They think the person used either gasoline or kerosene. It was spread around the outside of the building, where the walls meet the ground." He made a square tracing motion with the hand that held his cigar. "It caused the outside walls of the building to catch fire immediately."

"Oh, God," Maggie felt her stomach clench with fear and worry. She stared at Jack, her eyes wide, "I'm so worried about my guests."

Jack remained calm, his years of dealing with the near-daily crises in one business venture or another coming in handy. "Tell me who you think is responsible. Do you have a theory?"

Maggie looked over at Elliott and made a slight motion with her head, asking him to answer for her. She felt sick and unable to speak.

Elliott began to explain the inquiries he and Maggie had made and their theory that perhaps the accidents and fire had been caused by someone wanting to force Maggie into selling the inn. As he did so, without looking at her, he reached out and found her left hand on the arm of her chair. He placed his right hand over it and curled his fingers around her palm, not squeezing, just resting there, present. Letting her know he was with her. The movement was instinctive. Automatic. Like a practiced motion that comes from muscle memory. Maggie felt the warmth and comfort of Elliott's hand and relaxed slightly, her spine sank back into her chair and she exhaled deeply.

Elliott shared his recent encounter with the Keith brothers, the details of which Maggie hadn't heard yet. And he told Jack about his and Maggie's concerns about Inna Petrov and her mother, and their alibi that turned out to be a lie.

And while Jack was attentive and interested, never once changing the subject but following each line of thought thoroughly and coming up with new questions that Maggie and Elliott hadn't thought of, ultimately he had no new information to add. He agreed with Grace that development of the land on Juliet Island had become more competitive, especially in the past few years as the world economy continued to rebound from the 2008 recession. But he had not heard a single whisper of anyone specifically aiming to unseat Maggie and take the land and the inn that belonged to her.

"When Petal told me you two were coming for dinner tonight, and why, I made a few discreet phone calls to some of my site managers and other colleagues." Jack swirled the amber liquid in his glass and watched it for a moment, "But I didn't hear one mention of anyone who might be suspect." He looked directly at Maggie, "I'm sorry, Mags. I wish I could offer more information than that."

Elliott's hand was still holding Maggie's and now he gently squeezed it. She gave her host a faint smile, "Thanks, Jack. I appreciate you looking into this for me."

He smiled back at her and continued, "Here's what I can do. Bear is the coach of the high school football team, as you probably know. He's going to ask his boys to take turns patrolling your property each night, until we figure out what's going on."

Maggie made a little gasp of surprise. She immediately regretted it. She pulled her hand out from under Elliott's to wipe a couple of tears that appeared in the corners of her eyes. Her right hand was otherwise occupied with her wine glass. "Really?" she said, "That seems like too much. What will the boys' parents say, about them being out all night?"

Jack pulled himself up from his slouching, dude-like posture and leaned forward, his elbows on his knees. He met Maggie's eyes and held them, "Maggie Archer, you are a very important person on this island, whether you realize it or not. You employ members of the community. You bring tourism to the island and help the economy. You invest back into that economy by using the goods and services of people like Elliott's sister, not to mention the Libertas vineyards." He smiled at her, "And we all care about you."

Maggie began to cry in earnest now. Sparrow leapt up and found a box of tissues and brought them to Maggie, who felt like a fool. She'd cried more in the past twenty-four hours than she had in the past twenty-four months.

Jack continued, "Bear and I have cleared it with all the boys' parents. The boys will be in pairs on their shifts, so one can sleep in the vehicle they bring and the other can patrol for a couple of hours or so, and then they'll switch. Each night there will be a new pair until they run through the roster, and then the pairs will start at the beginning again."

Maggie snuffled into her tissue.

"We won't give up on you, Maggie. You're not alone in this. We'll figure it out. Whoever set that fire is going to regret it, not least because it proves the accidents at your inn have not been accidents. Now we know there's something going on, and we can figure it out and make it stop."

Sparrow, who had perched herself on the arm of Maggie's chair put her arm around Maggie's shoulder and pulled her in close. The group was quiet for a moment, while Jack's words settled into Maggie.

A piercing shriek came from upstairs that startled all the adults in the living room, who were so deeply engrossed in their conversation. Maggie blew her nose and then heard light footsteps on the stairwell. Jelly burst into the room, totally naked, except for a wedding veil attached to her head by a pink, plastic tiara. She danced across the floor on tiptoes and leapt into her grandmother's arms.

"Granny, tell me that princess story," she said, "the one where the princess tricks the dragon and saves the prince."

Twenty-Seven

THE NIGHT AIR WAS COOL. Maggie pulled her sweater around herself a little tighter and shivered.

"Are you cold?" Elliott fiddled with the controls on his truck's dashboard, turning up the heat.

The lights of the truck lit up the road ahead of them like a narrow, private tunnel. Juliet Island had no street lights and the light pollution was minimal. As they had walked from the Libertas front porch to the driveway, Elliott noticed the star-filled sky and it reminded him of nights spent sleeping rough in the national parks. He had always felt most at peace during those trips. They were not easy, but they filled him up in a way nothing else had, before or since. He loved the autonomy his parks job had offered him, and the ruggedness of it. After a childhood spent in a large city, some part of him always felt as though he was coming home when he walked and rode horseback through some of the most remote areas in Canada. His mother had been embarrassed by his job, he remembered as he had glanced up at the Juliet Island sky. She thought working 'out-of-doors,' as she called it, was beneath a well-educated man.

"You could do anything you wanted to, E," she used to plead with him, "Why *parks*?"

"You're right, Mom," he would say back, "I *can* do anything. And I'm doing this."

When Heather had begun her campaign to get Elliott to stop working away from home, Elliott's mother jumped on board that cause like it was the last train leaving the station. The pressure had been relentless. He had resisted it, thinking the two women would get distracted and quickly move on to something else. But his wife had surprised him, and hadn't let up. With Sarah fueling the campaign, all Elliott's mother had to do was stoke the fire. Eventually he had collapsed, resigned but resentful. Rather than saving his marriage, Sarah's choice to force him away from the job he loved actually damaged it further. Irreparably so, it turned out, though she never even came close to admitting that fact.

The velvet blackness of Juliet Island was taking him back to his parks days as he drove Maggie home. She was quiet, processing the evening, he assumed. It had been a good one, he reflected. The level of chaos reminded him how grateful he was that he and Sarah had not had children. Not that he objected to the idea of producing offspring one day, should the circumstances and timing prove right. But parenting was obviously incredibly difficult and he couldn't imagine doing it as a single dad, even part-time. Elliott was touched by Jack's offer of assistance to Maggie, and he was glad, now that he was leaving the island, that there was someone else who would help her and keep an eye out for her. The Libertas' were obviously good people. He checked inside himself, assuming that the weight he felt about leaving the island would have lifted, now that he knew Maggie was protected. But it had not. It sat there, dark and cold in his stomach. He turned his mind away from the feeling and played with the heat controls again.

It occurred to him with a jolt that this might be the last time he saw Maggie. He was planning to take the 10 a.m. ferry the next day, Thursday, so that he could spend a few days getting settled into the apartment he'd rented from a buddy in the downtown Vancouver neighborhood called Yaletown. He needed to move what few worldly goods he had out of storage and he'd have to arrange a truck for that and perhaps finagle a few of his friends to help him. No doubt the fathers and husbands among them could be bribed with a few cases of beer and a few hours spent in the company of other men, lifting heavy objects and swearing good-naturedly. He'd have to be packed and out of Libby's place by 9 a.m., and no doubt his sister would slow down his departure, filling his passenger seat with bags of bread and boxes of sweet treats, not to mention a few tears. She put on a tough act, but she was a softie underneath the independent exterior.

He considered all this as he drove. Perhaps it was better to say goodbye to Maggie tonight. She knew now that she was not alone and Elliott felt sure that must be shoring her up after a tough few days. They could part as friends, after an evening where she clearly felt supported and loved. He thought Maggie had been smart and wise to share her feelings with him earlier in the day; he felt no uncertainty about what she might have wanted from him. She obviously wanted to remain untethered. *Me too*, he said to himself, *this way is for the best.*

They came around a long bend in Wellington Street and Elliott began to slow the truck, thinking Maggie would want to be dropped off at the inn to make a last check that everyone was tucked in for the night. But when she noticed the truck downshifting she stirred in her seat and looked at Elliott, "Could you take me to my place, please? The other driveway?"

"Sure," he said and sped up again slightly.

Driveway found, he turned in, the lights showing him the way down the narrow path to Maggie's cabin. He stopped the truck and hopped out, coming around to Maggie's side to let her out. He opened the passenger door, and she turned in her seat and climbed out, landing lightly beside him. He had a few goodbye words organized in his head and was just about to say them when she reached up, without warning, and placed her arms around his neck. She pressed the length of herself against him and leaned in and kissed him. He was stunned, frozen for an instant. But then he decided this must be her way of saying goodbye. He wrapped his arms around her waist and pulled her into him even closer.

They kissed for a long time. Softly at first and then with slightly more urgency. Maggie hooked one foot lightly around his calf. After several long minutes filled with nothing but the taste and smell of each other, she pulled back slightly and stared into his eyes, their faces almost pressed together.

"Don't go home tonight," she said.

This was not at all was Elliott was expecting. He didn't know what to say. She had been very clear with him earlier that day about not wanting to be hurt when he left if they'd slept together. He was so shocked, he didn't say anything.

"I mean it," she whispered to him. "I know what I said earlier but I've changed my mind. Come inside."

Elliott kissed her again, reaching up and touching her hair that was falling past her shoulders. When they broke apart, he put his mouth close to one of her ears and whispered gently, "Lead the way."

Twenty-Eight

THROUGH THE TREES THE BRAKE lights of Elliott's truck flashed when he got to the end of the driveway. Two small red squares amid a mass of brown and green. Then they were gone.

Maggie sighed deeply and stood gazing at nothing for a long while after the truck had disappeared. Finally, after many minutes, Ruby came careening around from the back of the house, her morning investigation of the nocturnal activity in her territory complete. She dashed up to Maggie and sniffed around her feet, wagging her tail at nothing. Maggie bent her knees and crouched down. The dog came and licked Maggie's face and then dropped down onto her back in the dirt, presenting her belly to be rubbed.

"It's easy for you, isn't it Ruby? You just love everyone." She rubbed her dog's chest and tummy for a few minutes and then stood up.

The dog continued to loll, her forelegs bent at the knee. She gazed up at Maggie with adoring, pleading eyes, hoping for a few more seconds of rubs.

"Come on," Maggie said. "We both need breakfast."

At the word 'breakfast' Ruby leapt to her feet and hurried toward the inn, where her food dishes were kept. Maggie walked behind the dog's zig-zagging trajectory, deeply lost in thought and memory. She unconsciously touched her lips, remembering Elliott's kisses.

He had been just as she'd imagined he would be; an attentive and generous lover. He obviously had a deep appreciation for women's bodies and had, through his caressing touch and sometimes gentle, sometimes urgent kisses, let her know that he valued the experience she was having as much as he valued his own. They had made love twice the night before, and then once more, just as dawn was breaking and the light outside the windows in Maggie's bedroom was transforming from black to dark blue. They had showered together, which made Maggie giggle now as she walked. That was something she had never done before.

She didn't completely understand why she changed her mind about sleeping with Elliott before he left the island. She turned this question over in her mind and decided it had something to do with how loved and supported she had felt the night before at dinner with the Libertas family. And also that she felt Elliott was on her side the entire night, her partner in the mess that was the recent events at the inn. Something about the two of them telling the story to Jack and Petal caused Maggie to feel less alone. She realized part-way home from the dinner that she wanted to prolong that feeling.

And now it was gone. She did feel awful, as she'd known she would. Her emotional state was a curious mix of elation and delight from the night before, and grief and sadness at the loss of the first man she'd felt anything for in living memory. She knew the next few weeks, and possibly months, would be a roller coaster for her. She had known that when she stepped down from the cab of the truck into Elliott's arms. But she'd made the decision within herself knowing what the consequences would be and realized she was willing to live with them.

Ruby waited for her, panting and smiling, at the kitchen door. She pulled it open and went inside, hearing the comforting rumble of breakfast conversation among the guests and the clink of dishes and cutlery. Chris was there, keeping the orange juice and coffee flowing and making sure the granola containers and fruit bowls were full. She said good morning and then went about preparing Ruby's breakfast.

Once the dog was chowing down with her usual gusto and enthusiasm, Maggie made herself a latté at the cappuccino machine and took her mug through to the front desk. Sparrow was there, checking a couple of guests out who, Maggie guessed, were aiming to take the 10 a.m. ferry. *The same one Elliott will be on,* she thought, and then chastised herself. *None of that.*

She said goodbye to them as they collected their bags and headed out the front door, and sat down in the chair beside Sparrow's.

The young woman, dressed today in a loose, flowing flower-patterned dress with a small, faded jean jacket on top, turned to Maggie, holding a piece of paper in her hand. She took one look at Maggie and said, "You got laid!"

"Shhhh!" Maggie glanced around, making sure there weren't any guests close by.

Sparrow leaned in closer and made a quiet squeal, "I knew it! My mom was right. You two *are* meant to be together."

"He's gone, Sparrow." Maggie took a sip of her coffee, "He's moving to the city. I won't see him again."

Sparrow considered this, her eyes fixed on Maggie. She sat up straight in her chair and firmly set the paper she'd been holding down on the desk, "I don't believe it."

"It's true."

"How could he do that? He knows he loves you."

Maggie was shocked. She stopped with the coffee cup halfway to her mouth, "He what?"

Sparrow nodded, absolute certainty in her eyes. "After you guys left last night, my mom made several energy observations about you two and that was one of them. He knows it but he's reluctant to tell you."

"Oh, for heaven's sake, Sparrow. I thought you didn't believe in your mom's energy readings."

"I just say that to bug her. She's right ninety-five percent of the time."

"Well," Maggie put her cup down on the desk and picked up the pile of mail that was waiting for her, "this is an example of the five percent where she's wrong. We had a nice time last night, but Elliott is gone. He was always totally upfront with me that his plan was to leave the island as soon as he could. His life is elsewhere. And mine most definitely is here. End of story."

Sparrow made quiet disbelieving noises in her throat and turned back to the computer.

The women worked quietly together, side-by-side. Maggie opened mail and made piles of documents that needed attending to. She logged into the second computer and began checking her email, something she hadn't done for days. There were notes from vendors wanting to confirm orders and from the mother of the bride whose wedding had been cancelled, apologizing again. As Maggie worked, her mind drifted off, remembering Elliott's touch or something he'd said the night before. His back as he walked to the bathroom, long and strong and ending in the cutest butt she'd ever seen. His dark brown eyes that watched her so carefully, with a mix of curiosity and delight. His laugh, which rumbled up from somewhere deep in his chest, and rewarded her when she'd said something witty or clever. The way her head fit into the crook of his shoulder perfectly, as if it had been made to lie there. He was ticklish; at one point she ran her hand down his side from his ribs to his hip and he'd squealed like a ten-year-old girl. Maggie had laughed so hard she was breathless. He had been embarrassed at first, but then joined her in laughing. She thought the fact that he could laugh at himself showed a strength of character that she appreciated. He didn't have a crystal ego.

She shook herself out of her latest daydream and stood to go make herself another latté.

As she rose, she noticed Sparrow had the Trip Tips site up on her screen. "How are the reviews these days?"

"Pretty good, for the most part. Someone mentioned the fire, though."

"I guess that was inevitable." Maggie made her latté and grabbed two muffins from the tray on the kitchen counter. She set one in front of Sparrow. "What did they say?"

"Here, look." Sparrow rolled her chair to one side so that Maggie could read over her shoulder.

The Cormorant Inn was a disappointment from the word go. The food is decent, although nothing too write home about, as some others on hear have mentioned. Our room was fine, although not as large as promised. And the worse part was that a fire broke out while we were their. One of the guest cabins burnt down, endangering all the guests in the lodge and causing lots of drama, not too mention a sleepless night.

"Well," Maggie sighed, straightening up, "aside from the atrocious grammar, this person is not totally wrong about the havoc the fire caused that night. Although I don't agree that anyone in the lodge was in danger. And the comment about the food is just sour grapes. Greg is the best chef on the island."

"This person has left more than one review and they're never positive."

"Really?"

"I recognize the avatar. That's a picture of the actress who was in Gunsmoke. My dad has that show on DVD. He watches it obsessively."

Maggie peered at the screen, "What's an avatar?"

"Seriously?"

"Yes, seriously. Enlighten me. You know I'm a Luddite when it comes to computers."

Sparrow touched one finger to the screen, "It's that little square picture. People choose them to go along with their user name."

"And they choose photos of other people?"

"Sometimes. You can have a photo of yourself as your avatar, but it's a bit more private if you just pull an image off the internet. People often use their favorite actors or characters. Cartoons or other images. It doesn't really matter what you use."

"Huh." Maggie thought for a few seconds, "And this person has left more than one review about the inn? All negative?"

"Yup. Pretty much. Care Fish Mom."

"What?"

"Care Fish Mom. That's her user name."

"Bizarre. Can you pull up all this person's reviews so they're together?"

"Sure." Sparrow tapped at the keyboard for a few seconds until the screen in front of her changed. A list appeared with four reviews, all one star out of five. Down the left side of the screen, beside each review was the avatar that Sparrow had pointed out.

Maggie read them through, pulling chunks off her muffin and chewing them while she read. The reviews began in September of the previous year and the most recent one was from Tuesday.

"This person really doesn't like it here. Why do they keep coming back?"

"Excellent question."

Maggie sat, deep in thought, staring at the screen. The inn had many guests who were repeat customers. They were her favorites. Over the years they had become almost like members of the family. Many had made a special trip to the island so that they could attend Reg and then Betty's funerals, grieving with Maggie and offering their support. There were couples who had celebrated every wedding anniversary at the inn. There was one man whose parents used to stay at the inn every year, when Maggie was just a small child. Now he brought his wife each August for their end-of-summer getaway.

Four negative reviews was one thing, but four negative reviews from the same person was crazy. Maggie tried to wrap her head around who could be returning to the inn, again and again, only to leave these bitter and bilious reviews. She felt a stirring of feelings of betrayal. Someone was being friendly to her face, but complaining about the inn online. It made no sense.

She shook herself, wanting to escape the thoughts that were circling in her head with no solution to the question of why. She sat down in her chair, grimacing at Sparrow, "I'm at a loss. I don't know what to say about that."

"Haters gonna hate," Sparrow said and clicked the mouse so the Trip Tips page disappeared.

"Yes, but why come back if you hate it here?"

"Masochism?"

Maggie snorted and turned back to her pile of papers. After a few seconds she glanced over at Sparrow again, "Debbie Reynolds," she said.

Sparrow scrunched her nose at her boss, "Huh?"

"That avatar thingy is Debbie Reynolds. I don't think she was in Gunsmoke. She was in Singin' in the Rain, though."

Sparrow pulled up a website that said IMDB at the top left corner. She typed for a few seconds and then said, "You're right. It is Debbie Reynolds. I thought I recognized her from Dad's show, but..." she typed a little more, "That was Amanda Blake. Black and white, man, it's hard to tell people apart."

Maggie snickered, "You're so young. She's Carrie Fisher's mom."

"Who? Amanda Blake?"

"No, Debbie Reynolds."

"Who's Carrie Fisher?"

"Princess Leia. Star Wars."

"I never saw that."

"You're kidding me."

"Nope. Never saw it. Bear couldn't get enough of it, though. He had one of the blue sword things."

"A lightsaber."

"If you say so. And a bunch of little action figures. One looked like it was wearing pajamas. And when he was a teenager he built a model of one of the ships that was about this big." She held her hands out almost three feet apart. "He was mental about all that stuff. I think that's why I didn't watch it. I didn't want to give him the satisfaction."

The morning passed slowly for Maggie. She tried to focus all her attention on the tasks and paperwork that needed her input to try and distract herself, but her mind wouldn't cooperate. She found herself, many times, staring off into space, images and feelings rolling through her. She'd try to shut them off, but they'd return. She made small talk with the guests who wandered by for a chat, or who came to check out. Her heart wasn't in it though and she felt phony pretending to talk to them when her mind was so far away.

Finally just before 1 p.m. she gave up. Her stomach had been rumbling for a while.

"I'm going to make a sandwich. Do you want anything?"

Sparrow, who seemed to be in the back end of the inn's website, if the gibberish on the screen was any indication, shook her head 'no' and kept typing.

As Maggie made her sandwich in the kitchen, she heard voices outside. She cut the sandwich in half and, carrying half in each hand, backed through the kitchen door to the sitting area outside. It was Carol and Greg she had heard. They were sitting on the picnic bench top, their feet on the seat below them. They were pressed together from hip to knee, and smoking a joint.

"Uh, oh," Greg said as Maggie approached, "it's the boss. You better swallow this." He passed the joint to Carol.

"No way. That would be a tragic waste of pot." She inhaled and held her breath.

Maggie sat down in a Muskoka chair opposite them and took a bite of her sandwich, "You two are going to get me arrested."

"As if," Greg said, "Frank Nelson is one of my best customers."

"You're dealing? Jesus. I'm watching my life swirl down the drain."

"Not dealing exactly." Greg took the joint back from Carol. "I just grow it for 'personal use,'" he made hand quotes, "but when Frank and I smoked up at the Canada Day barbecue last year he thought it was awesome. So he buys from me occasionally."

"Good grief."

"It is good!" Greg adopted his most persuasive tone, "This is the one place on the island now that *won't* get busted for possession." He smiled and winked at Maggie.

Carol watched Maggie throughout this exchange. Now she spoke up, "You had a sleepover."

Greg laughed "No way, boss!"

Carol didn't look away from Maggie, "Right?"

"Right." Maggie thought she must be as transparent as a ghost, if everyone could see the events of the night before written on her face.

"Awesome, dude!" Greg was clearly happy about this turn of events. "Who was it? That doctor Freeland chick? She's super hot."

Carol swatted at Greg's head but he ducked just in time.

"What?" He looked back and forth from Maggie to Carol.

Maggie finally took pity on his clueless expression, "No, Greg. Not Doctor Freeland. A man slept over last night."

"A dude?" The chef looked even more confused, but recovered quickly, "Cool. Who's the lucky fella?"

Maggie didn't answer. She bit into her sandwich and chewed purposefully.

Carol smiled at her friend. "Elliott Simon," she said to Greg.

"Who?"

"Libby from The Bakeri's brother. You met him after the fire."

Greg nodded, "Awesome."

Maggie looked at him, squinting in the sunlight that came through the trees beside them, "Do you know who Carol means?"

"No. Not really. But that's ok. I'm just happy for you."

The trio sat quietly for a time. Greg and Carol finished smoking their joint and Maggie finished her sandwich. They were all enjoying the warmth of the sun and the quiet. Maggie thought back to her conversation with Sparrow.

"Hey, do you guys remember when we started having accidents here at the inn?"

Carol furrowed her brow, "I guess that depends on what you define as an accident and what you think is suspicious."

"That's just it, isn't it? Looking back, I think stuff might have been happening for a while but we just wrote it off as normal. Unsuspicious."

"When do you think it started?" Carol put her arms behind her and leaned back.

"I remember that the first time I had the thought that something was behind a problem we were having was when that pillar candle was lit just before Christmas."

"I don't remember that."

"Don't you? We had put the Christmas decorations out the week before and we had that candle on the fireplace mantle. But it was never intended to be lit. It was in one of those big glass vase things." Maggie made a motion indicating size and shape, "Remember? And the glass part had been put on one of the coffee tables and the candle had been lit, so it was an open flame on the mantle, below the big wreath."

"Oh, right. And those guests found it when they came in late."

"Right. It was super late. We had all gone to bed. But the Millers had been at a dinner party with friends and they got back at close to three am. It was just lucky they went into the Great Room before they went upstairs. They blew the candle out and I wouldn't have even known, but they mentioned it to Sparrow at breakfast the next day. They knew that we wouldn't intentionally leave a candle burning."

Greg was lying back on the picnic table top, humming quietly to himself. But then he surprised Maggie by speaking into the quiet. She thought he wasn't paying attention, "What about that meat that was left out?"

"Right!" Maggie sat up a little straighter in her chair, "When was that?"

"October, I think. No wait. September. I remember because it was my mother's birthday and I was leaving to go to Nanaimo on the day it happened. Her birthday is September 10th."

Maggie couldn't see Greg's face, just his knees and calves. "And you swore you hadn't left it out."

"Of course I didn't," Greg sat up and looked at her, "Who do you take me for? Some pot-smoking slacker?"

Greg actually was a pot-smoking slacker. At times, anyway. But he was also meticulous and fastidious about his kitchen and a very hard worker when it mattered to him. The meals at the Cormorant Inn proved that it mattered to him every day. He ran a tight ship and had fired more than one aspiring chef because he couldn't stand people who didn't respect the cooking arts. He played up the slacker aspect of his personality, sometimes a little too much. It had taken Maggie awhile to see the genius behind his surfer dude act, but once she had, she knew Greg to be loyal and committed to his craft. She sometimes wondered why he worked so hard to pretend not to care about his work. Perhaps his surfing and ganja buddies would tease him about it.

"Of course not, my darling," Maggie soothed his ruffled feathers, "but at the time I wondered if one of your underlings had left it out. But you asked them all, right?"

"I did. They all swore up and down they hadn't done it. And

I believed them. Still do, in fact. Because it's my kitchen and I am always the last to leave."

This was true. It was one of Greg's rules and he never broke it. He might sit outside and have a puff while the minions were cleaning the kitchen after the dining room was closed, but when they were done and heading home, he was the one who gave the kitchen a once over and turned out the lights.

He continued, "So if that meat had been out before we closed up shop, I would have seen it."

Maggie's eyes wandered over to the spruce and cedar trees that bordered the little garden area. Several thoughts were roiling round in her head, and she wasn't comfortable with any of them. She grasped at the tails of several ideas, but they slipped away from her, like salmon in a stream.

From far away she heard the sound of Carol's voice, but not the words.

"Pardon me?" She turned her head back to her friend.

"I said, I wanted to hear the details of your night of sin, not rehash the inn's troubles."

"Sorry," Maggie smiled, a warm flush appearing on her face, "some things I keep to myself."

The best way Maggie found to unknot herself was to take a walk on the long, curved beach that her inn overlooked. When Greg and Carol roused themselves to go in and begin working, Maggie gathered Ruby and grabbed a windbreaker from the staff closet in the back hallway. She and the dog walked through the inn's main parking lot and curved to their right. Ruby knew where they were going, of course, and charged ahead of Maggie onto the sloping cedar bark path that led down to the beach.

It was a relatively calm day on the ocean. The waves came to shore lazily, as though they almost thought they had better things to do. Ruby trotted ahead in her looping pattern, sniffing kelp fronds that had been washed ashore, and anything else that caught her eye. Overhead, the ever-present gulls made faint, half-hearted cries, matching the ocean's lazy mood.

One reason Maggie enjoyed walking on the beach when she was troubled was that it had the effect of emptying her mind. Today was no exception. She was able to focus on the sights and sounds, so dear and familiar to her, and yet always changing. She liked how the beach was never the same from one day to the next. The sand shifted, the driftwood was moved around by the waves. It was a change that was manifested not by human hands, which was what Maggie loved about it. Sure, in the summer one could observe the remnants of sandcastles left by industrious children that created mounds the beach might not otherwise see. But most of the change was nature-made. The power of the wind, rain, waves and sun never stopped impressing Maggie. The beach and the shoreline changed shape and appearance continually. They reminded Maggie that nothing stayed the same for very long, not even her troubles.

Ruby led her mistress all the way down to the far end of the beach, the guest cottages owned by her neighbor on her left and the ocean on her right. The pair walked as far as the rocky outcropping that defined the end of this beach and then turned to walk home. By the time they reached the inn's parking lot again, just over an hour had gone by and Maggie felt refreshed and her head felt a little clearer. Two thoughts that had been specters in the back of her mind had formed ever so slightly and she felt a pressing need to ask Sparrow a few more questions about the reviews on Trip Tips. She was pleased because Elliott had popped into her head only twice every minute on the walk, as opposed to twice a second earlier in the day.

Her rubber boots crunched on the gravel as she walked toward the inn, deep in thought. On her right a flash of color caught her eye. She turned to see a bright red convertible pulling into the parking lot. It had a soft top and a personalize license plate that said, 'VROOM.'

Clever, Maggie thought sarcastically.

Then she noticed a flash of blond hair in the driver's seat and realized it was June Brier. She was happy to see the widow out and about for the first time since she'd arrived at the inn. Their eyes met and Maggie waved. June waved back and then the car curved away into the long-term lot.

"Show me those trip reviews again, will you?" Maggie put her hands on Sparrow's shoulders and spun her toward the computer screen. Ruby drank loudly from her water dish under the desk.

"All of them?"

"Just the ones with the Debbie Reynolds thingy."

"Avatar."

"Whatever."

Something urgent was tickling the edge of Maggie's brain but she wasn't sure what it was.

Sparrow pulled up the Trip Tips site and with a few keyboard strokes and clicks of the mouse she had the list of four reviews by themselves on the screen.

Maggie leaned forward and peered at the screen and then stood up straight again, her face pale and her expression shocked.

Sparrow turned in her chair and looked up at Maggie. "What?"

"Look at the time that review was posted. The one about the fire."

Sparrow leaned into the screen, "Monday, May 11. 10:52 p.m. it says."

Maggie met Sparrow's eyes as she folded down into the chair beside her.

"What?" Sparrow said again, "I don't get it."

Carol had appeared in the kitchen doorway, her coffee mug in her hand. Her intelligent eyes, slightly reddened, looked at Maggie and Maggie could see she had figured it out, too. "The fire didn't start until early Tuesday morning," Carol said to Sparrow, "How did the reviewer know there was a fire unless they were the ones about to set it?"

Twenty-Nine

"I'M CONVINCED IT'S A DEVELOPER or someone from the island who wants this land who's doing this."

Maggie had poured a measure of scotch into her coffee mug and was sipping at it, a frozen look on her face, her eyes wide and glassy.

"Why?" Carol pulled up a folding chair and the three women sat huddled in a small circle, whispering slightly when guests walked by.

"I think that whoever is posting those negative reviews is the person causing the accidents. And that that person isn't a guest, but someone pretending to be."

"Are people allowed to do that?" Carol looked at Sparrow, "Haven't there been cases where people have been sued for placing false negative reviews on rival business sites? Like a restaurant that posts crap reviews for another restaurant in their neighborhood, so that business is driven away from their competitor and hopefully toward them."

"Sure," Sparrow said, "that happens. I've heard about a couple of cases that have gone to court but I'll bet it happens even more than we realize. People can be horrible online. They think the anonymity makes it okay to be shitty to others."

The three women were quiet, thinking.

"But you and," Carol hesitated at using Elliott's name but then forged on, "Elliott couldn't seem to find any information about anyone who might be trying to get you to leave."

"You're right." Maggie sucked her teeth for a moment. "All we found out was that the Petrov ladies don't have any witnesses to where they were the night of the fire. Even though they said they did."

"And my dad said he couldn't find any whispers about it either," Sparrow said. "He's a pretty well-connected guy."

"He is. You're right," Maggie bumped Sparrow's knee with her own, affectionately, "But he's not omniscient. There could be someone he doesn't know about or some new development firm that has its eye on the island but hasn't shown its hand yet."

"True." Sparrow didn't sound totally convinced.

"It's the only explanation that makes sense." She began counting off the reasons on her fingers, "One, we know for sure from the guest book and all the other online reviews that our guests love us. Two, every other guest who leaves a review on that site, uses their real name. Look," she pointed at the computer, "Ron Arnold. He was here last week. Liz Schwartz; she and her husband, Ken, come here every spring. Madeline P. That's got to be Maddie Page who came on that girlfriends' retreat last month." She turned away from the computer and looked at her friends, "No one leaves an anonymous review except this Debbie Reynolds character."

"Care Fish Mom," Sparrow interjected.

"Right. Care Fish Mom. Oh!" Maggie laughed, "I get it. Carrie Fisher's mom. That's what Care Fish Mom means."

Sparrow made a dismissive sound, and spoke under her breath, "Stupid. Who needs to be that clever with an avatar?"

The three women batted around ideas for the next half-hour. They considered who else, besides the people Maggie and Elliott had already thought of and the contacts that Jack Libertas had, might want to ruin the inn's business. Carol proposed, among other things, someone with mineral rights to the island who had discovered a vein of gold in the rocks beneath the Cormorant Inn.

"Be serious," Maggie said.

"Sorry," Carol said, "But it feels a bit frustrating. What else could it be other than someone wanting to develop this land? 'Follow the money.' Isn't that what they always say in the movies? And the money, in this case, is a direct result of how this piece of land is situated and how someone else could exploit it with a larger hotel and more cabins and, hell, even a marina down at the beach." She fixed her gaze directly on her friend, "Elizabeth Margaret Archer, you are sitting on a gold mine and you don't even know it. Someone is trying to force you to fold up your tent and move on. Probably because they know that if you sold while the inn was doing well, the price would be a king's ransom. Your instinct last week when you posed that theory was right. I'm sure of it."

Maggie leaned back in her chair and clicked the mug she was holding against her front teeth, "I dunno. Something is feeling off to me now. There's something going on that we're not seeing."

"You said a few minutes ago that you were convinced it was a developer."

"I know but...something's bugging me. I can't put my finger on it."

"I'll put my finger on it then." Carol took a sip of her coffee and then continued, "I promise you, when you dig to the bottom of this you are going to find some greedy land-grabber with dollar signs where his pupils should be. Those nasty Keith brothers are tops on my list of suspects."

"Land-grabber?" Maggie asked, smiling despite her concerns, "Is that a thing?"

"It is now. I just invented it."

"I dunno." Maggie thought about this. "It's possible. They certainly are nasty. But it seems slightly out of character for them doesn't it?"

"What do you mean?" Carol asked.

"I'm not quite sure. It's a feeling. The Keiths are not subtle. They're overt. They're bullies."

Sparrow nodded, understanding. "Right. This stuff is much subtler than that. The accidents that could be just that. And the negative reviews somehow don't strike me as their style either."

Maggie nodded, "Exactly. I don't think the Keiths have it in them to be that sneaky. They've only got one tool in their toolbox, so to speak. They are sledgehammers; they go at everything in a straightforward way. I can't see them being subtle enough to cause accidents."

The front door to the inn banged shut and a voice came from above the trio, "Excuse me?"

All three women startled slightly, so engrossed in their conversation they had tuned out the world around them.

Maggie stood up, "Yes, Mrs. Brier. How can we help? How are you doing today?"

The new widow looked worse than she had on Tuesday night. Her hair was lying lank around her shoulders and her eyes had deep rings the color of eggplant around them. Maggie kicked herself that in the past two days she hadn't checked in with her bereaved guest. She had been so caught up in her feelings about Elliott and their amateur investigation that she had been neglecting her duties as host. The stress of the fire hadn't helped either, of course.

"Maggie, did you say the other day that you would be willing to take me out to shoot a few photographs? I'm feeling like I want to get out and get some fresh air."

June's request was reasonable and Maggie had offered to do just what she was mentioning. But Maggie gritted her teeth slightly, resenting the intrusion into the bubble that had formed around her, Carol and Sparrow. She wished the moment hadn't been broken and that they could continue tossing around theories. Something they tripped over might make sense. Maggie felt, not for the first time, a gnawing desperation to save her home and her livelihood. She felt these things were slipping away from her and any time not spent focusing on how to solve this mystery were moments that were speeding her toward ruin.

The tickle in Maggie's mind became like an itch that needed to be scratched. She thought it might drive her mad if she stayed inside and let it buzz around in her head. Maybe some fresh air and taking her mind off it would allow it to speak to her in a clearer voice. "Of course, June," she said. "Would you like to go now?"

Thirty

MAGGIE TRIED NOT TO LOOK at the ferry that moved silently through the water. It was the 10 a.m. to Tsawwassen on the mainland and it reminded her of Elliott's departure. She allowed herself briefly to wonder if he would think of her, as she knew she would think of him, often and with tremendous fondness. And, she suddenly realized, quite a bit of grief.

"Did you hear me?"

Maggie shook herself out of her reflection and pushed aside the ache in her heart. "I'm sorry, June. What did you say?"

"I said did you know this island was where my parents honeymooned?"

"I didn't. What year would that have been?"

June shared the story of her parents' holidays on Juliet Island in the mid-1970s, but Maggie was only half-listening. Something about the sight of the ferry jostled whatever was bothering her about the mystery of the accidents at the inn. She could feel an understanding creeping closer, but it wasn't quite there yet. She tried letting it go, and focusing on June, to see if she could coax it out of the shadows, like a shy cat.

Maggie's focus returned to June, who was saying that she had been conceived on the island.

"You're joking," Maggie said, smiling.

June smiled back, just slightly. It was the first time Maggie had seen her smile since her husband died. "I'm kind of an honorary Canadian," she said.

"Did you vacation here as a child?"

"No, by the time I was a toddler my father's fortunes had turned and we weren't in a position to afford holidays. He was in venture capital, and that business is like riding a roller coaster. One minute you're up and the next you're down. We never knew from year to year if we'd be living on the street or riding in limousines. Mostly we were somewhere in between."

June and Maggie were walking along a narrow trail that led away from the Cormorant Inn property and along a bluff that overlooked Raven channel. The path wove in and out of trees, sometimes leading them over bare rock and sometimes leading them down little gullies where pine and cedar trees grew out of the rocks at odd angles. Both women had brought their cameras, and June stopped and focused her camera on the view from where they stood. Maggie waited while the shutter whirred, looking out over the dark water. The sky was completely clear. Off in the distance were the green mounds of South Pender Island sticking up out of the water.

"Is that what brought you and Arthur back to Juliet? The attachment your family had to the place?"

June turned and the pair began walking again, "Yes. I had never been here myself, but when Arthur and I were first married he suggested we come up and see what the island was like now. He had heard the stories of how happy my mum and dad were when they came here." She paused for a moment and then carried on, "Our marriage was going through a rough patch at the time and I think Arthur thought the peace and quiet here might do us some good."

"Did it?"

"Not really. Even though it is quiet here, he always found a way to be wrapped up in his work. So he tended to go off to a restaurant or the library where he could find a WiFi signal and work for hours on end. I didn't see him any more than I would have at home."

Above her, Maggie heard a chickadee calling to its mate and then the return call from several feet away. She and June were in the trees now. They climbed up a little wooden staircase that someone had built into the rocks to make the going easier. The path then led them out onto another bluff that overlooked a tiny private island with a small dock at the water's edge and a house peeking through the trees at the far right side. June wandered over to the cliff edge and stood looking out at the sea and the small island.

"You have everything here, don't you Maggie?"

Maggie wasn't sure what the question referred to but she agreed with the sentiment. "It is an amazing place."

"No, I mean you have *everything*. You had parents who loved you. And you have a purpose in your life – the inn and your guests. You don't have a care in the world."

This statement puzzled Maggie given all that seemed wrong in her life at the moment. She struggled to find the right thing to say to this woman who was obviously in so much pain about the loss of her husband. "Every life has its sweet spots and its challenges, June. I don't need to tell you that."

"But your life doesn't have challenges," June had raised her voice slightly, as though she was angry.

Maggie turned away from the view and looked at her. June's face was contorted in anger, like a storm that had blown up out of nowhere.

"Is that why you killed your husband?" Maggie asked, her stomach tight with knots. "Because he couldn't give you a perfect life?"

A cloud of shock passed over June's face and was almost immediately replaced by a look of smugness and disdain. "When did you figure it out?"

"I put the pieces together just now." Maggie looked out over the water and saw that the ferry had nearly disappeared from view. It was a small black and white dot about to disappear behind Pender Island. "The ferry jogged my memory. Something had been bothering me and then I realized what it was. You told Constable Nelson that you arrived on the Saturday ferry, which meant you couldn't have been here when Arthur fell to his death. But I was on that ferry early Saturday morning. It's the only one that day. And you weren't on it. I just realized that now when I saw your red car in the parking lot. I would have noticed it on the car deck that morning. It stands out in a place where most people drive decades-old beaters that are held together with duct tape and prayer. You came to the island on Friday perhaps? But stayed somewhere else and made a show of arriving at the inn on Saturday. Have I got that right?"

Some of the smugness was wiped off June's face and the look of anger ratcheted up to fury. "Just like I said. You've got everything. You've even got me figured out." June turned away and made a disgusted noise. When she turned back her eyes were full of tears. "How long had you been sleeping with my husband?"

This Maggie did not expect. She almost laughed but stopped herself just in time. June was completely serious. Maggie sought for a way to emphatically explain that was not the case. "June, please believe me. Your husband and I were not having an affair."

"As if," June spat. "He kept encouraging us to come up here. There had to be only one reason to do that. To get in your pants. Your type of woman disgusts me. Can't you keep your hands to yourself?"

She was pacing now in a tight trajectory like a tiger in a small cage. Maggie thought about arguing with her but realized it wouldn't matter. The woman was clearly unhinged. Somehow she had fixated on Maggie as the source of all the problems in her life. If she couldn't reason with her, Maggie thought she might be able to at least get the truth from her.

"Is it you who's been sabotaging the inn?"

"This hunk of junk?" June flailed one arm out, gesturing back toward the inn. "It was pathetically easy to cause problems here. All your local yokels working placidly here are so dumb they wouldn't have noticed if I'd set fire to the kitchen right under their noses."

Maggie felt herself reacting to this, wanting to protect her brood and her inn's honor. But she stayed quiet, not wanting to stem the flow of information from June. "Why?" she said quietly.

"At first I thought that if I caused enough problems Arthur wouldn't want to stay here anymore. But no. He kept insisting we come back." June whirled and glared at Maggie. "That's when I knew you were sleeping with him. Why else would we come back to this godforsaken place?"

"So you kept at it."

"You're goddamned right. I thought maybe if I did enough damage to your reputation that the inn would close and then we could go somewhere else for once."

So the sabotage had nothing to do with development, Maggie realized. It only had to do with misplaced jealousy. *How ridiculous that this woman with a wealthy husband and a house with a pool, a housekeeper and a gardener would be jealous of me*, she thought. With my failing business and my thirteen hour work days. And now, my broken heart. Maggie sighed and then pressed on, wanting what was happening to be over. "Did you push your husband or was it an accident?"

Now June began to cry in earnest. She swiped angrily at her tears. "I didn't mean for him to fall. I just wanted to get his attention. He was being such an ass. Denying that he was sleeping with you. I just wanted the truth."

"It was the truth, June," Maggie tried again, despite knowing she would fail to get through.

"Bullshit!" June spat. "Why else would he want to continue to come up here? Why else would he drag me away from my home and my..."

Maggie thought she was going to say friends, but instead, after searching for a moment June said, "...life."

"Maybe he thought you were happy here. Maybe he wanted to show you that he cared about your family's connection to Juliet Island."

June made a huffing sound that Maggie couldn't interpret. She was still pacing, her camera swinging and bouncing around on her chest with the violent turns and twists of her body. Maggie thought that if she wanted to get June back to the inn so she could call Constable Nelson, she'd have to find a way to calm her down.

Just as she thought this, June whirled again and looked at Maggie with renewed fury on her face. A thought had obviously occurred to her. Her eyes were wide and staring, and the deepening craziness in them made Maggie nervous for the first time. "And now," June was practically screeching, "you have a *new* boyfriend. You couldn't wait five minutes after my husband had died before you started up with someone else. I couldn't believe it this week when I saw you slutting around with that idiot fireman, or whatever he is. Why is everything always perfect for *you*?" The last word was screamed, and without warning, June launched herself at Maggie.

Maggie didn't even have a second to realize what was happening before the woman tackled her, bringing them both to the ground. The wind came out of Maggie's lungs in a rush when her back hit the rocks with a sickening thud. She heard her camera crunch as well.

June was on top of Maggie, swinging with both arms, trying to connect her fists with Maggie's face. Maggie deflected with her forearms while also trying to wiggle out from under June's body. But the widow was having none of that. After a few more swats with her fists, she climbed off Maggie's legs and began pushing Maggie toward the edge of the bluff. With a sinking feeling in her stomach, Maggie realized June intended to push her off the cliff, doing away with her as she had done with her husband.

Maggie scrambled wildly, pushing back at June's attempts to roll her toward the cliff edge. She managed to roll over and sit up on her knees. June buffeted her head with wild blows that Maggie tried to duck away from and was mostly able to avoid. She felt the toes of one of her shoes slip and realized she was mere inches from the edge of the cliff. June got a strong hold of one of Maggie's arms and began pushing and twisting her. Maggie felt herself restricting her own movements because she was afraid if she flailed around too much she'd end up throwing herself off the cliff's edge.

The fight had probably only been going on for ninety seconds or so, but to Maggie it seemed an eternity. She was getting desperate, and her breath was coming in short rasping bursts when she wasn't grunting with effort.

Her camera was still swinging around on her neck, hurting her when it bounced off her chin or chest. Maggie suddenly realized what she had to do. Mid-struggle she slipped the camera's strap over her head so that it came away from her body. Then she took a chance and slowed everything down.

She was kneeling with her bum resting on her calves and she could feel that now her feet, not just her toes, were hanging off the edge of the cliff. Below her she could hear the ocean's eternal whisper as it washed ashore. Her stomach did a little queasy flip when she thought about how long the drop was down to the rocks at the water's edge.

She stopped struggling, letting her arms go limp. June stopped too, for an instant, a confused look on her face. In this split second, which was the only chance she was going to have, Maggie gripped the camera lens as tightly as she could with her right hand. Out of the corner of her eye she saw movement at the edge of the forest and then a shout.

June turned but Maggie didn't. She kept her eyes locked on her assailant, waiting, hoping the woman who had already murdered once would change her mind about this time. But when June's face turned back to Maggie's and their eyes met, Maggie knew her wish was in vain. June's eyes were ablaze, perhaps more than ever. And whatever she had seen at the edge of the forest had clearly made her even more determined to do away with Maggie. She lifted her hands, palms out, and Maggie could see she was going to make one final push and send Maggie plunging to her death.

Maggie swung as hard as she could, the camera swinging in a wide arc aiming for June's temple. Whether it would make it there before June's hands connected with Maggie's shoulders was the only question Maggie had.

Thirty-One

THE PARTY HAD BEEN GOING on for several hours and even Ruby was exhausted and fully sated. The brown dog lay sleeping under an oak tree at the edge of the clearing, her feet twitching slightly as she dreamed.

Guests and staff alike were sitting at the tables that had been brought outside from the dining room. A long catering table with folding legs nearly sagged under the weight of all the food placed on it. Chef Greg had contributed two roasts, along with his famous garlic mashed potatoes. The rest of the food, including salads, vegetable dishes, and a tofu log that no one but Sparrow was eating, had been brought by the hotel guests and island friends who now sat laughing and talking loudly with one another.

Maggie looked around her at the familiar faces, all beaming, and wondered how she had gotten so lucky. She felt a pair of arms go around her waist as someone sat on the bench seat beside her.

"How's your head?" In an uncharacteristic move, Carol gave Maggie a light kiss on the cheek as she sat down.

"Not bad. Still a little sore."

Maggie sustained a variety of cuts and bruises during her tussle with June Brier, not to mention a black eye. She didn't recall June connecting with that eye specifically, but the event was such a blur that she wasn't surprised she couldn't remember. She was stiff and sore everywhere, and new patches of purple bruising were showing up on her legs and arms at an alarming rate.

But she was alive. And that couldn't be said for the previous person who had run afoul of June; her late husband, Arthur Brier.

"So tell me again," Carol said, chewing on one of Libby's sourdough buns, "if you figured out it was June who killed Arthur, why did you go with her on that walk?"

Maggie shrugged, not really sure herself. "I hadn't figured it all out yet. The realization about June's car didn't hit me until we were out on the bluff, walking." She thought for a few moments. "And even though I had started to wonder about her, because of the Trip Tips comments, I wanted to be wrong. I can't imagine the kind of pain June must have been in to try to kill her own husband."

"You're too understanding, Mags. That bitch is as crazy as a shit-house rat. You were so lucky to get away with just a black eye."

Off to one side of the clearing, the young constable, Brandon, was leading a few revelers in song, strumming Eagles hits on his battered acoustic guitar. Maggie watched Sparrow dancing a waltz with her dad. Francis and Nathan were dancing as well. The gathering was a celebration of Maggie's safe return from her walk with a murderess and the fact that the inn would hopefully be sailing into more prosperous times, now that its saboteur had been sent to a jail on the mainland.

When news of Maggie's 'adventure' (as she called it) with June on the headland bluff reached the general population of Juliet Island, which, as usual, took about 2.3 seconds, the island community moved Maggie to tears with their generosity. The idea was floated to set up a GoFundMe page to pull the Cormorant Inn out of its current debt-ridden state, pay off the roof repair bill, and to make some other much needed repairs and improvements. Sparrow and her technical genius had been pressed into service, and the page was up and running before twenty-four hours had elapsed after Frank Nelson handcuffed June Brier. The fund now exceeded its target, and every time Maggie thought about it, her throat caught with emotion.

Maggie leaned over and put her head on Carol's shoulder. Her friend wrapped her arm around Maggie's waist and held her tight. Maggie still felt very fragile and burst into tears several times a day. Dr. Freeland, who had examined her after the 'adventure' said that this was normal and that Maggie should be very gentle with herself for the coming weeks, and even months.

In the immediate aftermath of the attack on the bluff, Frank Nelson questioned Maggie for what seemed like days, but was probably only an hour or so. He wanted to know how Maggie discovered that June was the culprit in what the coroner's office had determined was the accidental death of Arthur Brier.

"I wasn't looking for a murderer," Maggie confessed, though she wasn't sure Frank believed her. "I was trying to figure out who was sabotaging my inn. But it turned out one person had done both those things."

"And it wasn't a developer or the Keiths trying to ruin your business?" Frank looked skeptical.

Maggie shook her head. "Honestly, Frank, I think it all came down to jealousy. June Brier is a deeply unhappy woman. My guess is she's spent her entire adult life trying to find a man who would fill the empty places inside her. Someone who would make up for all the lack she feels in herself. Did you know Arthur was her fourth husband?"

Frank shook his head.

A question occurred to Maggie then. "What happened to her other husbands, by the way? Are they dead or did she just divorce them?"

"I've asked the LA County sheriff's office to look into that and let me know, but I haven't heard back yet. We may never know. They may not feel it's important enough to get back to a remote Canadian RCMP detachment."

But the sheriff's office surprised Frank and called him back the next day. All of June Brier's pervious husbands were still alive. Arthur was the only one she had killed.

In jail, June was swearing Arthur's death was an accident. That he had tripped when he and his wife were walking on the bluff. She wasn't able to explain why she had concealed the fact that she'd been on the island that day and had pretended to arrive at the inn the following day. It was at that point that she began aggressively asking for a lawyer.

"She's having a psychiatric assessment, though," Frank said to Maggie. "The woman is clearly troubled, if not clinically insane. She won't stop talking about you."

Maggie scrunched up her face.

Frank continued, quietly though, breaking this news gently. "She's actually blaming you for Arthur's death."

"What? How can she possibly…?"

"Like I said. She's nuts."

Maggie shook her head, remembering. "When I think back to the Saturday when Elliott found Arthur's body…I went up to see June afterwards and she seemed pretty normal then. Grieving, of course, but also angry. I attributed that to her reaction to the news. Everyone reacts to loss differently." She looked up at Frank. "She was dressed and coherent and even had makeup on. But after that…" Maggie shook her head, "she seemed to go downhill pretty fast."

Frank shrugged and sighed, "I don't know, Mags. She may have been running on adrenaline at first, and it may have taken a day or two for what she'd done to sink in with her. I don't think we'll ever understand what was going through her head. Thankfully," he added as an afterthought.

Carol spoke up from Maggie's side, interrupting her memories. "By the way, what was all that business about the nasty reviews on Trip Tips? Do you think that was June as well?"

Libby was sitting on Maggie's other side. She took a bite of her hot dog and listened intently.

Maggie nodded. "I think so. We'll have to go back and have a more detailed look at the timing of the reviews, but I bet you they'll either coincide with June and Arthur's visits or they will have been posted very shortly after."

"I get that, but what made you think that after seeing the avatar of the lady from Gunsmoke?"

"It wasn't the lady from Gunsmoke, remember? It was Debbie Reynolds. A million years ago, she was married to Eddie Fisher."

"Right," Carol and Libby nodded, following along.

"And you know how for a while there I was addicted to late night talk shows." Maggie looked at Carol when she asked this.

"Yes. Jay Leno was your secret boyfriend."

Maggie nodded. "Well, there was this amazing interview with Carrie Fisher once on The Late Late Show."

"With Craig Ferguson," Libby piped up, chewing. "He was so funny."

"Right. That interview is hilarious, and Carrie explained that her father and Elizabeth Taylor had an affair. Eddie ended up leaving Debbie for Elizabeth."

Maggie's head swiveled back and forth from Libby to Carol. They both looked puzzled.

"So?" Carol finally said.

"So. Debbie Reynolds was cheated on. When June came to the front desk late Tuesday night when I was working, she was clearly high from sleeping pills. When Greg and I took her up to her room, she rambled on about several things, among them being a cuckoo."

Carol rolled her eyes, "She got that part right."

"I couldn't figure out why she kept calling herself a cuckoo, but when I saw the avatar and remembered Debbie Reynolds, I wondered if June meant 'cuckold.'"

Carol's face was blank. She didn't understand.

Libby filled her in, "A cuckold is someone who's been cheated on. Usually a man. But I guess in this case, June applied the word to herself."

"What a ridiculous word." Carol reached across Maggie and took some potato chips off Libby's paper plate.

Libby wiped her mouth on a mangled paper napkin and looked at Maggie, "But when she asked you to go for a walk and take photographs, didn't you realize she was dangerous?"

Maggie sat quietly for a moment. "It was a spur of the moment decision. I can't defend it. Perhaps I was foolish."

"Perhaps?" Libby sounded a little annoyed.

Maggie patted her arm. "I'm okay. It all turned out okay. Partly thanks to your brother." Maggie turned in her seat, craning her neck. "Where is he?"

Elliott was flipping burgers with Greg on the industrial-sized barbecue, wearing an apron that said 'Kiss the cook.' Maggie did just that.

"Hello, you," Elliott said, smiling at her.

"I'm going to go rest for a bit. I'm pooped. I'll come and find you in a little while."

Elliott looked hesitant. Greg elbowed his sous chef in the ribs, "Go with her. I'll give you the rest of the afternoon off."

Elliott untied his apron strings and pulled it over his head. As he and Maggie walked toward her cabin, he handed the apron to Brandon. "Take over, Maestro."

Brandon saluted, put his guitar down, and walked toward the barbecue, looking pleased to have something to do.

Elliott wrapped his arm tightly around Maggie's shoulders and pulled her as close to him as he could.

"Are you getting used to island life yet?" she asked.

"You mean in the last thirty-six hours? Not quite, but I'll get there."

It had been Elliott that June had seen running toward them on the bluff. He had returned to the inn just after Maggie and June left. Sparrow, sensing romance and oblivious to the danger Maggie was in, sent Elliott after them. A decision that proved both fortuitous and fortunate.

Luckily Maggie's roundhouse swing, propelled by the weight of her camera, had connected with the side of June Brier's head just before the murderess had pushed Maggie off the cliff. June had dropped to the ground like a sack of hammers and Elliott had pulled Maggie up into his arms and away from the cliff's edge.

"Did you miss the ferry?" was the first thing out of her mouth.

Elliott barked out a laugh that was a half-sob. It was so like Maggie to be worried about someone else despite the danger in the previous moment.

He pulled her into his chest and didn't let go for many minutes. Maggie was shaking and wouldn't stop for several hours. He rubbed her back and smelled the fruity shampoo she used in her hair.

After a long, peaceful moment together, Maggie's ragged breathing began to slow. She pushed away from his chest. "Really, Elliott. Did you miss the ferry?"

Over the ensuing two days he rarely left her side.

Maggie, so pleased and grateful that Elliott was with her to help her through the aftermath of the fight with June, hadn't broached the subject of when he would be leaving. The celebratory barbecue felt like the completion of the dark and dangerous time in her life. The inn would be saved and her employees were safe. For the moment, all was well.

The pair walked through the woods that surrounded the inn, heading toward Maggie's cabin. Maggie took a deep breath, knowing that now she would have to face up to the fact that Elliott must want to be getting on with his life.

She approached the subject from a slightly sideways angle, "Are they holding your job for you?"

Elliott glanced down at her, his face serious.

Uh oh, Maggie thought to herself. *Be brave.*

Elliott cleared his throat, as though he was nervous, and said, "Ms. Archer, I have a business proposal for you. How would you like a business partner to help run the inn?"

Maggie stopped walking and turned to look up at him, questions in her eyes. This was not the answer she'd been expecting.

"A business partner?"

"Well," Elliott hesitated, "maybe slightly more than that." He began to smile.

Maggie's heart leapt into her throat. She took another breath, trying to remain calm. "Did you have anyone specific in mind for this....'partnership'?"

Elliott put his hands on her shoulders and pulled her closer to him, so they were standing almost pressed against one another. "I had an idea of someone who might fit the position."

"Really? Who?"

Elliott shrugged, pretending to be casual. "I thought I might show you my resumé. It turns out I'm on the hunt for a new job."

"You are? What about the architecture firm?"

"Environmental engineering."

"Whatever."

"Well, I thought about it and let's face it, I wouldn't last five minutes in an office tower."

Maggie nodded, smiling wider now. It was true she had never been able to picture him in a suit and tie.

He continued. "Let me help you with the maintenance of the inn. I'll be working outside in a natural setting, which is my happy place. And working on a project that has meaning. Not just chasing a dollar in the city." He took a deep breath and added, for insurance, "You'll actually be doing me a favor. Saving me from the concrete jungle."

Maggie's mind was still whirling with all that had happened in the last few days, and now this offer from a man she thought she would never see again was making her heart want to leap out of her chest. She was at a loss for words.

Elliott waited for her to speak. When the pause in their conversation widened, his brow furrowed. He wondered if he'd offended her by talking business. He had been trying to find a clever way to tell her he loved her.

Finally he couldn't stand the tension any longer, and said, "What I'm really saying is, 'Maggie Archer, will you be my girl?'"

Maggie's eyes filled with happy tears. She nodded emphatically. Elliott leaned down and took her face in his hands and kissed her.

Your Free Mystery

We hope you enjoyed your stay on Juliet Island.
Please return again soon!

For updates about new releases, including the next Juliet Island novel, as well as exclusive promotions and giveaways, visit the author's website and sign up for the VIP mailing list at: www.AlexandraAmor.com

You'll receive a free cozy mystery when you do!

About the Author

Alexandra Amor is the award-winning author of a memoir about ten years she spent in a cult in the 1990s, as well as the Town Called Horse mystery series, the Juliet Island Romantic Mystery series and four animal adventure novels for middle-grade readers.

Each week, Alexandra hosts a podcast for mystery readers where she interviews mystery authors about their books, characters and inspiration. Most of the guests on the podcast have at least one novel available for free. Listen in and find great new mystery authors and books! Learn more at www.ItsAMysteryPodcast.com

Alexandra lives on the west coast of British Columbia and spends her spare time fantasizing about living on Juliet Island.

Learn more about her books, including the next Juliet Island Romantic Mystery, at www.AlexandraAmor.com

Acknowledgements

Huge thanks, as ever, to my family for all your love and support. And to my dear friends (you know who you are) for your encouragement and love.

Thank you to the Dream Team, Janet, Valerie and Joel, for your comradeship on the author journey and for holding me accountable. You guys rock!

Beta read by Maia Sepp
Copyedit by Dawn Nassise
Proofread by Angie Ramey
Cover design by Books Covered
Print design by Streetlight Graphics

57639978R00171

Made in the USA
Charleston, SC
18 June 2016